FALLING THROUGH CLOUDS

FALLING THROUGH CLOUDS

a novel

by Anna Chilvers

Bluemoose

First published in 2010 by
Bluemoose Books Ltd
25 Sackville Street
Hebden Bridge
West Yorkshire
HX7 7DJ

www.bluemoosebooks.com

British Library Cataloguing-in-Publication data
A catalogue record for this book is available from the-British-Library

Hardback   ISBN 10: 0-9553367-6-7
            ISBN 13: 978-0-9553367-6-8

Paperback ISBN 10: 0-9553367-5-9
            ISBN 13: 978-0-9553367-5-1

Printed and bound in the UK by Short Run Press, Exeter

To Johnny, Lorry Parks

Chapter One

There was a guy across the aisle. He was gazing at the tabletop, and he didn't look up even though I was staring at him quite hard. After Reading he finished his fourth can of beer and went off to the loo. I stopped trying to read my book and looked out of the window at the countryside passing by. Cows, brown and white, May blossom hanging over the black water of a slow river, rooks circling above a ploughed field. I wished we'd bought some beer. He'd finished four cans and it was only one thirty.

I was on the train out of London with Dad and Marcus Sullivan – who is Dad's colleague, my university lecturer and also, unbeknownst to Dad, my lover. I was meant to be going off to Egypt on an archaeological dig for the summer, but the trip was cancelled at the last minute owing to unstable politics. We were travelling to rural Wiltshire where my parents lived. I was trying to read *Atomised* by Michel Houllebecq. I was finding it hard to concentrate.

When the guy opposite stood up I got a waft of stale sweat and alcohol. It didn't turn my stomach. It made me want to nuzzle my nose into his armpits. It made me want to drink until I fell over and was sick. He had greasy hair and his clothes badly needed a wash. He was wearing an old leather jacket that was scuffed white around the elbows and collar. I wondered if Dad and Marcus would notice if I moved across the aisle to sit with him. Or if they'd care. But then an old lady who'd just got on settled herself at his table with a magazine and some homemade sandwiches. He didn't seem to notice her when he returned.

They were both going all the way to Plymouth. The conductor was a mutterer, checking the tickets and reading them under his breath – Exeter yes, Reading yes, Plymouth yes, Exmouth,

1

change at Exeter. When he got to them it was Plymouth yes, Plymouth again, and his voice rose a fraction as if he was pleased to get two the same in a row. I wanted him to say snap. I looked at the guy, hoping to exchange a smile, but he didn't look up. Dad handed the conductor all our three tickets together and he hummed as he scribbled on them with a biro, yes, yes, yes. The greasy guy left his ticket lying on the table where the conductor put it.

Marcus was sitting opposite me, next to the window in a rear facing seat. Dad was next to him by the aisle. Marcus has really long legs and his knees kept bumping mine under the table, which might have been accidental at first. But then I felt his foot sliding up my leg and he'd slipped off his shoe. He was in the middle of a rant about the parallels between Gilgamesh and the Odyssey – in fact he was making a point I made in one of my essays last term – and he didn't even glance at me. I knew that turned him on. Last year I would have reciprocated, snuck my foot into his lap and had a feel to see how much. But now I couldn't be bothered.

The old lady had got out a flask and was rooting around in her bag for something. Whatever it was she couldn't find it. She sighed and looked up and her eyes scanned the carriage, across to me with my book. I lifted it up in front of me so she could see the picture on the cover of a young girl in her underwear. She didn't react. She looked across to Marcus and Dad deep in conversation, along the aisle and back until her gaze fell on the man opposite her. She paused for a moment, then leaned forward.

"Excuse me, would you know if I can get any milk on this train?"

His eyes widened a little, then he smiled.

"You might be able to get some from the buffet car."

I looked at him in surprise.

His voice was pure Home Counties, full of grammar school and cricket on village greens. He could read the news for the

BBC. The lady with the bun showed no surprise though, only mild distress.

"Oh! I did want to avoid using the canteen."

She looked up the carriage to where someone was coming through the doors with coffee and a paper bag of sandwiches.

"Is it that way?"

He nodded, then leaned towards her. She must have been right in the force field of his beer breath, but if she was tempted to flinch she controlled it well.

He said, "I'll get you some, I need more beer anyway."

He came back five minutes later with a carrier bag of beer, which he put on the seat next to him, and a handful of plastic containers of milk which he gave to the woman.

Marcus's foot was at the top of my thigh now and he was wriggling his toes nearer to my crotch. Soon he would find the hard bit of the seam in my jeans and push against it so it rubbed. He sometimes did that in seminars, under the table, when there were other students there, or even other tutors. Once he'd even made me come, right there in the seminar. I'd had to bite my lip and clench my thighs and buttocks as hard to the seat as I could not to show it. He always managed to keep his mind on the subject in hand though. After, I'd go to his office and he'd lock the door and we'd fuck on the floor, or sometimes on the chair or the desk if he could clear enough space. I wondered how soon he was hoping for a fuck this time.

Mum was meeting us at the station, and when we got home we'd all have some tea, then Dad would drag Marcus off to his library until dinner time. They'd chat more over wine. So I suppose it would be after that, when Mum and Dad went to bed. Unless he was hoping to get a quickie in the bathroom somewhere along the line.

His toe found the seam and pressed hard. I stood up suddenly.

"I want a beer. I'm going to the buffet."

Marcus quickly dropped his foot back to the floor. He and Dad both looked at me.

Dad said, "We'll be there soon. Won't it wait?"

I shrugged and walked away down the aisle.

I changed my mind about the beer when I got to the buffet car. I looked at the books and magazines. I wondered why I was so angry with Marcus. It's not as though he'd made any promises. I always knew it was just fucking and just for fun.

Last year we giggled like silly children in the narrow bed I've had since I was seven. I thought it was hilarious sixty-nineing with my teddy sitting on the pillow. Afterwards he made it talk in silly voices and I got my old rag doll to answer back. We had sex in the garden too, not far from Mum and Dad's bedroom window, and he had to put his hand over my mouth to stop me shouting out. That whole fortnight was edgy and exciting, and I supposed that's what he was hoping for again.

But this dig in Egypt had changed things. We'd been going to go together. Just me and him. He was leaving his wife and kids behind and going away with me for the summer. When it fell through, I thought we could do something else – it's not as though the world is short of archaeology. We could have gone to South America or China or anywhere. The world of the summer was our oyster. I even asked him to go to Glastonbury with me. But he said it would be too difficult. His wife would get suspicious. My Dad had invited him to come and spend more time on the book they're writing together (and have been doing for five years now), so we could have some fun there. Like last year.

Last year. Fuck! Last year was last year.

The loudspeaker coughed into life and the conductor's voice announced that we would shortly be arriving at Westbury. I walked slowly back along the train to our carriage.

Marcus and Dad were standing up, pulling on their coats and lifting luggage down from the rack. I reached up to get my own suitcase, but Marcus stopped me.

"I'll do that."

I put my book in my bag and slid my arms into my jacket. We were pulling into the station and I could see Mum's green quilted figure at the far end of the platform.

The old lady was talking to the man with the leather jacket.

"But now Mother's dead I thought it was time to see a bit more of the world."

She bit into an egg sandwich and the guy nodded and smiled. For a second his glance flickered my way, but it didn't hold.

Marcus was following Dad down the aisle, carrying my suitcase as well as his own bag. I had to go. I looked back when I got to the end of the carriage. The guy was cracking open another beer. He pushed a can slightly towards the old lady and said something. She shook her head.

On the platform Mum was hugging Dad, then Marcus. I stepped forward and she hugged me too.

"It's good to see you, darling."

Marcus was on the other side of me, and he put his hand on my bum and squeezed. Then they were all three walking off along the platform, taking my luggage with them. I looked at the train, and through my reflection in the window, I could see the guy with the leather jacket. He was watching me.

The guard blew a whistle, and I didn't stop to think.

Ten seconds later the doors had closed and the train was pulling out of the station. Marcus was nearly at the end of the platform. He hadn't turned round. I watched him as we passed.

Chapter Two

When I sat down in the aisle seat the old woman looked across at me and laughed.

"Hello again, dear."

"Hello."

The guy took a swig of his beer and didn't look up, but I thought there was a hint of a smile around his lips.

"Can I offer you a sandwich?"

I refused. The old lady wanted to chat but I didn't want to discuss what I'd just done. I didn't even want to think about it yet. I got my book back out of my bag and held it in front of my face. I'd only bought it because the blonde girl on the front reminded me of a picture of me when I was sixteen, in my bikini and wearing too much make up – but it was alright. For the next part of the journey I immersed myself in the book, blocking out all other thoughts.

Near Exeter I looked across. The guy and the old lady were both asleep.

He was absolutely still, not a muscle on his face moving, each eyelid smooth and clear as an egg. Between the dirty hair and unshaven cheeks they seemed vulnerable, unmarked. The eyes they covered were deep and wary, even suspicious, but the lids were soft brown, veined faintly with blue. I wanted to lay my fingers on them.

They slept right through the bustle and noise of Exeter, where lots of people got on and off, and right on down the coast of South Devon. I tried to read, but there was too much distraction. The sun shone on the sea making it sparkle with silver and blue. There were stretches of sand that rolled for miles. The lady was snoring quietly. The man was so still I wasn't sure if he was really sleeping. At Teignmouth we headed inland, into green farmland, lush with dairy cows and farmhouses selling cream teas. It was so far removed from the seedy world of *Atomised*, I put my book on the table and watched.

Just past Totnes the man sat forward in his seat with a start, his eyes wide open and full of panic, his face white. He focused on me in confusion. I smiled but that didn't help. He looked so frightened and vulnerable I thought he was going to cry, so I spoke to him.

"You were sleeping. It was a dream."

Slowly his eyes relaxed and then he smiled too. For a couple of miles we pretended to take no notice of each other. But every time I looked up, he was looking too, and after a couple of times he stopped looking away.

"Fancy a beer?" he said.

I nodded.

He grabbed the carrier bag and moved across. We both cracked a can open and he leaned forward, opposite me, his elbows on the table.

"I'm Gavin."

"Kat."

He grinned suddenly.

"Your boyfriend's going to be pissed off."

"He's not my boyfriend."

We looked at each other and I knew I should say something else, but the moment went on too long. There was amusement in his eyes, and my stomach kicked a little. I wondered if he was mocking me. He spoke first.

"Where will you go?"

I wanted to say, how about you and me go to a hotel for a few days. He didn't have the air of someone with urgent plans. Or a girlfriend. Now he was closer the smell of his clothes was pungent. I wanted to explore the gulf between his voice and his hygiene. I wanted to lick his eyelids.

"I have a friend in Plymouth."

He nodded.

"What about you?" I asked

"I thought I'd try and paint. You know, by the sea. I've never done it before."

"What, by the sea?"

"No, painting. I've never painted before."

"Oh."

I looked at his hands, one holding the beer can, the other palm down on the table. His fingers were long, and fine black hairs grew between the joints. He wore a wide silver band on the first finger of his left hand, and on the back of his hands there were a number of small circular scars. Around each of his wrists was a black handkerchief.

"So what makes you want to paint now?"

"I thought it would be relaxing."

"Devon's a good place to relax," I said.

Then we talked a little about Devon and Cornwall and places we had been. He was onto his next can. The conversation was like a screen hiding what we really wanted to say – do you want me? Yes. Let's do it then – it was getting irritating.

"Are you planning to stay long?" I asked

Suddenly he frowned.

"I don't know."

I waited for him to say more, but he didn't.

Then he said "Sorry, I'm keeping you from your book."

"No you're not."

But he sat back in his seat and was silent. His face was closed again. I wanted to say something, to continue the conversation, but his body language was wrong. He looked out of the window. I wondered if he regretted talking to me, and we both sat in silence.

Soon after that the conductor announced we were arriving at Plymouth. The old lady woke up and looked around her, getting her bearings. She looked at the empty seat opposite her and then across at Gavin sitting at my table, and a look of understanding crept into her eye. She smiled to herself.

You're wrong, I wanted to tell her. Look at us. We've not spoken for ten minutes, and he hasn't even looked in my direction. We're as far apart as if we were at different ends of the train.

She was packing her things away in her bag, and I pulled mine onto my lap. Apart from the beer, Gavin didn't seem to have any luggage.

The train pulled into the station and we made a little procession down the carriage, her then me and Gavin behind. She had a large suitcase in the racks at the end and I offered to help her with it on to the platform.

As I pulled it the handle got stuck in the rack above.

"Here, let me."

Gavin leaned in to help, and suddenly our faces were close. He smiled and the look in his eyes was warm. My face burned hot.

On the platform, Gavin found a trolley for the lady's luggage and the three of us left the station together. She headed for the taxi rank, and while the driver loaded her stuff into the boot she thanked us and wished us luck. Neither of us asked her, luck with what?

Then she got in and the taxi drove off, and we were left standing together outside the station.

"I'm going this way," I said, pointing to the right.

"Me too."

We walked together in silence. He had his hands in the pockets of his jacket. He didn't look at me. I wished he'd smile again. I wished I knew what to say.

When we reached the main road I said, "I think I'll wait here for a bus. It's a long walk to my friend's house."

I stopped walking and so did he. He half turned towards me and shuffled a bit from one foot to the other.

"OK. I'm going for a quick drink. Over there."

He nodded across the road and I looked. There was a pub, grubby and narrow between two shops, no signs, no decorations, the sort of pub you walk by without noticing.

"OK."

He loitered for a moment longer. There was a bus approaching.

"Bye then."

"Bye."

He smiled briefly then dashed across the road. As the bus pulled up the door of the pub was just closing behind him.

Kirsten was home, but she was packing. The next day she was off to India with her boyfriend. I didn't even know she had a boyfriend.

"You know. Matt. I met him last summer when we were braiding."

Kirsten and I spent last summer travelling around resorts in Devon and Cornwall braiding hair for tourists. Mostly it was little girls, on holiday with their families, but sometimes teenagers wanted it done, and sometimes blokes would come over from the pub and ask to have their hair braided as a joke. Most of them were idiots and we sent them packing, but there were a few sweet guys who ended up with silk and beads in their hair. We even invited one or two back to the tent. Matt was one of them.

"Yeah, I remember. I didn't know you saw him again."

"He phoned me as soon as I was back home. We've been together ever since."

She was folding t-shirts and putting them into her rucksack.

"Do you think one spare pair of jeans will be enough?"

"I don't know."

She rolled the jeans and stuffed them sideways next to the t-shirts, then picked up some shorts and a bikini.

"I haven't got any clothes with me."

She looked at me sharply, then dropped the shorts and sat down next to me on her bed.

"What are you going to do?"

I shrugged.

"I can't believe you did that. What will Marcus think?"

I shrugged again, a bit I-don't-give-a-fuck.

"I wish I could see his face when he realised you'd disappeared."

"Pompous git!"

Kirsten started laughing, and before I knew it I was too. Then we were rolling around on the bed remembering things Marcus had said and done over the last couple of years and pissing ourselves. We laughed for a good fifteen minutes and then slid off the bed, weak and gasping.

"You can borrow my clothes. I'm travelling light. Help yourself."

Kirsten waved a hand towards her wardrobe.

"Thanks."

"You can borrow my van as well if you like. The tax has run out, but it's MOT'd."

"Great."

"And the braiding box too if you like. In fact, it's in the back of the van."

"Kirsten, you're fantastic."

"Well, sorry I'm running off and leaving you. It'll be weird doing it on your own."

"I like being on my own."

"I know, but camping. It's more fun if there's two of you."

We sat and stared at the floor. It was littered with things Kirsten was taking with her to India. Guidebooks, a couple of novels, sun cream, towel, notebooks, pens, walking boots.

"Oh I forgot. We're taking my tent with us. Sorry."

"It's OK. I'll get one."

Digital camera, sunglasses, headache pills, sickness pills, contraceptive pills, sundress.

"Tell me about the guy on the train. The one you got back on for."

"I didn't ... I just didn't want ..."

"I know you couldn't bear another two weeks with Marcus. You told me that. But why decide then? Don't tell me this mysterious stranger had nothing to do with it. Where is he now?"

"In a pub near the station. At least that's where I left him. But ..."

"Don't you want to see him again?"

"I don't know. He was moody and sullen ..."

"But he got you really hot anyway."

I squirmed a bit then looked up and Kirsten was looking at me.

"Why don't you go and see if he's still there? You don't want to regret it forever. He might be the love of your life."

"Kirsten!"

"Even if he's not, you could get a good shag out of it. And if he's not interested you can come back here anyway, so nothing to lose."

"Don't be ridiculous. He won't be there. He was only going for a quick drink."

Kirsten didn't say anything. After a few moments I looked up and she was looking at me, waiting.

He was still there. I tried to get Kirsten to come with me, but she had too much preparation for her journey. She drove me down and dropped me off outside.

The pub wasn't very busy – a couple of regulars chatting at the bar, a crowd at a table, all men except one, a woman in her fifties, over made-up and chain-smoking, and then some solitary drinkers looking neither left or right.

Gavin was right at the back in the shadows at the table nearest to the toilets. He didn't see me when I walked in. I stood at his table for a good thirty seconds before he looked up.

Luckily he recognised me. I could see that in his eyes straight away, although I couldn't tell if he was pleased or not.

"Kat!"

"I changed my mind. I will have a drink after all."

He stared at me, and I remembered he hadn't actually invited me, but I kept on smiling until he smiled too.

"Sure, what would you like?"

He bought me a beer and we sat together in silence. I began to hate Kirsten for suggesting this.

"Did you find your friend?"

"Yes. She's going to India tomorrow."

"Oh."

"It's OK. She's lending me her van. And I'm going to buy a tent."

He nodded. He was smiling, and I wondered again if he was laughing at me.

"What about you? Where are you going to stay?"

He shrugged.

"Dunno. Thought I'd wait and see what offered itself."

He was definitely laughing now. But it was OK, it was more conspiratorial than mocking. I felt as though he were egging me on.

"You can come with me if you want."

He looked completely different when he smiled.

"What size tent?"

"Oh, probably tiny. But there's the van too. You could sleep in the back of that, just until something better comes up. If you like."

Chapter Three

In the end he slept out in the open field. Both the van and the tent were too small, too enclosed for him, they made him edgy. He said he wanted to breathe the fresh air.

He took an old car rug from the back of the van and rolled himself up in it and lay on the ground next to my tent, with only a bin liner between him and the damp earth. I lay inside the tent in my new sleeping bag listening to his breathing. He was so close we could have been sharing a double bed. Only I was inside and he was out. I was quite pissed.

After the pub we'd both gone back to Kirsten's. I slept on her bedroom floor and he slept on the sofa downstairs. She was very curious, and so were her parents. But they were about to drive to Heathrow. So in the morning, after some coffee and toast, we made ourselves scarce and headed first to the post office to buy car tax, then to a camping store for a tent. Gavin paid for the tax, but I wouldn't let him buy the tent. I suggested he buy himself a sleeping bag too, but he said he wanted to travel light. Then we drove out east towards Kingsbridge, heading for the sea. We found this field, only half full as yet. The woman asked how long we'd be staying and I said a week for starters. Gavin said nothing.

We got the tent up then walked into the village, found a pub and stayed there until closing time. We played pool, ate chips and drank pints of beer. I don't remember how many. But walking back up the lane I hung on to his arm for support, giggling as I lurched towards the high hedges. He laughed too, but he didn't have any trouble walking in a straight line. At the camp I went off to the toilet block. By the time I returned he was rolled tight in the rug, only the top of his head showing. I stood at his feet and said goodnight, but he didn't respond.

On Saturday, the start of half term, the tourists would come flooding like ants down the A38 into this seabound foot of the country, with their dogs and dinghies and children baying for ice-creams, loose change heavy in their pockets. If I was going to do hair braiding, that was the day to start.

In the meantime I thought I'd relax walking by the sea, just chilling out. Gavin didn't want to come. He didn't seem to want to paint either. The first day he walked into the village with me, and I left him at the pub door just as it was opening.

I found him still there when I returned that evening. I'd had a real wash-clean sort of day. It was sunny, but there was a strong breeze from the sea, which blew my hair back from my head and blasted me with salt. I walked fast along the coast path, my body gulping up the miles after its long London college incarceration. I arrived at the pub scrubbed and salted and full of exercise. Ready for a beer.

Gavin hadn't moved all day and the air had settled around him like a dark blanket, sodden with alcohol fumes and cigarette smoke. When I saw him across the pub he looked like a refugee who had given up hope, the glass of beer in his hand the only thing he had to hold on to.

I sat down next to him and he looked up. For a moment I don't think he recognised me, then something lit in his eye – just a pinprick – the faintest glow of welcome, and he smiled.

We drank in silence for a while. Then I gave him a stone I had found on the beach. It was smooth pale grey, the size of a milk-bottle top and had a hole worn away in the middle.

"A memento of my day," I said

He held it in the palm of his hand and felt its weight, rolled it from side to side.

"It's beautiful. Thank you"

I grinned, pleased with myself.

I said, "Have you got anything for me?" and immediately wished I hadn't. He'd bought me a beer for god's sake.

But after a moment he said, "Yes, I've got a story for you. Let's get some more beers in first."

A few minutes later I sat down across the table from him. I wanted to watch his face while he was talking. We both had our hands on the table and our fingertips nearly met.

"Once upon a time there was a girl."

"What was her name?"

"Her name was Anna."

I moved my fingers so they touched his, our fingertips pressing together on the scratched glaze of the table. He was looking down at his beer as he spoke.

"Her father was the ruler of the land, and she lived in a palace whose grounds were enclosed by a high wall and the entrance was closed by heavy locked gates."

"Did she ever go out?"

"She never went out."

"So she was a prisoner?"

"She was a prisoner, but she never thought of herself as a prisoner. She had everything a girl could want. Clothes, books, toys, ponies to ride and puppies to play with, delicacies from all corners of the world and servants to wait on her from dawn until nightfall."

"Did she have any brothers and sisters?"

"Not then, though some were born later."

"Was she lonely?"

Our fingers walked in closer until they were linked. He pressed against mine with his tips, one finger after the other in sequence, and looked up at me.

"No, because she had a playmate. Her father had taken many prisoners during his wars with neighbouring countries. One of these was a boy, the son of a prince, who her father had kidnapped. As he was royal and a child, he was allowed to play with Anna and attend her lessons and run with her in the palace gardens. They became inseparable friends."

"Did he have a name?"

"His name was Lot. As they grew older, their feelings began to change, and by the time Anna was thirteen she knew she was in love with Lot. She told him, and he said he loved her too, and they vowed never to be separated or to love any other.

"Anna's father was too wrapped up in his affairs of state to notice that the two children had grown up, and they were still allowed to roam freely in the palace grounds. It wasn't long before their racing games and rough-and-tumbles became something else entirely, and when Anna was fourteen she found herself pregnant with Lot's child."

"Wouldn't it have made political sense to marry them off, joining the two countries in matrimony?"

A wall light behind Gavin illuminated the left hand side of his neck and shoulder. I could see grime in the tiny lines of his skin above his collarbone. I imagined licking the dirt away, the gritty feel on my tongue, the tenderness of his newly clean skin.

"By then their fathers were sworn enemies. And Anna knew that she couldn't keep this child in the palace grounds. She had to hide it from her father."

"What did she do?"

He slid his left hand forward so our palms met, and wrapped his fingers around my hand. His was warm and dry.

"She hid the pregnancy, with the help of her maidservant, by binding her body and wearing loose clothes. Only the three of them knew. And when the baby was born, it was Lot and the maid who delivered it."

He drank from his beer, and so did I. I had to use my left hand as he had a firm grip on my right which I didn't want to break.

The seconds went by, a minute, two. He was lost inside his thoughts, his gaze concentrated on the table. I wanted more. I was scared of losing him.

"What happened to the baby?" My voice was almost a whisper.

He looked up quickly, realised how hard he was gripping me and released his hold – our fingers still touching, the pressure gone.

"There was a visiting merchant. Anna asked him to take the baby away to his own country. She and Lot both gave him their rings for the child when he grew up, and a parchment giving the details of his birth. The baby was smuggled out of the palace grounds the next day."

"How sad."

"Yes. It was sad."

"What happened to Anna and Lot after that?"

He looked at me oddly, as though I'd asked the wrong question.

"I don't know. I never heard what happened to them. Only the baby."

This became our pattern. I walked the coast path, and Gavin spent the day in the pub. In the evenings I brought him something of my day – a shell or a starfish or an anecdote, and he told me more of his story. I found myself, as I strode along the cliffs in the sunshine, looking forward to the dark smells of the pub, to Gavin's voice wrapping its tale around me, to the feel of his hand holding mine. And it seemed to me that he only came alive when I appeared, as though his day was spent waiting, biding time.

But it couldn't last forever. Friday night the pub was crowded and we had to shout to hear each other.

"I'm going into Salcombe tomorrow," I said

"Salcombe? To walk?"

"No, work. The tourists are arriving. Haven't you noticed the campsite's filling up?"

"Yes, the enemy's approaching," Gavin said.

"Not enemies. Punters. Do you want to come?"

I didn't think he would. There had been no more talk of painting since we arrived. He had shown no inclination to do anything except drink. But he said he'd love to.

When I got up the next morning there was no sign of Gavin. Usually I was up first and he was still lying there in the rug covered with dew. I'd give him a poke with my toe to wake him up. But today, nothing. I looked in the back of the van and his rug was there rolled up as normal. I decided to go for a shower and worry about it afterwards.

When I returned he'd just finished making coffee over Kirsten's little camping stove. He'd had a shower, washed his hair and shaved. He was barely recognisable.

"I didn't want to scare off your customers," he said.

He looked at me and smiled just as I was taking a swig of coffee, and I swallowed too quickly and burned my throat. He looked so different. With the hair removed from his face he looked younger. I'd guessed his age to be somewhere between twenty-five and forty-five, but now I could tell he was nearer to thirty than anything. His skin was smooth and pale, and running along the left side of his jaw was a scar, about three inches long. I had an impulse to run my forefinger along it – or my tongue – but I took another scalding sip of coffee instead.

"Do you want to borrow a t-shirt?" I asked him.

But he was happy as he was. As we drank coffee his hair dried in the sun and the breeze lifted it from his shoulders.

"I think I'll get a haircut," he said.

He found a charity shop too in Salcombe, and bought a couple more t-shirts and a pair of combats. That night, after a long day on the harbour front, we went to the village pub for chips and beer. The barmaid didn't recognise him.

The next two days were just as busy. Salcombe was thronging with tourists and all the little girls wanted braids in their hair. Some remembered me from last year. A good trick at the end of the day was to turn a few away – sorry, I'm packing up now, you'll have to come back in the morning. And they did. A few customers waiting at the beginning of the day got you noticed, which ensured a steady stream. By the end of Sunday my fingers ached.

Monday was a bank holiday. We sat on an Indian throw on the waterfront. I had a little fold-out stool to sit on while I worked – it got me at about the right height for most of the heads I had to work on. Gavin, when he was there, hung around watching, dangling his legs from the sea wall or wandering up and down. He wasn't there all the time: he explored the town and the pubs, and came back to me now and then with gifts – a cone of chips, a can of beer, an ice cream.

Around ten o'clock I noticed there was a similar set up a couple of hundred yards away. A blanket on the ground and a couple of hippy looking girls surrounded by a throng of children. Gavin went to check them out.

They were doing henna tattoos, and soon we got a relationship going. I'd send my customers on to them and vice versa. Any girl who'd only had the hair braid or only the tattoo wasn't going anywhere with their parents until they'd completed the set. It was even busier than the previous days.

When we packed up we all went for a pizza together. The girls were called Mitch and Nathalie and they were here for the week too. Nathalie had a line in hippy clothes, which she was planning to bring down later in the summer. The three of us swapped stories and laughed a lot, but Gavin was pretty quiet. He didn't offer any information about what he was doing there, so neither did I. A couple of times I saw Mitch or Nathalie cast a curious glance at him, but he didn't look back, only down into his beer. I suppose they thought we were a couple.

Tuesday Gavin fetched coffee and doughnuts from the harbour café as soon as we arrived. He handed the sticky bag to me.

"I need to go online. Is there an internet café?"

"I don't know." I bit into a doughnut and the jam dribbled down my chin. I licked it away and saw that Gavin was watching me. "There'll be a library. You can get internet access there."

He nodded, satisfied, and soon after he disappeared for the rest of the day.

Mid-afternoon I noticed there were a couple of guys hanging around with Mitch and Nat. Last year Kirsten and I had loads of hangers-on, but this year it wasn't happening. I was either with Gavin and seemingly attached, or on my own, which doesn't seem such fair game as two girls together.

Mitch and Nat were getting pretty friendly with these two. Soon they'd had their hands tattooed and Mitch sent one of them over to me for a hair braid. They both had baggy jeans and shoulder length hair, and they were having a party that evening to which they invited us all.

Gavin turned up at around five. He looked edgy and tired, and for once he didn't smell of booze. I told him about the party and he shrugged.

"Whatever."

Chapter Four

I knew he was dangerous. There was something at the back of his eyes, something wavering, unsteady, a flame that a gust of wind might catch. And if it caught, anything could happen – anything might catch fire. Or the flame might just go out. I had no idea what that gust of wind might be – if any words or actions on my part might be the trigger or if it would come from somewhere else. But I knew it was desperately important that the flame stayed alive. Something about it moved me more than anything ever had.

Sometimes I looked at him when we weren't speaking, when his eyes were focused on something I couldn't see, and I felt a burning inside right from my groin to my throat. It was sexual desire – yes, I wanted him like I'd never wanted Marcus – but it was more than that. A need to cry and a desperate hunger, and something tender too. I wanted to enfold him, to cup my hands around the flame to keep it safe. Maybe even blow on it gently and feed it with oxygen. He was dangerous and vulnerable, and I was playing with fire.

We drove out in the van that evening, the four of us, following the two lads in their beat-up Mini Metro. They took us to a farmhouse on the side of a hill sloping down into a valley. Where the valley ended a couple of miles away, you could make out a triangle of blue sea. The fields were dotted with brown cows and cowpats, and music was already blaring from an enormous wooden barn next to the house.

Inside, the barn was edged with straw bales for seating. A few people were sitting, in groups or on their own, most of them drinking beer from bottles and cans. There was an enormous space cleared as a dance floor, but no one was dancing yet. Outside someone was starting up a barbecue.

Mitch and Nathalie and the two lads settled into a corner with some beers and one of them started rolling a joint. Gavin stood a few feet away from them watching. If it wasn't for him I'd have sat down with the others and relaxed, but he was uncomfortable.

"Want to go outside for a bit?" I asked

He nodded.

Outside was a yard bordered on two sides by outbuildings, including the party barn, and on another by a red brick farmhouse. The fourth side had the entrance to the lane with a big wooden gate held open by a pile of bricks. There were a few pieces of farm machinery lying around. Gavin and I climbed onto the back of a flatbed trailer and sat watching the barbecue.

"Do you mind? Coming here?" I asked after a while.

Gavin shrugged.

"It doesn't matter."

"It does matter if you're having a bad time."

"I'm the one tagging along."

He leaped down from the trailer and walked over to where beer was stacked up at the barn entrance. He grabbed two fourpacks. Walking back, he looked up and gave one of his rare and sudden smiles, then he swung himself up next to me.

"May as well get pissed and enjoy ourselves."

He opened a can and passed it to me. I was grinning.

"I like having you around."

"I know you do. I'd piss off if I thought I wasn't welcome."

We looked at each other, and for a moment I thought he was going to kiss me. I was ready for it. More than ready. But he didn't. It was like a shutter suddenly came down and his eyes blanked out, although he was still looking at me. He was tense again, fiercely tense as though he were gearing up for a fight, thinking aggression into all the parts of his body. He didn't move at all. Then he smiled, but it was a different smile, a horrid mocking, cynical smile that I couldn't look at and I turned away.

We drank in silence after that. He was drinking fast, making up for all the beer he hadn't drunk earlier in the day.

The party was filling up, and now there were cars and vans parked way down the lane. The daylight was fading and the music getting louder. Through the barn doors we could see quite a few people dancing.

"Do you want to dance?"

He didn't, so I went on my own, and spent the next hour or so having a good time in the barn with Mitch and Nat and anyone else who cared to dance with me. I glanced in his direction every now and then, and he was still there sitting on the trailer with his beer. After a while some other people joined him, but he didn't appear to be communicating with them. Next time I looked he'd gone.

I left the dance floor and wandered into the farmyard. It was full of people now, and I couldn't see if he was there or not. I decided to get us both some food from the barbecue. Neither of us had eaten for hours. I got two burgers and a pile of potato salad and beans all on the same plate. I grabbed a couple of forks and paper napkins, then wandered back over to the trailer to scan the yard.

"You looking for that guy in the leather jacket?" asked a girl.

I nodded.

"He went in there."

She pointed to the building behind her, a stable with closed doors and filthy windows. There weren't any lights on.

I pushed the door with my foot and it swung open easily.

"Gavin!"

I could see there were empty stalls, and some dark shapes that could have been tools or pieces of machinery. It smelled of cows, but there were none in here at the moment. There was a stack of straw bales to the right of the door.

"Are you Ok?"

The door shut behind me and suddenly it was pitch black.

"It's me. I've got some food if you want some."

There was a rustling noise and then he grabbed my arm and the plate of food fell to the floor. He pulled me hard so I was forced up against his chest. I was too surprised to resist. He pushed me against the pile of straw. With the other hand he grabbed my hair and pulled my head backwards and kissed me. I say kissed, but it wasn't like any kiss I'd had before. He was pressing his mouth so hard onto mine that my teeth were cutting into my lips. His tongue thrust into my mouth and his stubble rasped hard on my face.

I tried to pull back. I whispered, "Gavin, that hurts."

"Shut up."

His voice was angry and harsh. He started to pull at my clothes. I could feel spikes of straw pushing through the cotton of my shirt into my back. He pulled the shirt loose and tried to kiss me again.

"No!"

I pushed him as hard as I could and managed to slide out from between him and the straw.

I stumbled to the door and fell out of the barn, back into the party. Someone had decorated the yard with fairy lights and they had come on while I'd been gone. Purple and pink and white. All around the top of the party barn, and the house, and along the fence by the lane, wrapped round and round like twinkling barbed wire. There were none on this side of the yard, which was in comparative darkness.

I walked over to the gate and stood looking out over the fields towards the sea. There weren't so many people outside as before. The barbecue was dying down, and people were gravitating towards the music. The big barn thrummed with energy. I liked it that they were in there and I was out here. I liked the green tinge to the dark, and the warm black silhouettes of the cows as they munched the grass. I could hear crickets whirring in the hedge.

I've no idea how long I stood there. It might have been ten minutes or an hour. By the time Gavin found me my feet had gone numb with cold.

He stood next to me and leaned on the gate in the same way as me, his elbows resting on the top bar, his chin on his fingers tips. I could feel the warmth of his body only a foot away.

"I'm sorry."

I could tell he was looking at me, but I didn't look back. I knew that the sea wasn't visible anymore now that darkness had fallen, but I was desperately trying to make out its horizon in the V-shape of the valley's end.

"Want some of this?"

He held out a bottle of whisky, open, a quarter already gone. I took it and drank from the bottle, a gulping mouthful that sent a shock of heat through me from my mouth to my stomach. A cow was coming towards us along the hedge, head down, nuzzling the grass. I could hear the tearing sound as it ate. I could hear Gavin's short unsteady breaths. The music from the barn seemed distant and irrelevant. I took another swig from the bottle and the warmth started to spread through me. I moved my feet.

"Let's get out of here," I said

I looked at him now. He was watching me, and his face looked more vulnerable than I could have imagined. I drank more whisky, then handed him back the bottle.

"Come on."

He smiled uncertainly.

"Look…"

"Shut up," I said.

In the van I had another slug of whisky before starting the engine. I managed to manoeuvre out of the farmyard entrance and we crawled down the track back to the main road. It was late and there wasn't much traffic about so it didn't seem to matter much how well I drove. A few miles later I was doing about fifteen miles an hour in the middle of the road when we met a car coming fast round the bend. I missed it, but suddenly my heart was pounding and I couldn't drive any more. I pulled into a gateway and grabbed the bottle off Gavin.

I gulped so fast it was a moment before I could speak.

"I can't go any further. We'll have to stay here."

Here was a trading estate on the outskirts of Kingsbridge. Gavin got the blanket out of the back of the van and we climbed over the gate into a car park. There were planted areas round the edges, shrubby bushes surrounded by bark chippings, but no grass. Gavin spread the rug under a weedy birch tree and we sat down with the whisky bottle. There was still over a quarter left.

The moon was up now, nearly half full and rising over the squat square blocks of the buildings across the tarmac. Gavin and I sat back to back and passed the bottle between us.

When it was empty he turned round, nudging me with his shoulder so that I moved too and we were facing each other. Then he kissed me again, and this time it was a real kiss. I felt warm right through my body, which might have been the whisky. But as I lay back on the rug and Gavin's head blocked my view of the moon, I knew it was more than that.

I was woken by the sound of a delivery lorry reversing into the car park. It was light, but still early. I lay watching the bulk of the vehicle manoeuvre into the delivery bay of the store opposite, and thinking about the night before. Sex with Gavin was good. Although my limbs were stiff with cold, I could still feel the warm glow of whisky and pleasure. And something else too. A nagging image that added to other things about him which so far I'd ignored.

Gavin had never removed the black handkerchiefs from his wrists. Even when he'd cleaned himself up, they'd stayed in place, and I never questioned it. But last night, as our bodies moved together, one of them had slipped, and I'd caught a glimpse in the moonlight of the ragged scar that it hid. It encircled the whole of his wrist. Like the mark on his face it was healed, but slightly pink rather than the silver colour scars take on over time. It wasn't long since these wounds had been inflicted. In that moment, before passion distracted me, I thought it looked like the result of a burn.

It was time to talk. I sat up and turned to where Gavin was sleeping behind me, but he wasn't there. There was a dip in the rug where he'd been. I looked around the car park, but couldn't see him. I sat still for a moment, trying to take no notice of the sudden cold. Then I remembered the van. He must be in the van.

I gathered the rug around my shoulders and climbed over the gate. He wasn't in the front, so I threw open the back doors. Empty. I climbed into the driver's seat, telling myself he must have gone to find breakfast, and found the note.

It was written in pencil on a screwed-up paper bag which he'd flattened out.

Kat, sorry about everything. I don't want to fuck your life up too. I wish I'd met you earlier, Gavin

Chapter Five

Gavin wants to creep around the edges of the airport, away from people, but he makes himself keep walking. His legs feel stiff and over-jointed. Everywhere he sees Bertrand. Bertrand in baggage handling, Bertrand in arrivals and in the departure lounge too. Bertrand is in the gents where Gavin cannot piss in the urinals anymore but has to go inside a cubicle. Bertrand is in W H Smith buying some cigarettes and waiting outside the airport for a taxi. When Gavin goes through customs, Bertrand places a hand on his shoulder and turns him round. But it isn't Bertrand. Only a customs official handing him his wallet, which he's dropped. Gavin looks at his wallet uncertainly. It is yours? asks the official, seeing Gavin's puzzlement. It is.

Once this wallet was as familiar to Gavin as the knees of his jeans or the toes of his desert boots. Now he looks at it as though his favourite tennis ball from way back, age ten, had suddenly landed in his hands. In the main hall some workers are dismantling a Christmas tree.

He sees Bertrand walking fast towards the exit, striding with familiar purpose. He looks back, but Gavin isn't sure any more that it's really him. He knows it can't be. Bertrand is dead. Gavin feels the heat of threatening tears. Wonders if he might vomit. He concentrates on breathing through his nose. This is Heathrow Airport, and here men don't cry or throw up on their shoes.

Sometimes Aggie comes to the flat. Gavin looks up and she is there, her face full of concern. Sometimes she brings him sandwiches, or cooks him food. Mostly the kitchen is too full of bottles. Full and empty. Gavin stays in the flat and drinks, because outside he sees Bertrand. Aggie says, have you eaten since I was here last? He doesn't know when that was. Did she come yesterday or before the weekend? He keeps the curtains closed against the daylight and there is no difference between day and night. Once Aggie raised her arm above her head to stretch and Gavin cowered and whimpered like a baby.

She wants him to go and see someone. She says don't worry I'll come with you. He's an expert. He understands what you've been through. He can help you. When Gavin says no, she is angry. You can't stay here in this flat forever, drinking yourself to death. You have to make an effort to help yourself. Gavin stops listening and turns back to his computer screen.

He spends a lot of time on the computer. He surfs the net. He looks at everything. Shopping sites and gossip pages. Chat rooms for Star Wars fans and travellers in China and would-be suicides. Porn of every variety: teens, bondage, horses, rapes. He looks at the victim's face to see if it's real. It rarely is. Once he put Bertrand's name in a Google search and pages of stuff came up. He clicked on one and there was Bertrand's face smiling at him from the screen, his thin red hair slicked back, his domed forehead shining. That time he was sick. It's the only thing that's touched him so far.

Aggie brings the expert to visit him. She doesn't tell him beforehand, they just turn up. Gavin is wearing the same jeans and t-shirt he's been wearing for weeks. He realises he must stink. The expert sits in the armchair opposite Gavin and asks him questions. Aggie is in the kitchen making tea. Gavin wants to tell the man to piss off, but finds some buried resource of politeness. He didn't realise he could still communicate normally, but hears himself answering the questions.

I've lived here for five years. On and off. My work has taken me away a lot.

Aggie brings me food. But mostly I order what I need on-line and they deliver.

I can't leave the flat.

I don't know. It might not be like this for ever. I can't think ahead.

I couldn't write anything they'd want to read.

Aggie comes in and gives them mugs of tea then sits in a chair by the window, out of their conversation.

It was Aggie who asked you here. Not me.

Gavin is angry. The man is sitting in his chair drinking tea as though this were his consulting room. And Gavin was getting by OK. The nightmares have been fewer recently, since he's taken to drinking whisky. If he can pass out rather than falling naturally to sleep, they tend not to come.

Do you have nightmares?

I'd like you to leave. And you too, Aggie.

Yes, I know what you're doing. But if I want your help I'll ask for it. Now piss off.

Aggie tells him it's over four months since he returned to the UK. She says people are asking about him. People from the newspapers. They want to know if he'll be coming back. If he is able to write anything about his experiences.

When she's gone, Gavin sits in front of the computer and thinks about the future. For some reason he's still here. His body is functioning and he's still young. Perhaps Aggie is right and he should start to think about a life outside of this flat. But when he tries to think what that might be there's white noise between his ears.

He opens his inbox. He hasn't checked his emails since he returned, and there are hundreds, especially from around the time he got back. He scans down the list, wondering whether to just delete the lot. A lot of it is unsolicited. Random offers of goods for sale – printer cartridges, Viagra – appeals for aid, questions from curious news junkies who've managed to get his email address. And messages from family and friends that he can't bear to read.

He is about to click on empty when he sees a message, just over half way down. It was sent in February and now it's nearly May. The sender's name is GK. Bertrand's brother. The title of the message: A man of honour keeps his word. Gavin breathes deeply.

Once he would have claimed to be a man of honour. It was his belief in truth and honesty that led him into journalism. Uncovering truths that others strove to hide gave him a sense of personal as well as professional pride. His work made him comfortable with himself, even when it put him in the way of danger.

But everything has changed. He has looked into his own heart and found nothing there. When fear loomed close enough, honour deserted him without a backward glance.

He knows this is true because he has seen it with his own eyes.

His hand shakes as he opens the message.

>> Dear Gavin, I know that Bertrand held you in high regard. He told me he had invited you, and that you had agreed, to spend New Year with us at our family home. Unfortunately the course of events made this impossible, but I would like to extend the invitation once more for the New Year to come. GK <<

He wouldn't be asking if he knew the truth. Gavin knows he should decline. He should write and explain everything, but he can't. The truth is sometimes too painful to look at.

>> I'll be there. Gavin<<

These are the first words he has written for over a year.

Next time Aggie comes round Gavin is pacing up and down. She doesn't comment, but as she unpacks the food she's brought she keeps giving him curious looks. Gavin can tell she has hope. In any difference she looks for signs of recovery. He could disillusion her. Tell her the man she thought he was, the brother she wants back, is gone forever. Because in reality he never existed. He was a mirage that disappeared in the desert heat. But Gavin says nothing.

He checks his emails for a reply. Sometimes he limits this to two or three times a day, but mostly he can't keep away for more than an hour. So far there's nothing. He deletes everything else and leaves the box empty.

Since his return he has avoided all newspaper reports, television and radio broadcasts. He never looks at the news pages on the internet. The few times Aggie has tried to talk to him he shut her up. He doesn't know how the world perceives him or Bertrand. Or what story will have been fed to Bertrand's family. Even whether or not they got the body back. All he knows is they haven't been told the truth.

Bertrand was close to his brother. In those first days with the unit, he emailed him every day, and didn't hide any of the stuff that was going on like he did from his girlfriend. Some of the others kept blogs as a way of holding on, a place to write out the insecurity and fear which had no place in their official reports. Emailing GK was Bertrand's version of a blog. He never told Gavin what the initials stood for.

He tries a night without whisky and it takes him to a different place than he expected. He is lying on his stomach on the ground and his legs are itching in the heat of his protective suit. They still believed back then in imminent chemical attack. Bertrand is next to him, supported on his elbows and holding his camera ready. The ground shakes with the rumble of explosions, and the sound echoes back in harsh layers, slicing the hot air. Soldiers are shouting. Further off are other human noises, screams of anger and pain.

Gavin and Bertrand get to their feet at the same time and are running. This is important, something that has to be captured.

A sergeant stands in their way yelling at them to get back, but they ignore him. Bertrand has his camera up to his face, ready to start shooting. There is smoke and heat, and sand fills the air, getting into their eyes and their clothing. Gavin feels more afraid than he has ever felt before.

He wakes sweating. It is a few minutes before the force of the dream hits him. They could have died that day, running foolishly into the crossfire. Instead they got some of the best footage taken during the whole time with the unit. That night in the shelter they were exultant, high on adrenalin and the joy of survival.

Gavin wishes he could stay in the dream forever. Awake, he sees how hollow their excitement was. How little the victory.

Three weeks later the reply comes. When he opens the mailbox and sees it, he tells himself he knew it would be there. He has looked so many times and been disappointed, but this time there was a buzz of expectation.

He knows he's fooling himself.

The message is titled – Your Mission, Should You Choose to Accept.

>> Gavin, thank you so much for accepting my invitation for New Year. You have no idea how much it will mean to us, you being a close friend of Bertrand's. We can get in touch to arrange details nearer the time.

I would like to ask you an enormous favour. Bertrand once mentioned that you have family living in the South West, and I wondered if you're likely to be down that way between now and New Year. It's just that I have a note from a small business notifying Bertrand that an item he ordered is ready for collection. Very ambiguous, I know. I'm trying to tidy up his affairs, and wondered if you could pick it up for me. I'm away from home at the moment, but can email the address to you a week on Tuesday when I return.

Thank you again, GK <<

GK has misunderstood. The family holidays in Cornwall were part of Gavin's childhood. His aunt died years ago, he has no family there anymore.

He thinks about his reply. He doesn't want to tell GK that he's wrong. He doesn't want to refuse.

Gavin has not left the flat for five months, even to walk to the end of the street.

He knows if he asked Aggie she'd jump at it. She'd want to go with him.

This is what makes him decide. The idea of escaping from Aggie.

Once his mind is made up he can hardly bear to stay. It will be ten days before GK sends the address. He cannot sit in one place. He paces the rooms. He stands and stares out of the window.

Aggie visits and comments on his agitation.

Are you sleeping? Are the nightmares back?

He stares at pigeons in lines on the rooftops and doesn't answer.

After four days he's had enough. He walks out of the flat with nothing but the clothes on his back and his wallet. He lets the door slam behind him, knowing he doesn't have the key.

Chapter Six

He's been in the dark so long he's afraid of the light.

He remembers regaining consciousness and opening his eyes to blackness, closing them and finding no difference. Tape binding his mouth, forcing his lips between his front teeth. He makes a noise in his throat, swallowing down the bile of panic, and an answering moan comes out of the dark. Bertrand too. Gavin's hands and feet are bound and there is pain in his limbs and back. He tries to shuffle into an upright position, but the sound of his movement seems too loud and he stops, not wanting to attract attention. He doesn't know where they are, what sort of place they're in, if there are guards outside or if they've been abandoned. He briefly considers the possibility that they are buried alive, but banishes the thought.

In those first few hours he questions everything, and examines every possibility. Beneath that he is aware of dehydration. Now and then his throat closes convulsively, and he swallows, aware of the danger should he allow himself to vomit. He tries counting a minute but can't judge the speed of the numbers. When he reaches sixty it seems such a small piece of time. He continues, and the numbers become a backdrop for the images that flood back in. The grinding roar of planes banking and turning. Then the impossible sound of an explosion, shooting flames and black smoke. Men running, burning, their mouths open in screams of agony. Gavin's brain turns off the sound and the scene unfolds in silence. He sees the jeep, the American flag hanging from its side, and at that moment it represents nothing but escape. Bertrand is with him, and they leap in together, Gavin behind the wheel. Other vehicles are escaping up the north road, but there are bodies in the way. Gavin would have to drive over them to escape at any speed, so he takes the road east, not knowing where it leads. The smell of burning flesh follows them, and he pushes hard on the accelerator. A mile, two. Space between them and it. Bertrand's face is grey, expressionless. A gun lies across his knees, snatched from a dead soldier as they ran past.

But when the attack comes he doesn't use it. Gavin slams on the brakes and Bertrand lets the gun fall to the floor with a clatter. A group of masked men fill the road. Some point their guns straight at Gavin and Bertrand. Others run to the jeep and tear open the doors. They are shouting in a language Gavin recognises but doesn't understand. When the two men don't respond they yell and raise their rifles. Gavin sees them black against the blue sky. Then just black.

In Salcombe Library, sitting in front of a computer screen, Gavin moves his lips as he counts. Nine hundred and fifty-nine, nine hundred and sixty. A screen saver bounces across the screen. He notices the librarian is looking his way so he moves the mouse and the page flashes up in front of him again. BBC News archives, report of friendly fire incident. Six dead, thirty injured. No mention of any missing. They weren't supposed to be there, him and Bertrand. No one noticed they were missing because no one knew they were there in the first place.

He hasn't had a drink today. Something has shifted in his head. He has been away from the flat for six days and he hasn't seen Bertrand.

That first day, in the street and in the station, he thought he'd done the wrong thing. The daylight was glaring, noisy and full of life. Everything could be seen. The light was inescapable, just like complete blackness which clings and gets into every part of you. In his flat these last months he has never drawn the curtains or turned the lights out completely. He has lived in the half-light.

But even out here in the daylight things can be hidden. At the train station people walk by him without looking, not even a passing glance. He buys a ticket and it is given to him, no questions asked. The boy in the ticket office looks bored. Gavin imagines leaning into the glass and saying to the boy – do you know what I did? I killed my friend. Killed my friend. The boy would shrug and give him the ticket anyway.

His mind is probing thoughts which he'd closed off. He can't stop it. I killed my friend. Just words. He is detached, there is no emotion in them. But they're words his brain hasn't allowed up to now. If he were to follow them they would lead into blackness.

The librarian isn't looking any more. Gavin opens his emails and the message is there from GK as promised.

>> Thank you so much for doing this, I do appreciate it. Don't know what the parcel is, probably not important. But nice to clear these things up. There's nothing to pay, it just needs collecting, from Merlin's Cave (!), ...<<

The address he gives is in north Cornwall. Time to move on.

Dawn has begun and the first birds are starting their song. The air is grey and light, not yet infused with the colours of morning. He leaves Kat still sleeping on the car rug, her body curled against the early morning chill, her face smooth and childlike. Before he leaves he kneels and watches her breathing. He places his fingertips lightly on her cheek and she sighs in her sleep.

He hitches a lift with a lorry leaving the retail park. It takes him to Plymouth, and from there he gets a train to Bodmin. He buys a bottle of whisky, then heads out of town northwards, walking the lanes between hedge banks ten feet tall. There are orchids and wild strawberries growing amongst the grass at their base.

Sometimes the hedges seem to close in on him and the road narrows. He can feel their height sealing him off from the fields beyond. He drinks from the bottle and looks up at the sky. Occasional trees and houses, tall enough to show above the hedge-line, help him calm his breathing. At a crossroads a pair of dogs run out of a farmyard barking and stop him in his tracks.

By late afternoon he can smell the sea.

Early evening in Camelford he buys fish and chips, then heads off again, northeast. He sleeps in a field downhill from a wind farm. He can hear the rotors going round, a gentle rhythmic roar, and tries to find it soothing. He thinks he can also hear the rush of the sea. Lying awake beneath a starry sky he thinks about Kat and wonders if she's sleeping yet. He wishes he could reach out his hand now and touch the tent fabric, as he has on other nights, aware of her body only inches away. He sits up then and drinks until he falls unconscious. During the night a spider makes a web between his face and the grass, and if a grazing sheep noses at his leg, he doesn't stir.

Merlin's Cave is a gift shop for tourists. It's shelves are stuffed with Arthurian statuettes, tarot cards and pieces of crystal; wind chimes and Celtic jewellery hang from tree branches attached to the ceiling, and there's a table piled with books about ley lines and natural medicine. The air is sweetened with incense and whale-song, and it's busy. In front of the counter are buckets and spades in heraldic colours.

Behind the counter is a middle-aged woman with long faded hair wearing a blue Indian-style dress. Gavin can feel her eyes on him as he leafs through a book on myths of the green man. He hasn't shaved. He has no written note from GK authorising him to collect the parcel. He doesn't know how to approach her.

The woman's eyes turn sharply as a child knocks a trinket sideways on a shelf. The way she tells the child to be careful reminds Gavin of the sergeant in the unit. The child is cowed and slinks behind his parent. This isn't the right time.

As he replaces the book a noise starts up from the back room, a low-pitched buzzing. The woman reaches through a bead curtain and pulls a door to, and the sound stops. Gavin is frozen with the book half back on the shelf, still supported by his hand. Then he lets go allowing the book to fall to the floor, and quickly leaves the shop. He can hear the woman tutting as the door closes.

He has learned things about himself from Kat. If he shaves and washes and wears clean clothes he can pass for a normal person. No one has recognised him from pictures in the news. He can hide just as well out in the open as he could in the flat. But if he sleeps rough and looks like a tramp it's harder to get what he wants. He knows the woman in Merlin's Cave won't be persuaded to part with Bertrand's parcel.

He books into a bed and breakfast and has a long soak in the bath.

The bath is nearly long enough for him to lie with his legs straight and his shoulders submerged, but not quite. His knees are just below the surface, and if he lifts them they raise out of the soapy water like pink whales. He smiles. This is something from before. Lying in the bath, letting the heat of the water soften his muscles, the steam open his pores, he can almost trick his brain into forgetting. He tries choosing the memories, taking control.

Meeting Bertrand for the first time in a London restaurant. A busy Friday night. Bertrand is waiting in a dark corner with a book on the table. They'd chosen the book when they talked on the phone as a way of recognising each other. Gavin has a copy in his pocket too. He touches it with his fingers.

Bertrand is wearing corduroy jeans and a striped shirt, open at the neck. They have to talk loudly to be heard above the din, but no one overhears or looks their way. They could have been discussing a night out or a football game. Bertrand has a friend who can help them, someone he's worked with before. He will arrange a safe house for them on this side of the border while they check out the situation. Their best bet is to find someone with a goods lorry who can smuggle them in. If you pay there are people who are willing.

They eat pasta and drink red wine. Bertrand is wearing a silver pendant that glints in the light of the table candle. It's a pentacle on a chain. Gavin's mind flicks forward to the moment before Bertrand died, he was wearing the pentacle then. He's lost control. He sits up in the water and grabs for the soap.

The May bank holiday is over, but the town is still busy. There might be work going. Gavin worked this coast before, when he was seventeen, staying with his aunt in the summer holidays. Then he went out on the fishing boats, chatting to the tourists on the early morning pleasure trips. They liked him. He was well spoken, knowledgeable and friendly with children. Their teenage daughters liked him too. The fishermen were pleased because he kept the customers away from their equipment and they didn't have to talk to them. He got fish to take home to his aunt, and a sleep in the afternoon before going out to the pubs to check out the teenage daughters.

He doesn't think he'd cut it as a tour guide now though. He tries a few bars, but none of them are hiring yet. His other summer job that year was in a tattoo studio. Most of the time he made the tea and cleaned the machines. Once or twice when the studio was closed the tattooist let him have a go. The marks are still there on his thighs, hidden lightly by hairs. The guy was called Mel, and now Gavin thinks about it he remembers a girlfriend, a mousy girl called Sheila, who was into astrology.

He walks past Merlin's Cave looking for another entrance and sure enough it's there. A faded sign on the side of the building, Merlin's Tattoos, and an arrow directing customers round to the back.

Gavin walks into the room behind the shop and Mel is there tattooing the arm of a boy barely old enough. He looks up briefly from his work and nods to Gavin to take a seat. He's enormous, bald on top with a ponytail behind. His tattoos are all of dragons. They're crawling out of his shirtsleeves and his neckline, bejewelled, breathing fire behind his ears in green and red. He wears a number of crystals hanging on different length leather thongs around his neck. Gavin thinks of Sheila on the other side of the bead curtain and tries to picture them together but can't.

When he finishes with the boy Mel turns to Gavin. He doesn't recognise him. Gavin asks for a tattoo of a pentacle on the back of his hand.

Chapter Seven

"Was the baby a boy or a girl?"

"A boy. The merchants were sailing to a busy port where they had business. They found a wet nurse, a native of that city, and took the child with them. There was a young lad on the ship, still a child really, on his first voyage, who took a great liking to the baby as it reminded him of his younger brothers and sisters left behind at home. He spent all the time he could playing games and making faces to amuse the baby. The sailors let him off with light duties as they could see his usefulness in keeping the baby quiet.

"When they arrived at the port, the merchants went into the city to conduct their business. Most of the sailors dispersed in the town, looking for wine and women and relaxation. The wet nurse went to visit her family, leaving the child alone on the ship with the boy."

"Something dreadful's going to happen. I know it."

"Listen and you'll find out. The boy and the baby had a lovely time, playing and laughing, but eventually they got tired, and both fell asleep. The baby in its cradle and the boy on the floor beside it.

"Now, in that town there lived a wealthy merchant called Viamund. Just the day before, his wife had given birth to their first child, a boy, who had lived for only five hours. Viamund was distraught. His wife, who had barely survived the birth herself, was sleeping, and Viamund had been walking about the town since dawn. When he reached the port he saw the ship, newly arrived, and thought he would introduce himself to its owners, in the hope that doing a bit of business would take his mind off his personal troubles.

"When he saw the baby, guarded only by the sleeping boy, he didn't stop to think. He tucked the cradle under one arm, and in the other he took the casket containing the gifts which Anna and Lot had given to their child along with the parchment detailing his birth. The poor boy, asleep on the floor, did not stir, and neither did the baby wake.

"Viamund took the child home to his wife who received him joyfully. They named him Surcote. They knew he had another name, given by his real parents, but they never told him what that name was. They brought the boy up as though he was their own child, and no one, including the boy himself, ever knew any different.

"On returning to the ship the merchants were horrified to find the child had gone, as they had promised to let Anna know of the details of the family they placed him with. The boy was stricken with guilt and grief. But although they searched far and wide, sending messengers throughout the land, they could find no trace of him."

I drove to the campsite and took the tent down. I didn't want to stay there any longer without Gavin. Then I drove into Salcombe for another day of tourist mayhem. Since I'd been up so early, it was only nine thirty when I arrived and it was still quiet. Even so, I couldn't bring myself to face anyone yet.

I bought some coffee at a stand and drove out of town along the estuary. Beyond the boatyards the inlet of water was still and flat like a lake with a wide band of grass between it and the road, planted with tall trees and benches set beneath. Across the water was an old clay pit, like a small fortress overgrown with rhododendrons. I parked the van and walked beneath the trees sipping my coffee.

There was no one about except for a couple of dog walkers with their dogs. At the end of the inlet there were two people working, a man and a woman, dressed in waders and bright yellow jackets looking in the edges of the water. I sat on a bench a few hundred yards away and watched them. I could just hear the sound of their voices over the water beneath the call of the gulls.

I wrapped my hands around the polystyrene cup and felt the warmth against my palms.

Kirsten was right. It wasn't going to be so much fun alone.

My head hurt from the whisky.

The sun was rising in the sky, reflecting in the water, but I still felt cold.

I wished I knew where he he'd gone.

Already I missed him like a limb removed.

By the end of my coffee I knew that I wasn't going to do any more hair braiding that day, or possibly any day. Like Kirsten says, there are some things you have to follow up, because if you don't you might spend the rest of your life regretting it.

Salcombe Library doesn't look like a library. It's in a row of houses with steps up to the front doors and white-railed balconies on the first floor. They are mostly made into apartments now, but once they would have been quite large houses. The library occupies the first floor of one of them. You go up the steps and into a lobby where someone keeps their bike – maybe the librarian. You can get up to the library by the stairs or a lift.

At the counter in the middle, a solitary librarian was busy putting new covers on some books. The shelves were in rows along each side, and there were two tables, one scattered with newspapers, the other bearing computers for public use. I didn't go up to the counter straight away, as I wasn't really sure what to ask. Even if Gavin had been here and the librarian recognised my description, what else could she tell me? She's not going to have been hanging over his shoulder watching him on the internet for clues.

I looked at the fiction books. Most of them were hardbacks with soft worn covers. Romances and adventures. The books I recognised from my own reading were thin paperbacks lost between them. I found a collection of short stories and took a seat at the table. I could kill some time reading for a while.

It was about twenty minutes later that Aggie came in. I didn't know that she was Aggie then of course. She was a tall thin woman wearing smart jeans and brown boots with a pink cashmere sweater and a silk scarf around her neck. She had dark hair pulled back in a severe ponytail and a voice that could cut through crowds. I looked up as soon as I heard her.

"I'm looking for someone who was in here yesterday."

The librarian looked confused.

"A library member?"

"No, a visitor. He used the internet. He emailed me. He said he was here in Salcombe library."

The librarian shook her head.

"I don't know ..."

"Do you keep any records? Could you tell me if he was here? If he's been back again today?"

"Sorry. We don't keep records of guests. If he was a member, his details would be confidential."

"I've come down from London, I got the first train I could this morning. He's called Gavin. Gavin Redman."

Aggie's voice cracked a bit as she said his name. The librarian looked distressed.

"I'm sorry. I don't know how I can help you. I suppose you could leave a message, in case he comes in again. But ..."

"He said he was moving on. He has long hair, and he was wearing a leather jacket. Do you remember him?"

"I'm sorry. I wasn't here yesterday."

I'd closed the book already, and now I left it on the table and went over to the counter. I stood next to Aggie.

"Are you Gavin's...?" I started but didn't know what to say.

She turned quickly and stared into my face for what seemed like ages. I held her gaze. Her eyes were grey and hard and I could feel my mouth filling up with saliva.

"I'm Gavin's sister," she said eventually. "Who are you?"

I swallowed in relief. His sister. I'd thought with her accent, and her expensive clothes, that maybe she was a respectable life he was running away from. Perhaps she was.

"Kat. I'm Kat. I met Gavin last week. We've been together. But now he's gone. I was looking for him."

The librarian looked from Aggie to me and back. She smiled.

"Look, if anyone comes in, fitting that description, I can ask. If you leave your details. But I can't promise."

"He won't."

Aggie wrote her name and phone number down on a scrap of paper and gave it to the librarian. Then she turned back to me.

"Shall we talk over coffee?"

I had my normal black coffee, she had a cappuccino. I told her about meeting Gavin on the train, and how we'd spent the week together. I was careful to point out that he didn't sleep in the tent, and I missed out what happened at the party and afterwards. I showed her the note.

She took it in her hand and sat looking at it in silence. There were tears in her eyes. Then she said, "This is Gavin's handwriting."

"Yes. He wrote it."

"He hasn't written anything. He wouldn't even hold a pen."

She looked up at me now and the tears filled her eyes. One spilled over and ran down her cheek and she dashed at it with her hand.

"Since he came back, all he's done is look at that bloody computer. He doesn't even type on that. If he can't get somewhere by moving the mouse, he doesn't bother."

"Came back from where?"

She stared at me uncomprehendingly, then gradually with disbelief.

"You mean, you don't know who he is? He didn't tell you?"

"Only his name."

So she told me. She told me that Gavin was a freelance journalist who had gone to Iraq with a photographer called Bertrand Knight, and that they'd been captured. They'd been missing for nine months, from March until New Year, when Gavin had turned up at Heathrow Airport and phoned her to come and collect him. He wouldn't talk to her or to anyone, about what had happened. He'd stayed in his flat and refused to come out.

"It was in the papers but you won't remember it. It didn't even make the front page. If Gavin had had a story to tell they might have been interested, but he didn't."

"What about the other guy?"

She shrugged.

"Hasn't Gavin said?"

"He won't talk about it. At all. If you try he puts his hands over his ears like a child and hums with his eyes closed."

"God!"

We sat then in silence. I drank my coffee, but it had lost its taste. I remembered the times that Gavin would wake up suddenly in the night with a shout that woke me. The first time I crawled out of the tent to see what was the matter, and he was sitting straight up. I couldn't see his face in the dark. I said, are you OK? and he said, go back to bed. After that I didn't come out, but I always lay there listening, aware of him, ready in case I was needed.

"Of course, he has PTSD," said Aggie.

"What?"

"Post Traumatic Stress Disorder. He needs some professional help, or whatever's happened is going to keep on damaging him. He can't do it on his own. We must find him."

"Was he seeing someone about it?"

"No. He's refused. Absolutely refused to speak to anyone, just sat in his room with his computer. And now this."

She looked accusingly at me as if it was my fault, then seemed to realise and looked down again. She had a faint line of white foam on her upper lip from the cappuccino.

"Maybe this is best," I said. "What he needs. Some time out to get to grips with it himself."

"He needs treatment."

"Maybe this is part of his treatment. Sometimes you instinctively know what's best for you."

"You might as well say that someone with a broken leg should treat themselves by walking on it. You don't know him, not the way he was before. He's damaged, he's a different person."

She was crying openly now, the tears running down her face, catching and running into the corner of her mouth. I thought of the salt taste. She ignored the tears and gulped at her coffee.

"But you say he hasn't written anything up until now." I pointed at the note, "Isn't that a good sign?"

She didn't answer for a few seconds, and when she did it was with a question.

"Is he still drinking?"

"Yes, he is. It's weird – I've never known anyone drink so much without getting completely pissed."

"Well, quite apart from anything else, if he doesn't stop he's going to damage his liver. This thing is too much, Kat. He can't do it on his own. Did he give any indication of where he was going?"

I shook my head and Aggie sighed.

Our coffee was finished.

"Will you stay here?" she asked.

"No. I think I'll head back to London. I have a friend there I can stay with."

"I suppose I'd better come too. There doesn't seem to be anything I can do here."

She fished in her bag for her purse and pulled out an envelope, which she handed to me.

"Have a look at that," she said.

It was a photograph of Gavin. When I looked at it my breath caught in my throat and I nearly started crying. It was taken before. He was sitting on a chair in a garden, relaxed, with an intent look on his face as though he was listening to someone. The scar wasn't there, and he was cleaner, close shaven, younger looking. But the main difference was in his eyes. These eyes were full of confidence, bold even. He looked like someone full of energy and ideals, ready for a challenge, or ready to challenge anything. He was barely recognisable as the person I knew. I handed it back.

I said, "If he emails again, will you let me know?"

Aggie smiled.

"Yes," she said, then, "Thank you."

Chapter Eight

Gavin gets Bertrand's number from an acquaintance at the newspaper office. The editor is trying to get Gavin a placement as an embed with one of the regiments going out. There's a guy hanging around the office that Gavin's met once or twice before. He hands Gavin a scrap of paper when the editor is in the middle of a phone call. It has a mobile number, and the name, Bertrand Knight.

"If you don't have any luck, try this chap"

Gavin phones later, from his flat, explains the difficulties they're having.

Bertrand says, "Fuck that. Those fuckers won't let you see anything anyway. Come with me."

Gavin hasn't even told him his name.

"Don't you want to see some of my work, meet, see if we can work together?"

"If you like. Meet me at Pepperoni's, Rupert Street. 9pm. Bring a copy of The Fog by James Herbert. So I know who you are."

Gavin spends half the afternoon scouring second-hand bookshops for a copy of The Fog. He doesn't want to spend the money on a new copy. In the end he gives up and goes to Waterstones. In the horror section there are rows and rows of black books with red, white and gold print, dark green and purple coloured pictures on the spines and covers. James Herbert has two shelves to himself. Gavin didn't realise he'd written so many books. He read a couple when he was still at school, but they weren't really his sort of thing. In fact he's a bit worried about Bertrand's choice. Doesn't know if he wants to spend all that time up close with someone into horror books.

Turns out, Bertrand's never read it, or anything like it.

"I was at a friend's when you called, and it was the first book I spotted on his bookshelf. This is his."

He flips the book open and on the flyleaf is a message written in green ink: *To Jimmy, Happy 15th Birthday, from your girlfriend Cheryl.*

"I suppose I should have asked him," says Bertrand.

"Might have been a good idea."

"I don't read modern fiction. Don't understand it. Real life is unreal enough, don't you think? Like, who could think it up? Silicon boobs and sixty-four-year-old mothers and Michael Jackson. That's before you even get started on the real horror stuff."

"Like war?"

"War, rape, genocide, torture, mutilation, child abuse, fascism, poverty, starvation, beheading, stoning, dismemberment."

Bertrand sounds as though he could be reading the menu in his hand. His voice is light and steady. Gavin stares at him and Bertrand looks up to meet his gaze.

"I photographed the first Gulf War, Rwanda, Bosnia and Afghanistan. Red wine or beer? I don't do white."

"Red wine will be fine."

Gavin has worked with some people who think they know it all. They've covered stories in all parts of the world, seen atrocities, been in danger of their lives, and they think this gives them some sort of superiority. Not just that they're more experienced, more knowledgeable, but that somehow this gives them a moral high ground, makes them more worthy than younger reporters who haven't had the chance to get that experience.

Bertrand is probably ten years older than him, and certainly more experienced, but Gavin doesn't get the feeling that he's trying to pull rank. He hasn't asked Gavin anything about himself.

"I know someone north of the border. A journalist, although he doesn't write now. He owes me a favour. He'll help find someone to get us across. He'll put us up for as long as we need."

The waiter arrives with the wine and two glasses. Bertrand waves his hand when he asks which of them will taste it.

"Just leave it, thank you. What equipment do you have? Do you have a flak jacket? Chemical protection? Communications equipment?"

Gavin doesn't, but Bertrand waves his hands again.

"No worries, easily got."

Another waiter arrives with plates of steaming pasta. Bertrand begins eating straight away, bent forward, shovelling the food up to his mouth with his fork as though he were starving. He eats over half the plateful like this before pausing, laying down his fork and taking some bread from the basket on the table. He rips it in half.

"We can fly out later this week. I'll sort out tickets tonight on the net. Then we'll have to travel south to the border. Probably best to hire someone to drive us. Or we could buy a vehicle, then we could give it to Fred, my friend, as a thank you for putting us up. Yes, come to think of it that might be best."

He picks up his fork and shovels in more pasta.

"What do you think?" he asks through the food.

Gavin has hardly touched his. There is a knot of excitement in his stomach, which is making it hard for him to swallow. He wants to go out and cover this war, but hasn't really believed it would be possible until now. Although the editor has been persistent, Gavin knows it's pretty unlikely that he'll get a place as an embed. He's caused too much trouble in the past. Going it alone appeals to him, but scares him. He's planned routes, looked up the prices of equipment on the internet, pored over maps, but that's all. Bertrand doesn't even seem to think about the dangers. His enthusiasm is like a bulldozer.

"I haven't even said I'll come yet," Gavin says. "I've only just met you. I have no way of knowing if I can trust you."

Bertrand looks at him in surprise, his fork halfway to his mouth. Then he grins.

"OK," he says, "that's cool. Won't make much difference if I book the tickets tonight or tomorrow anyway. We've got to get the equipment before we can fly."

He pours the last of the wine into their glasses. Gavin picks his up and gulps at it. He breaks bits off a piece of bread. Bertrand has finished his food and lays down his fork. Gavin still has half a plate of congealing pasta that he can't eat.

"The night is young. Any ideas?" asks Bertrand.

Gavin swallows more wine. He tries to imagine the places Bertrand would go. The sort of people he'd hang out with. It's easy. In fact it's a wonder he's never bumped into Bertrand before. They probably share acquaintances, if not friends. But Gavin wants to unsettle Bertrand, take him out of his comfort zone.

"I have some friends we could hang out with. They're usually up for a good time. They'll be in the Fox until closing time."

"OK. Let's go."

Mark and Spider are over in the corner with a couple of girls Gavin has seen before. One of the girls is wearing a dress made of lilac satin, decorated with black lace. It's quite short – above her knees – and as she sits she keeps pulling at it to keep it from riding above the tops of her fishnet stockings. Her dark hair piled on top of her head is slowly falling down. The other girl is small and blonde, wearing a black leather mini skirt and a black vest.

"Hi," says Gavin, "room for a couple more?"

Mark looks up and grins.

"Hiya Gav. Sure, shove up will ya."

The girls slide along the bench into the corner, making enough room for another person. Spider is sitting on a stool, and there's an empty one next to him.

"Is that Dorrie's?" Gavin asks.

"Yeah, she's in the bog."

Dorrie is Mark's girlfriend. Spider is his best mate. All three of them wear old jeans and black t-shirts. Mark has a leather jacket and Spider has his hair bleached and gelled. Dorrie has short black hair in spikes and black lipstick. They share a squat in Camden where Gavin lived too for a while last year while he was doing a piece on homeless kids in London. None of them think of themselves as homeless, although their living room has holes in the floor and the bathroom has one wall missing. Surprising how quickly you get used to pissing into the loo with a vista of London in front of you. Some people Gavin knows would pay a lot of money for that sort of thing, though they would have some glass between.

He grabs a stool from another table and slots it in between Dorrie's and the bench. Bertrand sits next to the girl in the lilac satin. He looks out of place in here with these people. It's because of the colours he's wearing, Gavin thinks. Brown cords, cream, brown and orange striped shirt. It's the colours that are too clean and warm, not the clothes. Dorrie, when she returns from the toilets, is just as clean as him and Bertrand, but her tight black t-shirt is faded and her jeans are ripped showing the stockings beneath. Her boots have six-inch stiletto heels. Bertrand can't keep his eyes off her.

They are drinking beer from three-pint jugs. Gavin and Bertrand buy two more and fill up everyone's glasses.

"We're going to Luigi's after," says Mark, "wanna come?"

"Sure," says Gavin.

The two girls are called Eve and Tabby. Eve is the small blonde one, and Tabby in lilac and black. They seem pleased that Gavin and Bertrand have showed up. Means the night is looking up for them. Gavin knows the score. They're not selling it as such, but they're willing to give what you want in return for a good night out. No questions asked in the morning. He can see the signals going between them. Which one's yours? I'll have the one in black. No I will, the other one looks a bit weird and scary. No he's just wet, you'll be fine. He's not wet, I've seen his type before, gets a bit excited and turns into an animal. Lucky you. Not like that, he might want to do weird things, he's probably a pervert. God, what are you on Tabby? He's as harmless as a pussycat, look at his shoes.

Gavin realises this conversation is in his own head. He shakes it hard and swigs at his beer. Bertrand is leaning across him talking to Dorrie. He's not paying any attention to Eve and Tabby. His shoes are brown leather.

"Is Luigi's a night club?"

"Kind of. A drinking club."

"So no dancing?"

"You can dance if you want to."

"Will you?"

"Would you like me to?"

Gavin glances at Mark who's listening, a grin on his face. He knows Dorrie's a flirt, but believes that's as far as it goes. Gavin knows otherwise.

Bertrand is grinning too.

"Maybe."

Eve and Tabby are shuffling in their seats and emptying their glasses.

"It's nearly throwing-out time, shall we make a move?" Eve says.

Tabby presses into Bertrand's arm and looks up at him. "You can dance with me if you like," she says, "I love dancing."

"Oh, I'm not much of a dancer," Bertrand says, still looking at Dorrie, "I prefer to watch."

"Cheeky!"

Dorrie winks at him. She has nearly half a pint left in her glass and she knocks it back in one.

"Come on then, let's get this show on the road."

Luigi's is below some shops in a side street near the Embankment. There's a small sign above a black door and a bell to ring. A Swedish doorman opens the door to them. He smiles when he sees Dorrie and she gives him a kiss on the cheek. He looks over her shoulder.

"You'll have to sign your friends in," he says. "And no trouble tonight please."

This last comment is aimed at Mark and Spider.

The walls downstairs are whitewash over rough plaster and the place seems like a painted catacomb, poorly lit with lamp fittings here and there on the walls. There is a small room with an L-shaped bar and a couple of fruit machines and tables spilling through from another room through an archway, where couples and small groups sit drinking, their heads close together. The dance floor is in another room off to the left, glowing with red light. The DJ is playing loud rock music, but no one is dancing.

Bertrand buys everyone beer and double whisky chasers. Gavin dreads to think how much it costs. Spider goes straight to the fruit machine and Mark looks at the empty tables, deciding where they will all sit.

"Let's sit here," says Bertrand, putting his drink down on an empty table, "there's a good view of the dance floor."

Dorrie smiles at him and puts her beer down next to his. She knocks back her whisky before she sits down.

Mark looks put out. He likes to make the decisions. He looks at Bertrand and Dorrie sitting close together and giggling and Gavin wonders if he's going to make a fuss, but he doesn't, he shrugs and sits down on the other side of Dorrie. Gavin and the girls are left with the other side of the table. Gavin decides to make the most of it and sits down in between them.

After a while Gavin and Mark go to the bar for more drinks and the girls get up to dance. Gavin watches them while he chats to Mark. Mark is a pavement artist who makes his money drawing in chalk on the ground for tourists. He's good. Gavin asks how it's going.

"Not bad. It's always slower in the winter, but I'm getting better patches now. One on the South Bank that really brings in the dosh."

Eve and Tabby are dancing together on one side of the dance floor. Dorrie is on her own right in the middle. She is dancing suggestively, running her hands over her body, shooting sidelong glances at Bertrand. Gavin wonders who she's really doing it for. Mark has his back to the dance floor and can't see her. Once her glance slides over Bertrand and she makes eye contact with Gavin, but she looks quickly away.

They stay in the club for two or three hours. They've moved on to red wine and empty bottles litter the table. Mark and Spider are on the fruit machines, concentrated, elbows jerking in the orange lights. An hour ago Spider won fifty pounds, but it's all gone back in now. Eve and Tabby are dancing; Dorrie and Bertrand sit silently at the table gazing into their drinks. Dorrie looks as though she might collapse at any minute. They've all drunk a hell of a lot, and Gavin knows drink's not all she'll have had. Gavin staggers when he gets up to go to the loo, and steadies himself by putting a hand on Dorrie's shoulder. She looks up at him and smiles.

When he comes out of the loo she's waiting for him in the narrow passage at the bottom of the stairs. She wraps her arms round his neck and lays her head against him.

"Gavin," she says.

He tries to unwind her arms, but she pushes her body closer.

"Gavin, kiss me."

"No Dorrie. No. Mark's in there."

She starts to kiss his neck, little light kisses from his collar bone up towards his ear.

"Come on, Gavin. Why did you come back if it wasn't for this?"

She undoes his fly and slides her hand in.

"See, don't tell me you don't want it."

"That's not why ..."

Gavin sees a slight movement up the corridor before Dorrie's head blocks his view and she is kissing him, her hand moving on his cock. Thirty seconds, his tongue tasting the whisky in her mouth, before she is pulled roughly away and Mark is there, swinging a punch into his face.

"Bastard!"

Mark hits him again and he staggers sideways, crumpling into a heap as he tries to do up his flies. Then there are feet flying around him, more pairs than one. Mark and Spider and Dorrie in her pointed boots. He covers his head with his arms, but they stop.

"Come on lads, none of that in here."

He hears the doorman's Swedish accent, and then he is being lifted and half pushed half pulled up the stairs and into the night air. The hands on his arms are Mark's and Spider's. Dorrie is following behind.

"It's not the first time," she's saying to Mark. "He's a horny bastard. Always trying it on in the squat, when you were out."

"Shut up, slag."

They throw Gavin down in a doorway, and then the feet start in at him again. He tries to curl into a ball but Mark's boot in his face knocks him backwards. There's a blast of pain and he wonders if his jaw is broken, as the boot comes down again and blood pours into his eyes.

"Bastard! Fucking cunt!"

With every kick Mark lets out an expletive. Gavin covers his face with his hands. He can feel Spider's feet laying into his lower back, but Dorrie has stopped.

"Leave him Mark. You're hurting him."

Her pleading seems to be making Mark even angrier. The thuds rain down on Gavin's neck and shoulders. The blood has blinded him.

"Enough!"

The voice is sharp and authoritative. The kicking stops and then there is the sound of footsteps running away. Gavin feels someone rolling him over and wiping the blood from his eyes. It's Bertrand.

"You OK?"

"I'll live."

"You fuck his girlfriend?"

"Only once."

"Idiot!"

They both laugh, but pain snags in Gavin's jawbone and it turns into a gasp. Bertrand puts an arm under his shoulders and hoists him up.

"Come on. We'll get a cab back to mine and clean you up. We can open a bottle of whisky."

Chapter Nine

An ordinary room, bare, concrete floor, hard and cold beneath him.

Gavin watches Bertrand watching the guard.

The guard moves across the room and places a bowl of food on the floor beside Bertrand. Rice and peas. There is already a similar bowl on the floor beside Gavin.

The guard has removed the gag from Gavin's face and untied his hands from behind his back. He did this carefully, replacing the rope with handcuffs, securing Gavin's wrists one at a time. Now his hands are in front of him, joined with a piece of chain six inches long. The blood is rushing through his armpits and shoulders, his muscles readjusting themselves into their new position. It hurts. There's another guard just outside the door, he can see the edge of a boot and the end of a gun.

Gavin could speak now if he had anything to say.

The guard is removing the rope from Bertrand's wrists. His shoulder jerks and his arm moves forward. It might be an involuntary action, but the guard takes no chances. He holds tight onto Bertrand's wrist and snaps on the handcuff. He also kicks Bertrand's thigh with his heavy boot. Bertrand doesn't react.

The guard's face and head are covered with a black scarf. Only his eyes are showing. Bertrand watches this face intently. The guard will not make eye contact with him. Only when the handcuffs and chain are in place does he remove the gag from Bertrand's face. Gavin expects Bertrand to say something, or even to spit at the guard. But he does nothing. The guard leaves the room, kicking the door shut with his foot and snapping out the light in one fluid movement.

They are in blackness again.

There is the turn of a key in the lock.

Two cabs have stopped, taken one look at Gavin covered in blood, and driven off again. Others drive by without stopping. Gavin and Bertrand wander along the Embankment to Cleopatra's Needle. They lean against the wall and watch the water. The Thames is dotted with the reflections of orange and white lights, wavering, uncertain against the solid black of its flow towards the sea. There are a few boats moored, but nothing is moving.

Gavin thinks of the river as the skeleton of the city, always there, never changing, describing its shape, whilst the buildings and the people are the muscles and sinew, sometimes strong and vigorous, sometimes weak, atrophied, wasted. The river will last long after the city has gone, like bones in the earth telling a story of a body long dispersed. Strange that it consists of something so fluid as water. Gavin thinks there must be some deep meaning in that, something about fluidity and longevity, but his brain is too addled by beer and boots to follow it through.

"That would get the blood off," Bertrand says, nudging Gavin and pointing to the river.

Gavin laughs. "I'm not jumping in there. It's fucking freezing."

"I'll race you."

Gavin looks at Bertrand and sees he's serious. He's already stripping off his jacket.

"It's March. Do you know how cold it'll be in there? And filthy. You've no idea of the crap that gets thrown into that river."

"You chicken?"

Bertrand is taking off his socks and shoes. He tucks the socks into the shoes and puts them under a bench. Then he takes off his trousers and folds them neatly, laying them on top of his jacket. When he takes off his shirt Gavin can see the goosebumps. Bertrand hugs his arms across his chest and hops from one foot to the other.

"You coming or what?"

It's so cold they'll be in danger of catching hypothermia. And the drink will numb them. They won't know how cold they are until it's too late. The water is foul, full of oil from the boats, chemicals, sewage, litter, God knows what.

Gavin finds himself stripping off too. He piles his clothes in a heap on the bench. They're both standing by the Thames in central London in their underwear in the middle of the night in March. Down here by the Needle, they can't be seen by traffic on the road. But there are pedestrians here in the city, even at two in the morning.

"There and back. Loser buys the plane tickets."

Gavin nods.

On a count of three they both dive into the water.

The first impact with the cold is like having your skin sluiced off leaving the flesh exposed. The shock makes Gavin want to curl, let his body fill with the heavy blackness, sink to a place where the cold can't reach him. But instinct is strong and Gavin is a good swimmer. He stretches out his limbs, forces them into movement, tries not to think about the water that splashes against his face, leaking into his mouth as he turns his head to breathe. Every fourth stroke. Arms sweeping over head, legs kicking. One two three breathe. He is back at school, back in swimming lessons with the games teacher shouting out at the edge of the pool, all of the swimmers in unison. One two three breathe. One two three breathe. The concentration moves him onwards, keeps the cold at bay. While his limbs are obeying the rhythm, they can't freeze into stillness.

He can hear Bertrand to his left, a quiet splashing, the gasp of his indrawn breath, slightly behind Gavin's own. They are about neck and neck. It's a long way to the other side of the river.

By the time Gavin reaches it the air is raw in his lungs, each in-breath rasping with cold like sandpaper. Bertrand is a few strokes behind him. The rhythm of his limbs has become subconscious, part of the basic stuff he needs to do to stay alive. He wants to do a flip over and turn, flamboyant like an Olympic swimmer. But it isn't a swimming pool. The edges are ragged and shallow. He treads water and turns, sees Bertrand, wet and sleek, his head like the head of a seal in the water. Then Gavin is off again on the home straight.

He is well over half way when he realises something is wrong. The regular splashing which was following him has stopped. He looks back, and there's no sign of Bertrand. The water is still, lapping softly against the orange reflections. Gavin looks left and right, his heart tight in his chest. Nothing.

Then Bertrand rises up out of the water, terrifying, gasping. He is silhouetted against the far bank, water encasing his body, reflecting silver on black. There is a moment when he looms there, a river monster emerged from the deep, a figure from long-forgotten nightmares. Then he disappears again beneath the surface of the water. There's a rippling, then nothing, as though he was never there. As though someone had thrown in a stone, and the river had swallowed it, accepted it.

Gavin watches frozen in horror. Then he dives. Beneath the water is another world. A world of blackness where light filters through in narrow shafts from above. Gavin cannot see Bertrand, so he feels for him, dragging his arms from side to side against the weight of the water. He swims towards the spot where Bertrand was, five feet, ten, behind him.

They collide as Bertrand comes back up to the surface for the second time. A drowning person, how many times do they surface before they die? He mustn't let him go under again.

They break through together into the freezing air, Gavin holding on to Bertrand. He can feel the weight trying to pull him back under as though Bertrand's body has an agenda of its own, and now that this drowning has begun, nothing must get in its way.

Gavin gets his arms around Bertrand's chest beneath his armpits. His back is towards the shore. He must try to swim backwards pulling the weight of two bodies. It isn't far, but he's cold and tired. There is a private jetty, which he hopes he's heading for. He can't see where he is going.

He doesn't know if Bertrand is conscious. He's certainly not helping.

Eventually they bump into the jetty, and Gavin drags Bertrand out of the water onto the wooden platform. His body is suddenly so heavy that Gavin nearly slides back into the river. But he pulls him, inch by skin-scraping inch, over the edge.

Bertrand lies inert, his skin mottled blue and red, cast over with orange from the nearest street light. There is a string of vomit dangling from his lips. Gavin places his hand in front of his mouth, beneath his nose. There is warmth, faint, intermittent.

But they must have their clothes. They haven't swum in a straight line. They are fifty yards or more from Cleopatra's Needle. To get there Gavin will have to go up to street level, dripping in his underwear. The cold has him in its teeth; if he doesn't move he will be immobilised, useless.

He looks at Bertrand, who shudders and coughs up some water, then falls back into a slump, more dead than alive. He has no choice. He dashes up the wooden steps, over a small white gate, and up the stone steps to the pavement. A car rushes past him, and the noise of its engine is like the lash of a whip. He runs.

As he reaches the Needle another car passes, which slows, and there is shouting from the window before it speeds up again and vanishes into the night. The clothes are still there. Thank god the clothes are still there. Gavin pulls on his trousers and throws his jacket over his shoulders. He grabs the rest, his and Bertrand's, to his chest and returns.

This time no cars pass. Bertrand is still in the same position. Gavin tries to lift him by the shoulders, but it's impossible. He's a dead weight. He needs warmth. He needs medical attention. Gavin drapes the rest of the clothes across Bertrand's body, then searches for the mobile phone in his jacket pocket. Luckily there's still a bit of power left in the battery. He dials 999.

In the dark room, Bertrand is eventually the first one to speak.

"Did you see how young they are?"

Gavin's voice croaks when he tries to answer. Then he coughs and vomits. He tries to move his head to avoid hitting his legs, but he can feel the wet hotness seeping through his trousers, turning instantly cold. The smell is sour and unavoidable.

Bertrand continues.

"When I was in Bosnia, I saw women raped by boys who were barely old enough to hold an erection. They were children with guns. They don't know the difference between war and war games. It's all the same to them."

"How can you tell? Their faces are covered."

"Their eyes. They have fear in their eyes. They think they're making up the rules, but all the time they're worried someone is going to come and tell them off, and wrest the power away from them. They're afraid of us."

"They don't act like they're afraid. I'm afraid."

"You are afraid because you're in their power. They're afraid for the same reason."

They fall silent. Bertrand is talking in riddles that Gavin can't understand and this annoys him. He wants to talk about what they should do, if there is anything they can do, if there is any possible way out of their desperate situation. He knows there isn't. Bertrand's acceptance of their powerlessness infuriates him.

He hears a scrape on the stone floor, the chink of metal against china. Then a soft chewing sound, and the tap of a chain against the side of a bowl. Bertrand is eating his rice and peas.

Chapter Ten

"The boy grew up, much loved by Viamund and his wife, who never had any more children. No one, saving the boy's parents, knew the real circumstances of his birth. Viamund kept the casket containing the documents and rings hidden in a secret place."

Kat is holding Gavin's hand, looking into his face as he speaks. He can feel his voice coming out easily, smoothly, handling the words as though he were used to it. Talking, storytelling. His voice has not been used so much for a long time. Months, even years. He gives her hand a squeeze. It must be something to do with her, this girl with the pale blue eyes and open face, that gives him confidence. He remembers telling stories to Aggie's children and the rapt expression on their faces as they listened. Monsters, ghouls, tales of derring-do. He used to ham it up dreadfully just to make them squeal and giggle.

"When Surcote was a lad, on the verge of manhood, news came that the Emperor of Rome was trying to rebuild his city and his empire, after the devastation caused by a succession of wars. Viamund decided to try his luck, and removed his family and his household to an estate on the outskirts of Rome, from whence he began making himself indispensable to the Emperor."

"I don't like Viamund. He's a sleazeball."

Gavin shrugs and smiles.

"Whatever. But he did well in Rome, and so did Surcote. As the boy grew into manhood, he mixed with the young nobles at the court and trained and studied with them. He excelled in games and sport and soon became a favourite of the emperor."

"Anna would have been proud of him."

"I'm sure she would. Anna knew nothing of the whereabouts of her son. Things had changed back in her country. Her father was no longer in power. Her younger brother had taken over."

"I thought she didn't have any brothers or sisters."

"She did. They were born later, not long before her own baby was born. She had a brother called Arthur, and a sister too."

"So she was the sister of King Arthur?"

"She was."

"And this boy with the silly name, he was King Arthur's nephew."

"Yes. And King Arthur was beginning to get a reputation. News of his exploits had reached even Rome."

"So did Viamund let on?"

"Viamund fell ill. He realised he was going to die, and he didn't want take Surcote's secret with him to the grave."

"He told him?"

"He told the Emperor. He handed the casket into the Emperor's keeping, and asked him to look after this boy, who had royal blood running in his veins. Soon after that he died, and Surcote moved into the palace at Rome and became the charge of the Emperor."

"What about his mum, Viamund's wife? Was she still alive? Didn't she have something to say about it?"

Kat's face is indignant and suddenly Gavin wants to laugh. He wants to laugh and he wants to kiss her. He feels a bubble rising in his chest, a lightness that he hasn't felt for so long he has forgotten. He knows she can see it in his face, because she beams at him and holds his gaze steady with her own, waiting. In a moment, everything could change. He only needs to move closer, pull her gently towards him with a little pressure on her hand, and their relationship would be on a different footing.

He smiles.

"The books don't tell us. Maybe she went with him to the palace."

Not fair. She doesn't know what she'd be getting into. Don't want to mess her about, she's too special.

"So that's two mothers lost by the wayside already, and he's barely grown up. I'm not sure about this story Gavin, he's a bit careless with his womenfolk."

"That's what it was like back then. Use them up, throw them away. Pass them on to your friends."

She punches him on the arm and laughs.

"My turn to get the drinks in," she says.

He wakes from this dream of Kat, his legs twisted in the sheets of the narrow bed. He is covered in a light sweat, the result of the whisky he drank last night with Mel. Not too much whisky, by his standard, though Sheila wasn't impressed. She'd come down at two in the morning, when Mel's laughter had got too loud, and kicked Gavin out, taken her man off to bed with a dark face.

Gavin looks at the back of his hand. It is sore and red, marked with the scabby outline of a five-pointed star, enclosed in a circle. Now that he's awake he can feel it throbbing as the blood courses past the damaged veins. Given enough whisky, Mel had been willing to do it, although he had refused that first day in the studio.

"Sorry, no hands, no faces. Policy I'm afraid."

Gavin had left that time, but he'd returned, every day with the same request, until one day Mel had said, "I'm sure I know you from somewhere."

It was Sheila, coming through from the shop with a cup of tea, who recognised him now that he was clean and shaven.

"Gavin! Oh my god! How wonderful to see you. What happened to you?"

"Nothing yet. I've been trying to persuade this lump of a husband of yours give me a tattoo, but he won't."

Mel closed the shop and got out the whisky bottle. Sheila cooked them up a pot of lentil stew and they reminisced, going back fifteen years, remembering incidents in detail, examining the past with a magnifying glass. Ignoring the years in between.

Occasionally Gavin noticed Sheila looking at him curiously, but he evaded her, ripping into another tale about an exploit, a girl, a tattoo punter, from the distant past.

Around eleven Sheila went to bed. Mel didn't take much persuading after that to get the tattoo needle out.

Gavin rolls out of bed and unwinds the sheet from his body. He walks naked across the room and steps into the shower. The hum of pain in his hand is quite pleasant. He presses the back of his hand against his thigh and it intensifies. The water is scalding hot on the back of his neck. He places his right palm over the back of his left and squeezes. That's more like it. He increases his grip until the pain is almost unbearable. Almost, but not quite. He can't press that hard. He remembers the feel of the needle as Mel injected the ink under his skin. A buzz, an irritation. Not real pain. Real pain is something that breaks you down, unties the knots that make you who you are. The tattoo sort of pain you can bear up under with pride. Real pain dissolves pride instantly.

He rubs soap across his body and thinks of Kat. Kat in his dreams, holding him while he goes on unimaginable journeys. Kat sitting on the ground outside her tent, her pale hair shining, her legs bare and brown in the sun. The soft down that creeps up her thighs leading into darkness. He remembers shamelessly staring trying to get a glimpse of her knickers. Imagining the hot wet warmth. In his dreams, his hand follows his thoughts, and still she fiddles with the stove, heating the water for their coffee. It isn't until he's got two fingers inside her, three, that she turns to him, smiling, bringing her mouth to his.

These are the good nights. Since he left her there have been a few of these interspersed among the nightmares. And yesterday, the email.

Gavin has found a job at the big hotel up near the castle. He is general dogsbody. He empties the rubbish and loads the dishwasher, helps the caretaker with maintenance jobs. When he applied in person, the manageress looked him up and down, obviously thrown by his accent.

"What experience do you have, Mr...?"

"Enough. I'm looking for honest work for the summer that will pay for my board and lodging while I'm here. I'm not after a career in hotel work. I'm not as malleable as a sixteen year old. But I can work hard, and I will do any job you choose to give me, however menial"

It only took her a moment.

"OK. You can start tomorrow at 7.30am."

He has to miss breakfast at the B&B as the landlady isn't up that early, so he has decided to look for a room of his own.

After work yesterday he went to the library to look through the local papers and check his emails. There were several from Aggie with titles like *Worried about you, Please read this, Where are you?* He deleted these without reading them. There was also one from Kat, which he opened.

>>Gavin, I hope you don't mind me emailing you. I met Aggie in Salcombe after you left. She was looking for you (so was I) at the library and she gave me your email address. I'm back in London now. Didn't seem the same down there after you'd gone.

Obviously Aggie has told me some of your history. I understand your need to be alone, I don't want to intrude. I just wanted to let you know that I've never met anyone who made me feel like you did. We were strange together. Kind of like wary animals caged up together, but now I understand why that was. Don't let yourself get trapped. I know you need to work things through, but leave an escape route. You're not on your own – if you want me, I'll be there.

That last night was one of the best of my life, despite the bad start.

Don't feel you have to reply. I just wanted you to know how I feel.

Hope you're OK.

Love, Kat<<

Drying himself in the shower, he rereads the email in his head. He knows it word for word. In the library his finger hovered over the reply button, knowing she'd come if he asked. But he isn't what she deserves. He clenched his hand, squeezed his fingers until the bones cracked.

The sun is shining on the sea as he walks the coast road to the hotel. The fishing boats are still far out on the horizon, but making their way in towards the shore. The smell of salt and the cool early morning air take him back. He is almost carefree. He imagines that Kat is beside him, that they are holding hands.

A car appears suddenly round the corner, at speed. Gavin leaps for the pavement as the car swerves to avoid him. The driver is young, male, angry. He shouts at Gavin from the window.

"Fuckin' idiot. Walk on the pavement you wanker."

He hadn't realised he was walking in the road. He is shaken by the near miss, his heart is racing. But worse was the lad's anger, the way he dealt with the shock by lashing out. Gavin lights a cigarette and walks on with his head down.

At the hotel he is given the job of clearing an outhouse behind the kitchens. The chef wants to use it for storing supplies, but it's full of rubbish: old planks of wood from a refurbishment, boxes of soap past their sell-by date, a broken toilet, empty containers of all shapes and sizes. It's dusty, dirty work.

By lunchtime Gavin has removed everything to a skip. He is hot and his lungs feel as though they're full of fur from the dust he has breathed in. The outhouse is empty, but filthy. There is no window, the daylight comes in through the open door. In one corner there's a spill of oil from a can that has fallen over and leaked. He fetches a broom, some detergent and a scrubbing brush. After he has swept the worst of the dirt out into the yard, he gets down on his hands and knees and starts on the oil spill.

He has just started scrubbing when someone walks past outside, whistling tunelessly. As they pass, they knock the door to the outhouse, which closes with a slam, plunging Gavin into darkness. Instantly he is cold. He sinks into a crouch, his hands over his face. The door fits closely, an overlapping plank on the outside, cutting out all light. The blackness starts to creep in through the gaps in his fingers, in through his eyes and nose and mouth, into his lungs, into his blood stream. He rocks gently back and forth on his heels.

After many hours the blackness becomes less maleficent. It becomes soft, like velvet, hanging in drapes, a black cocoon. Gavin comes to dread the harsh intrusion of light.

He lies on his side, his eyes open, his hands between his thighs palms together. He stares into the blackness because he knows what will happen if he closes his eyes. He is afraid of the images his brain will throw at him. The darkness is his comfort and his friend, but if he allows his eyes to close it will turn against him.

His eyelids ache, his eyes feel as though he's rubbed them with sand. The darkness swirls with spirals of red; he can't tell where his eyes end and the dark begins. The red becomes blood, becomes pain. He can feel the welts, the slight stickiness of his clothes above the damaged skin, a few points where the blood has dried and stuck to the fabric. When he moves his clothes hang heavy from these new scabs. The pain courses through his back, his buttocks. His feet are burning. His chest is heavy as lead with the weight of it.

He no longer knows if his eyes are open or closed. He can hear Bertrand breathing, long ragged breaths, with spaces in between so long Gavin wonders if there is still life in him. They haven't spoken. Gavin can see Bertrand's face, filled with determination not to let them see his pain. A forced blankness, which is only convincing to someone unfamiliar with his features. Like them. They were infuriated, incensed. Bertrand must be in more pain even than Gavin. Gavin is interested to discover how he himself reacts in extreme situations. How short the length of his endurance. He thinks about this as though it were something he'd seen in a film, something removed from himself.

Time loses itself with no markers. Gavin gave up counting a long time ago. He doesn't know how long he's been lying here on his side. His body aches so much he can't move. He's cold. The blood on his clothes has stiffened. His eyes might be open or closed, he can't tell.

He doesn't know if the crack of light is inside his head or out of it. It widens, and suddenly his eyes are wide open, dazzled by the brightness. Blinded by fear. A black boot appears, dark trousers. A figure in silhouette against the glare of light. Gavin sits bolt upright and screams.

Chapter Eleven

The hotel manageress gives him a mug of tea in her office. Gavin is still shaking, has barely spoken a word. She tells him it's three o'clock; he's been shut in the outhouse for two and a half hours.

"Why didn't you shout? Someone would have heard you."

Gavin shakes his head.

" – the dark," his throat is tight and he coughs to let his voice through. "Sometimes in the dark, I forget where I am."

The manageress sits in silence for some minutes considering him. Gavin cradles the mug of tea, lifts it to his lips and lets the hot sweetness flood through his body.

Eventually the manageress speaks.

"You've obviously had a shock. Go home. Have you got friends here?"

Gavin nods.

"Well don't spend this evening on your own. If you feel well enough in the morning, we'll be pleased to see you. You're a valuable worker. But if you have any more phobias or problem areas, I'd be grateful if you'd let us know so we can avoid them."

Gavin gets to his feet.

"Thank you."

"It's OK. Sit here and finish your tea."

Despite the advice he doesn't plan to go to Mel and Sheila's, but he finds himself walking that way. Spend the evening with friends, the manageress said. Well, they're the nearest he's got, and he doesn't have to say anything about what happened.

There are no customers in the tattoo studio. Mel looks at Gavin's hand and tuts. Gavin hasn't had a wash since clearing the outhouse and there is dirt in the pores of his skin, in the folds of the scab, in a black line where the scab meets the inflamed skin. Mel gets out some antiseptic wipes. Holding Gavin's hand with his left, he uses his right to clean away the dirt. He is surprisingly gentle. Gavin watches the big hands, red and green with dragon heads, holding the white cloth which is cool on his skin. He remembers the needle.

"Mel, you missed your vocation."

Mel looks up. "Go on then, what'll that be?"

"You should have been a nurse."

"Funny you should say that. I've considered it before. Sheila too. We even got the college prospectuses and everything. Way back, before we got the shop. But then the premises were available, and we thought we'd give it a shot, and here we still are."

"A loss to the medical profession."

"It's not that different to what I do here. Lads who've had a bit too much to drink, and think a tattoo would be hilarious. We're just a bit earlier on in their evening than A&E."

"Do they get their tattoos?"

"Not if they're drunk. I'll never tattoo anyone who's really pissed."

The shop closes at five. Sheila comes through, and they move up to the kitchen. She empties soup into a pan from cardboard cartons, and puts it to warm on the gas cooker. Mel gets beers from the fridge, butter in a butter dish. Sheila cuts chunks of fresh bread and puts them in a basket in the middle of the table. The room is warm and bright, smells delicious. Gavin fiddles with the beer bottle.

"How's the room hunt going?" Sheila asks.

"It hasn't today. I came here straight from work. I'll get a paper tomorrow. Look in the newsagent windows."

"A friend of mine has a room."

Gavin looks up.

"It's empty. Hasn't been lived in. She has a shop on the front, outdoor gear, that sort of stuff. There's a couple of rooms upstairs. She uses one for stock, but the other is empty. She'd let you have it for next to nothing. But like I say, it's just a bare room. You'd have to share the loo with the shop."

Gavin thinks about the outhouse. Up to when the door slammed, he'd enjoyed clearing it, getting rid of the clutter. He is sorry he didn't get to clear up the oil, finish the job. He's wanted to see it empty, clear, clean.

"It sounds ideal."

"Well, if you're interested, I could take you round to meet her tomorrow afternoon, after you've finished work."

"Thank you."

What came after the door slammed shocks him. He thought things were improving. There are the nightmares, the shaking, the drinking. He knows there are memories he can't explore. Memories his brain won't even let him remember. But he's been coping. Since Kat, he's been coping. He is horrified that his brain can take him over like that.

Sheila places a bowl of soup in front of him and a spoon.

"Are you all right Gavin? You seem quiet."

He straightens his shoulders, pulls in his chair, smiles.

"Just tired. Busy day. Thanks for the soup."

He'd like to tell them what happened. Spend the evening with friends, the manageress told him. Let them know what happened, she meant, let them look after you. But he can't tell them, because there is too much. If he tells them about this afternoon, he'll have to tell them why it happened. Tell them the whole past. Start on that one story and the whole lot will come with it, and he can't do that.

What he needs is someone who already knows.

Kat knows.

Aggie has told her. He wouldn't need to explain anything to Kat. She knows, and she still wants him. She said, in the email *if you want me, I'll be there.*

He washes the soup down with beer. He could do with some whisky, but Mel seems a little fragile after last night, and doesn't offer to get the bottle out. So Gavin suggests they go for one or two in the pub.

Sheila raises her eyebrows, but Mel ignores that and they go.

The whisky warms him and after a while Gavin stops thinking about the outhouse. Or if he thinks about it, it is removed, unimportant. He can put it in the past, imagines that the hotel will do the same. Just a trivial incident. By closing time he feels comfortable, free of thought and emotion.

He walks back with Mel. The studio and the flat are in darkness.

"Can I check my emails on your computer? Just quickly. You have an internet connection don't you?"

He didn't know he was going to ask this.

And the next morning, when he wakes in his room at the bed and breakfast, the morning sunlight making a harsh gold line between the curtains, he isn't sure if what he remembers is what happened or just what he dreams of. He may have let his finger slip, let the mouse click on *reply*. Sent an email, with the name of the hotel, the name of the town. Nothing more. But he wouldn't have done that. Even after the whisky. He just wanted to read the words again, to know that Kat was there, that if he got stuck in a dark place, she would pull him out.

In the hospital waiting room, Gavin tries to sleep, lying across three chairs, his feet still on the floor. There are two stitches in his head, just by his eyebrow, where Mark kicked him. After they took Bertrand, they made him come down to A&E.

"It's not me. I'm OK. It's my friend I'm worried about."

But they took no notice and stitched him anyway.

He didn't tell them the whole truth. In the ambulance their first priority was to get Bertrand warm. He was breathing, just, but suffering from severe hypothermia, the paramedics told him. They wrapped him in woollen blankets, and a silver thermoblanket too. Attached him to a monitor to check his temperature and his heartbeat. Both weak, but definitely still there.

Eventually, as they neared the hospital, they turned to Gavin, sitting huddled in a blanket of his own.

"What were you doing?"

"He was drunk, and wanted to go for a swim. I tried to stop him, but when he jumped in I thought I'd better go in after him."

Why not tell the truth? It was like being at school and getting into trouble with your friends. Trying to shift the blame onto the one who can't defend himself. Gavin opened his mouth to tell them – no actually it was both of us. Both of us were behaving like kids.

But they'd turned back to Bertrand, to the job in hand.

At the hospital they'd rushed him off on a trolley to the emergency ward.

"Wait there," they said to Gavin, "someone will see to you soon."

And now, two hours later, still no word. Gavin is wondering whether to approach the nurse on duty at the desk, or whether to get some sleep, when suddenly Bertrand is there, standing by his feet, accompanied by a little blonde nurse.

Gavin sits up quickly.

"Bertrand! Are you OK?"

"They're letting me go home. In a taxi. I'm to keep warm."

The nurse speaks to Gavin.

"Your friend needs some sleep. I expect you both do. Go home, have a cup of hot chocolate, and go to bed."

Bertrand grins.

"I don't think I've got any hot chocolate. Will whisky do?"

The nurse wags her finger at him, amused.

"No, it won't. I think you've had enough for one night."

"OK matron."

"I'm not a matron."

Gavin watches with amazement. Nearly dead from drowning and cold only two hours ago, and now Bertrand is flirting with the nurse.

"Shall I book a taxi then?"

Bertrand replies without looking at him.

"Nurse...."

"Kimberley."

"Nurse Kimberley has already booked one for us."

She walks them out to the car park, holding on to Bertrand's elbow, although Gavin is sure he can walk without support, and holds the door open while Bertrand climbs in.

"No more skinny dipping, now," she says.

"Oh, it wasn't skinny dipping," Bertrand replies, "I kept my pants on."

She grins and slams the door closed.

"Cute," says Bertrand.

Bertrand's flat is in Holborn, three floors up above a row of shops. It is has polished wooden floors and a view from the lounge window that includes St. Paul's. First thing he does when they get in is get the whisky out. It's a sixteen-year-old malt. He pours two hefty measures into cut-glass tumblers and hands one to Gavin.

The room has a black leather sofa, drinks cabinet, some racks of CDs and a high-tech music system, a flat screen TV, and an almost empty desk. On the desk, a phone is flashing. Bertrand tells Gavin to make himself comfortable, then presses the button to listen to his messages.

The first is a woman's voice.

"Hey babes, where are you? I spoke to Gerry today, and he says he can get you some work on the New York Times. Safe work, in the US. Some demos or something – no war zones. Are you listening? I said, no war zones. I know you're up to something, and I don't like it. Remember, we agreed. You've done your time. Please, can we have a safe life for a while? I love you. I don't want to lose you in some pointless accident in somebody else's war. Call me. Gerry says he can meet us for lunch tomorrow."

Bertrand presses the delete button. The second message is a man.

"Hi Bertrand, got your call. Can do. Meet me tomorrow, twelve o'clock, my office."

He presses the button again. *Message deleted. No more messages.*

"That was the guy who can get us the equipment. You can come with me."

He doesn't mention the first message.

Someone is calling Gavin's name. He looks down from where he's perched on the top of a stepladder.

"Hello Gavin."

It's Kat.

"The woman at the desk said it would be all right if I came up. She said you're nearly finished."

She's wearing dark blue mascara and she's got a new stud in her face just to the right of her nose. It looks like a beauty spot and he feels immediately excited by it. He wants to greet her calmly and affectionately.

He places the paintbrush carefully down on the top of the paint can, which is sitting on the flat bit at the top of the ladder, and climbs down the steps. He stands in front of her.

She whispers, "Are you pleased?

He steps forwards and gathers her in his arms, smearing the denim of her jacket with wet paint from his hands as he squeezes her hard as he can.

"You bet."

Chapter Twelve

There were no curtains at the window to keep out the morning, so the light just came in, starting early because it was the summer. It didn't wake us because we weren't asleep. I could hear the sea down on the beach, crashing in wave after wave. It was a gentle sound, soothing, sexy. I could hear my heart beating as the blood rushed through my ears, fast from exertion. I could feel his heart pounding too, against my chest, *boom boom boom*, with the susurrations of the sea behind it.

The first light was grey, picking out shapes but no details. There weren't many shapes in this room. My bag, a few bits and pieces of Gavin's, a heap of our clothes on the floor. The shapes of us.

Gavin, his body spent, his head dropped forward onto my shoulder, so the nearest silhouette marked out by the light from the window was his neck and the back of his head. His hair was cut short, shaped into the indented curve where the skull meets the top of the spine. A man's haircut, soldier's, skinhead's, so short as to suggest aggression. The skin there is soft as milk. I touched it, and he rolled an inch on his forehead, smiled at me.

We'd barely stopped touching since he came down from that ladder at the hotel in his white overalls and nearly crushed me. After all those days spent in Devon, circling each other, never coming up close, it was as though the barriers had melted away. Walking through the hotel, through the streets, we held on to each other tight, stopping every so often to kiss. He licked my new stud from the outside and the inside. I'd only had it for a week and it was still quite sore, but I liked the feeling of the bar moving inside my flesh.

We went to meet Sheila, the woman helping him to find a room, and she brought us here, to this bare room with its window looking out onto the sea. The landlady didn't seem fazed by the sudden doubling of the number of tenants. She said we could move in straight away. She'd swept and cleaned the room earlier, and it was just bare. Bare whitewashed walls and a bare wooden floor.

Sheila said she'd got a spare mattress in the attic if we wanted it.

So, after a trip to Gavin's B&B to get his belongings and pay his bill, we went to Merlin's Cave and Tattoo Studio and Gavin introduced me to his friend Mel, a big tattooed man with a greasy ponytail and a friendly smile, who looked even bigger next to Sheila, his wife, who can't have been much over five foot. She was wearing a long green tiered skirt in a soft shiny fabric with a darker green tunic and an amethyst necklace. She wore flat black shoes, and her brown hair was long, unstyled, streaked with grey. She looked like a hippy witch gone to seed. Mel looked like an overgrown biker.

Sheila had eyes like a bird though. She kept giving Gavin sidelong glances when she thought he wasn't looking, and she stared at me as though I was planning to raid her nest. I wondered if she had the hots for him herself – she seemed like another generation, but she was probably only ten years older. But when I saw her with Mel, I realised that wasn't true. There was a tenderness between them – a surreptitious touch of hands when they passed each other, a hand draped momentarily across a shoulder, moments of eye contact a second too long – which showed real long-standing love. Besides, the looks she gave Gavin were anxious looks.

She cornered me in the kitchen at their flat while Gavin and Mel were shifting the mattress out of the attic.

"What's the matter with Gavin?"

"What do you mean?"

"You know what I mean. He's changed. Not just his age, more than that. His confidence, the way he looks at people. His reactions are really jumpy."

"I'm not sure ..."

I tailed away. His secrets weren't mine to give. If he'd wanted to tell his friends anything he could have done so.

Sheila leaned back against the counter and surveyed my face. She wasn't hostile, but I felt there was some sort of judgement being made.

"Look honey, I'm not asking you to be disloyal. I know it's not your fault."

I thought she did think it was my fault.

"I read auras. It's a gift I have. Yours is clear, honey, I know you're OK. But Gavin's isn't. Gavin has something in his aura so black it scares me. It's eating away at him. It wasn't there – not when we knew him before. He had a lovely aura then. Blue and sparkling, crystal clear. But that's all being poisoned by this blackness, and it needs to go. I know something about cleansing auras, but I need to know what put it there. He can't do it on his own, and you keeping quiet won't help him. If you love him you need to do something."

I stared at her and she held my gaze. I'd met enough people like her before, hippy dippy and well-meaning, and although they didn't bother me I never took what they said very seriously. But she'd hit the nail on the head with Gavin. Something was eating away at him. His memories, and something else too. Guilt? Shame? I didn't believe Sheila could help him by performing some esoteric ritual, but it can't hurt to have your friends rooting for you.

I was the first to look away. I looked at my hands, flicked my nails against each other.

"I don't know what happened – exactly. No one does. But it was in the papers, right back at the beginning of the year. Check them out on the internet. It will give you the background."

She gave me a small smile.

"Thank you."

"I didn't know him then." I scraped at the dirt under my thumbnail, not looking at her. "I only met him in May. But I'd say, although I know nothing about it, that his aura's salvageable."

"I'm sure it is." Her voice was sharp. "But not if it's left to itself."

She reminded me of Aggie, and suddenly I liked her. I wondered if Gavin knew how worried she was about him. Probably not.

There was the sound of something heavy sliding on the stairs and the men's voices as they manoeuvred the end of the mattress around the landing.

"If you're sticking around for the summer and you need a job, I could do with a hand in the shop."

I looked at Sheila in surprise.

"You don't have to give me an answer now. Think about it." And she smiled.

Gavin traced the outline of my lips with a lazy finger. I could smell the whisky in his breath, the cumin and salt tang of sweat on his skin. I ran my hand down his back, feeling the smooth skin between the ridges of scar tissue. He still covered his wrists – though he had replaced the dirty black rags with red sweatbands. He kept them on, even in bed. I wasn't going to mention any of this. If he wanted to talk, that was up to him.

He said, "I'm glad you came."

I laughed and kissed him on the lips.

"So am I. Thank you."

He poked me in the ribs and rolled over on top of me, peering down into my face in the grey light.

"That's not what I meant, you dirty bitch."

We kissed then, a desperate, needful kiss, wrapping our arms around each other, and pressing our bodies hard together. I wound my legs round behind his and pulled him closer. I could feel his teeth against my gums, the hard back of my stud scraping above my teeth, and I pressed my hand hard on the back of his head. My tongue ached, but I wanted more. I wanted to go deeper.

When he lifted his head the room had grown lighter, and the sky outside the window was stippled with tiny silver clouds like fishes. His face was still close enough for our noses to touch. His eyes were shadowed and dark in the hollows beneath his brows.

"Carry on with the story." I said.

"About Sir... Surcote?"

"Yes."

He rolled onto his side, by my side, one arm still behind my head, the other across my breasts. I tightened my grip of him with my thighs.

"Where had we got to?"

"His dad had died and he was with the Emperor of Rome, being trained as a knight."

"Oh yes. He did very well there you know."

"You said."

"He impressed everyone. Started winning contests and tournaments. Outstripped all his contemporaries, so they had to start pitting him against the older fighters, the experienced knights. And that way he learned fast. Learned lots of tricks from the old dogs, picked away at their experience, learning, second-hand, all the knowledge they had spent lifetimes gathering. He was quick, could put techniques together, assimilate. He became the best knight in the court at Rome."

I put my hand between his thighs where the flesh was hot.

"Sounds too good to be true."

"Oh, he was a sound knight and true. One of the best in history. It's not for nothing that his fame has lasted through the centuries."

"How come I've never heard of him then?

He kissed me on the nose and thrust his hips towards me so the end of his cock bumped against my stomach.

"Impatience! You have heard of him. You know Surcote wasn't his real name."

"Ok." I lay my head on his shoulder. "Ok, I'm listening."

"There was a big tournament, to which knights came from far and wide to test their prowess. Chariot races, one-to-one combat, duels. The idea was to find the best knight of all. Some of the knights were young and untested, others returning to show their strength after trials abroad. Surcote outmatched everyone and at the end of the Trials was named as the finest knight at the Imperial Court. The Emperor gave him a tunic of crimson silk, which Surcote declared he would wear with pride for the rest of his days. He also asked a favour of the Emperor."

"What favour was that?"

I ran my fingernail in a line from under his balls right to the end of his cock.

"He asked that he would be allowed to undertake the next trial of single combat against an enemy of the Emperor."

"And?"

I licked my finger and followed the same line again.

"Well, war broke out between the Persians and the Christians, and the leaders of the two empires decided that, rather than risking the lives of many, the matter should be settled by single combat between champions from each side. The Emperor was in discussions with his heads of state when Surcote burst into the chambers to remind him of his promise."

He was glistening. I slid down the bed and followed the trail my finger had made with my tongue. For a few moments he didn't speak and I could hear his breathing.

Then he continued. "The Emperor was reluctant to rest such responsibility on the shoulders of one so young, but he was a man of his word, and eventually agreed."

"Surcote set off across the seas to the Holy Land with an escort of one hundred men under the command of a centurion. But the gods were not with them on that voyage.

I looked up at him. "Gods? I thought they were Christians."

Gavin raised his eyebrows. "Whatever."

I slid the length of him into my mouth and out again.

"The sea was rough and they were tossed about like driftwood in the waves. Twenty five days they were lurching and listing, Surcote throwing up over the sides of the boat because, bold knight as he was, he had no stomach for the sea."

"Did his men all drown?"

"A storm blew up."

"But ..."

"A worse storm. And they were blown off course and forced to land on an island. The men lay about on the beach like sodden scraps of seaweed, retching and groaning as the winds tossed the ship at anchor in the bay. The night was dark and cold, and as he lay there listening to the trees of the forest behind, bending and creaking under the force of the storm, Surcote underwent terrors of the mind that far outstripped any physical trials. More than once he woke from fevered sleep with a scream on his lips."

By now the sky outside was bright and the square of the window was an entrance through which the daylight streamed, filling the white room and connecting it to the outside world. Our closeted cell of the night hours was gone for the time being. I watched Gavin as he spoke. The morning had swallowed the shadows, brought colour to his skin. His naked shoulders were brown and glowing; his face mobile and warm. I looked at his Adam's apple moving in his throat, his green eyes, his teeth glinting white as his lips formed the words of the story. I held my breath, watching his face for a flicker, any sign of danger. But he slid carefully on, past the night of darkness and nightmares, into the coming of morning.

"Daylight came, and with it Surcote's courage returned. The storm had abated and the early sunshine was warm and revivifying. The men needed food, so he gathered them into hunting parties and they set off into the forest to look for game."

I smiled at him, and for a moment he stopped, his gaze held by mine, his mouth stilled. His eyes returned the smile. I covered the back of his hand with mine, pressing on his new tattoo, and licked his cock again. He looked at me silently and then continued.

"Unbeknownst to them..."

"Uh oh!"

"Unbeknownst to them, the island was ruled by a cruel and powerful lord called Milocrates, an enemy of the Emperor of Rome, who had some months previously kidnapped the Emperor's niece and was holding her captive in his castle on the island. As Surcote and his men were busy bringing down their seventh stag in the forest, Milocrates' men burst upon them and demanded explanation of this theft.

I rested my head on the top of his thigh and watched him talking.

"Surcote explained that they were only taking enough to keep them alive, but the men were not satisfied and a fight ensued, during which all of Milocrates men were either killed or put to flight."

"There's going to be trouble!"

"You could be right. The men returned to their ship to find it had been damaged by the storm. It could be repaired, but it would take at least twenty-four hours. Surcote knew this was time they didn't have. When Milocrates' men returned to the castle with news of their skirmish, an army would be sent after them. It was decided that spies should go inland to assess the situation. Surcote volunteered to go, along with the centurion's brother."

"The excitement's getting a bit much. I think I need to go and pee."

Gavin grinned at me.

"Go on then. I'll make some coffee. Do you fancy some?"

"Yes please."

His cock was hard and knocking against my face. I put it in my mouth, slid up and down a few times, then looked up again.

"On the other hand it would be a shame to waste this.

"But you want to pee."

"It can wait. Might give it an edge."

Gavin pulled me up the bed so that my face was above his and held me there.

"You," he pushed himself into me, " are a bit of a wild-cat. I can see I'm going to have to take you in hand."

Chapter Thirteen

She is sitting cross-legged in the middle of the bed, a sheet wrapped around her naked body, holding the mug of coffee in two hands. Daylight is filling the room and she is bathed in brightness. Her hair shines, with a pale glow reminiscent of the moon's reflected light. She looks at him, then down at her coffee, hiding her huge pale eyes with translucent eyelids.

Everything seems to be slowed down, every tiny movement to carry a weight of meaning. He looks at her eyelashes, long, curled, still tinged blue with yesterday's mascara. They seem to caress her cheeks, and also to be flirting with him. There is an answering tug at the corners of her mouth, almost bending her lips into a smile, but she is resisting it, just as she is hiding her eyes. She lifts the mug to her lips and the sheet slides off her shoulders; she grips it to her sides with her elbows to stop it falling further. The coffee is black and very hot. She sips but lets in barely a drop. Still her eyelids are covering her eyes, her lashes dampening in the steam from the coffee. It has been a couple of seconds, but to Gavin, for whom a memory is being made, it seems much longer.

He feels as though they were at the bottom of a deep pool, and when she tosses back her head and opens her eyes wide at him, he almost expects to see her hair lift, undulating like weed in the water.

"Sheila's offered me a job."

Her voice is clear and strong. She's not in the same dream world as him. He makes an effort to break to the surface.

"Has she?"

"Yes, in the shop. For the summer. If I want it."

"And do you want it?"

She leans back, forgetting all about the sheet, which drops, puts the coffee mug on the floor beside the mattress and, in the same smooth movement, lies back. Her knees are bent up, one crooked over the other, so that her foot is waving in the air.

"I don't know. I think so. It depends if you want me around for the rest of the summer."

He's living in one part of his mind at the moment. He knows there are other voices shouting to be heard, but he's turned the volume down on them, he's not listening. More than anything he wants Kat to stay, and that's the only part he's paying attention to.

He lies next to her on the bed, on his front, supported by his elbows, looking into her face.

"I'd love you to stay."

She kisses the end of his nose.

"OK. I'll tell Sheila."

Her lips are pink and shining with moisture. He follows the shape of them with his eyes and, conscious of his gaze, her tongue darts out and back, like a lizard on a stone. He quickly lowers his head, covering her mouth with his own, his tongue following hers inside. She latches on to him with her body, arms and legs clutching him tight, and they roll, mouths clamped together, until she is on the top and she lifts her head an inch, her hair hanging around their faces like a curtain of sea grass.

"Are you going to carry on with the story?"

"I have to go to work."

"I won't let you go. Five minutes."

"I'll be late."

"I want to know what happened to the Emperor's niece."

"OK. But it will have to be the edited version."

"Go on then – edit."

Her lips are centimetres away from his own, he can feel her breath. His breath is her breath exhaled, and hers his.

"Surcote managed to get into the city. There was a great army being raised against them as the men from the forest had exaggerated their size."

"Men like to do that."

Coffee scented breath, and a sweetness the same as the taste of her skin.

"But Surcote was not satisfied with information, he decided to rescue the princess. He entered the castle, hidden among the men that were arriving to prepare for battle. He found his way to the lord's chambers where the princess was being held. There he found a man he knew, Narboar, from the palace at Rome, who had been captured along with the princess. Narboar escorted Surcote and his companion into the princess's presence."

"Was she beautiful?"

"Princesses are always beautiful."

"What did she think of Surcote?"

"She had seen Surcote before at her uncle's palace. She knew of his great prowess."

"She must have been excited."

"I'm sure she was. She told Surcote that Milocrates, the evil lord, had a special suit of armour and a sword that he always wore in battle. The story went that if anyone else were to wear that armour and carry that sword, then Milocrates would die at their hand."

"Did she show him where it was?"

"She did. Surcote took the armour and the sword, and the princess agreed to open the city gates at the opportune moment to let the Romans in. They decided to attack the city rather than wait for battle at sea, where their disadvantage in numbers would be obvious."

Kat has her elbows on the bed by his ears. She lowers her head and starts to kiss his neck, softly, her lips barely touching his skin. He can feel the tiny hairs rising to meet her breath, shivers like lines of mercury running down his shoulder bones.

"Carry on."

"Well, everything went to plan." Her tongue is tracing the edges of his ears, hardly touching, leaving the thinnest trail of saliva. "The princess opened the city gates, and the Romans set fire to the city. Milocrates discovered the theft of his armour and was filled with great doubt and despair. When he met with Surcote on the battlefield he knew his worst fears were about to be realised. He lashed out at Surcote, wounding him on the forehead, but the young knight was undaunted. As the blood trickled into his eyes, he struck out in anger," Gavin swallows hard, " and severed Milocrates' head from his shoulders."

"That told him then."

He stops speaking. Kat is lying across him, her head resting next to his on the mattress, blocking the light from the window. He can feel the panic rising. The weight of her is pinning him to the bed, her skin hot against his skin, her breath damp in his neck. There is the familiar tightening of the chest, the curdling of acid in his stomach. He closes his eyes and breathes. In slowly, out slowly. He doesn't want to spoil this moment.

He opens his eyes again and shifts beneath her, rolls gently over so they are lying side by side.

"Sorry, dead leg," he says. He kisses her softly on the lips before standing up. He gathers his clothes and begins to put them on.

"You're not going to leave it there?"

"I have to go to work." He wonders if she can hear the panic strangling his voice, and makes an effort to relax his limbs and his face, makes himself smile. "Anyway, best to leave you wanting more."

At work he can feel that his heartbeat is still too fast, too irregular. He is unwilling to let his thoughts roam free. He would like to think about the previous night, relive it, relish it. But there it is, that last moment with everything threatening to crash back in on him. He has to hold it back. If he can resist memory for long enough, maybe the bad memories will recede.

Maybe he can learn to live with the past. Maybe he can have some sort of normal life with Kat.

There is still half of the ceiling to paint. He is painting white on top of white. The old paint isn't dirty. There's no grime to speak of, it's just lost its brightness. As the new coat goes on, he can see the difference, can see, which he didn't really at first, that a new coat of paint was needed. He watches the wet shining new paint eating up the space, covering over the old white. The part he did yesterday has dried, but still holds the new gleam. That end of the corridor looks brighter than the other. He concentrates on the paint on his brush, the thick half-solid mass of the paint in the can, the bristle-shaped indentation on the surface of the paint, which quickly closes over. He prefers using the brush to the roller, although the roller is useful for getting the area covered. He feels more in control of the brush. When he uses the roller, looking up at the ceiling, he gets a fine white spray on his face.

A drip runs down the handle of the brush from the bristles and he wipes it off with his hand. The paint is sticky in his palm. He closes his hand into a fist and opens it out again. The paint has spread into the fine lines of his hand, but missed the deeper creases, making a veined white blotch in the middle of his hand. The flesh coloured lines showing against the white look indecent and vulnerable, like lips showing through a mask. He wipes his hand on his overalls, removing most of the paint, smudging the mark on his hand into uniformity.

He remembers their first night near the Turkish border, arriving in the dark after their long drive down from the capital. A black moonless, starless night. Bertrand's friend 'Fred' greeting them on the outskirts of the village, his friendship tainted with wariness.

The two of them had been friends and colleagues. They had worked together in Afghanistan, Fred the reporter and Bertrand the photographer. Now Fred has turned his back on writing, and everything that went with that way of life. On the drive down Bertrand told Gavin he didn't believe Fred could keep it up. That the pull of journalism was too great.

"He's a fucking good writer. And if he wanted to get away from it all and have an easy life, why live so close to the Iraqi border?"

But Gavin isn't so sure. He senses an uneasiness. Because of their shared past, Fred can't turn Bertrand away, but this is an intrusion into the fragile security he's making for himself. Although Gavin has never met him before, he senses that something fundamental has changed, that Fred is no longer the risk-taking adventurer that Bertrand described on the journey. Fred knows that he has to help Bertrand, but also he knows there could be a cost for himself.

They leave the car parked near an abandoned farm, hidden from the road. Later, Fred will come and claim it, when they have moved on to the next leg of the journey. They follow Fred, his shape barely distinguishable from the covering darkness, through the fields to his house – a low flat building of two rooms. There he reheats potato soup on a kerosene stove, steams rice, and they eat hungrily from bowls, sitting cross-legged on the floor.

Bertrand seems at ease. He chats to Fred about old times, past adventures, laughing out loud at near misses, uncontrollably at the memory of a time when they were captured, although only for two hours. Gavin watches. Fred is laughing too, but Gavin can see his laughter is forced. He wonders if Bertrand can see it. And if so, why he is so insensitive as to continue a conversation that Fred is obviously not enjoying. Bertrand is laughing so much that tears are running down his face.

Gavin goes outside to look at the darkness.

He finishes with the brush for the time being. Back to the roller. He climbs down from the stepladder and pours paint from the can into the paint tray. The paint is thicker than treacle. It pours slow and wide. He has to jerk the can up sharp to stop too much falling out. Slow to pour and slow to stop, the receding paint leaves a thick white veil on the outside of the can. He uses the roller to remove it, and then climbs back up the ladder, tray in hand.

He didn't mind darkness then. That night he enjoyed it. Better than the tension inside the house. Better than Bertrand's lack of awareness. He didn't go far, just a couple of hundred yards. Far enough for the voices inside the house not to reach him. It was warm, and the black night was comforting, holding him secure within itself, like a fly in amber.

Two nights later they are in the back of a truck loaded up with crates of tinned food. They are boxed into a space at the bottom of the pile. The journey is uncomfortable in the extreme. Some of the roads are uneven, and it seems as though the crates could cave in on them. It is so dark that Gavin can barely imagine the tips of his fingers when he holds his hand in front of his face. But even so, he has no fear. This is excitement. It's dangerous and the danger runs with the blood in Gavin's veins and thrills him.

The hand holding the roller has started to tremble. Gavin puts the roller down in the paint tray and lowers his arm, gives it a shake to get the blood flowing back. But the trembling doesn't stop, it gets worse, moving up through his arm and into his shoulder and neck. He climbs down from the ladder and lays the paint tray on the floor. He sits down next to it and hugs his knees to his chest, trying to squeeze the trembling into stillness. Then his whole body is shaking and he can feel wetness on his cheeks.

It isn't the darkness causing it. Those memories are safe to explore. It's the moment earlier when he nearly lost it in front of Kat, when the story he was telling got too close. He wants to go there, to probe, to assess the danger level. But his mind won't let him. Repels him like a negative magnet. He has no control. However much he wants the future to work, he is powerless against the past, which could creep in unexpectedly and fuck it up at any time.

Chapter Fourteen

"Who knows how long this time together will last. I love you. I think we should make the most of the time that we have."

Gavin's voice trailed away, leaving the tinkle of cups and saucers. We were in a café on the high street, sharing a pot of tea. We'd both just finished work for the day. My head was reeling.

I leaned over the table and grabbed his hand with both of mine, pulled it to my lips and kissed his palm. His skin smelled of turps and there were tiny traces of white paint. I kissed it again and ran the tip of my tongue along the heart line. He smiled at me, and I rested our hands back on the table.

"I love you, too." His smile broadened. " But why the doom and gloom? You sound as though you expect it to be over any minute."

He sighed and withdrew his hand. "You know. Things could go any way."

"Didn't you hear what we just said? Love, the big L-word. It means you stick by people. If shit happens we work through it together."

"I'd like to go for a walk with you on a moonless night."

"Moonless?"

"Yes. No moon. No stars. Just dark, you and me, and the moors."

"Haven't we gone off the subject a bit?"

"No. It's what I'm talking about. We should do the things we really want to do. Live on the edge. Make the time we have really special."

I grabbed his other hand just as he reached for the teapot.

"Hey sweetie, as far as I'm concerned we can live on the edge for the rest of our lives."

He started rubbing the palm of my hand with his thumb, a deep groove that linked straight to my groin.

"Does that mean you'll come to the moors with me next new moon?"

"Yes."

His eyes were looking straight into mine, and he was laughing.

"Shall we leave now and go back to our room?"

"Yes please."

Outside he grabbed my hand and pulled me down an alleyway between the café and the next shop. He pressed me up against the wall and we kissed. I pressed my mouth hard against his mouth, my body hard against his body. I could feel his cock against my hip. I slid my hand down into his trousers, and grabbed hold of it. Then he was fumbling with my skirt, pulling it out of the way, and suddenly he was inside me, and the world stopped.

I whispered into his ear, "We can't, someone might come."

He whispered back, "If you're lucky it might be you."

The next new moon was two weeks away. We spent those weeks working, walking, fucking, talking. Two of the best weeks of my life. Some evenings we went round to Mel and Sheila's and ate in their kitchen. Some nights we went to the pub, with or without them. But always we ended up back in our room, naked, bodies entwined, rolling and screwing until we hardly knew what part belonged to who.

One night, lying on my back on the bed, soaked through and heavy with post-coital bliss, Gavin reached over and put a lit cigarette between my lips. I lifted both my arms. With one hand I took the cigarette, and with the other I grabbed Gavin's wrist. Still without thinking, I pulled at the red sweatband with my fingers, revealing the hidden scar. The room became charged with silence, waiting. Gavin and I looked at each other. Without blinking, or taking my eyes from his, I brought his wrist to my mouth and kissed it. His face didn't show anything. I licked the scar, following its line with my tongue until his wrist wouldn't bend anymore. The scar completely encircled the wrist. I kissed it again and looked at him.

Eventually he spoke.

"It's a rope burn. My wrists were tied behind my back. They'd taken away the handcuffs and tied me with rope as a punishment. It was rough rope and they tied it tight. They pissed on me too, where my hands were tied, to make the rope burn worse."

It was like someone had dropped a stone on my chest. I was flattened. I had no idea. No idea what he'd been through, nor any idea how to help. I kissed his wrist again.

"I love you," was all I could think of to say.

We took the bus to Camelford in the morning and walked out of town and on to Bodmin Moor. We had sleeping bags and food, but not the tent.

It was the first time we'd been for a proper walk together. Before, in Devon, when I went walking he stayed in the pub. He was good to walk with. Our strides pretty much matched, and he didn't chatter. That suited me. We walked hand in hand, and light rain spattered our faces. We walked like that for an hour or two, by which time we were right out onto the moor.

The first part was along a rough track leading to a couple of remote cottages. Then a gate took us onto open fields grazed by sheep. The grass was cropped short, and the hillside strewn with grey stones and boulders. The sky was a lighter shade of the same grey. The path snaked across, brown and sharp and well worn. We walked faster here. It was easier underfoot than the pot-holed track. Halfway across the first field was a wet boggy patch set with stepping-stones. The mud wasn't very soft, as the weather had been mostly dry. We jumped from one to the next laughing and shouting to each other.

There were quite a few people about and, as the day wore into afternoon and the sky cleared to sunshine, there were even more. The fields gave way to open moorland, and the boulders were bigger. In some places there were standing stones. We didn't go up close to any because they were surrounded by groups of people with cameras. We stopped to eat near Rough Tor, sitting on a pile of boulders off to the side of the track. We sat on the far side from the path, where we couldn't be seen.

The stone I sat on was warm from the sun. I munched on bread and houmous and looked about me. Blue sky, moorland stretching in every direction, groups of white sheep here and there, and the bright squares of people's t-shirts, pink, red or blue, as they walked along the path in small groups. Sounds drifted through the air: voices calling to each other, laughter, the bleating of sheep. They were there, but separate from us. Sitting on these rocks, where we couldn't be seen, we had our little private world in the midst of them.

Gavin was sitting on a big rock, his knees bent up in front. He was wearing a black t-shirt, black jeans and DMs. His hair was cut short and close, and his neck and arms were quite brown. He had the red sweatbands on his wrists, and the tattoo on the back of his hand had healed. The black pentacle looked significant and vaguely menacing. Looking at him I felt that familiar melting and opening from the stomach down. I wondered how hidden we were from the road. He felt my gaze, turned and grinned.

"Gavin, can I ask you something?"

"Anything."

I couldn't ask him anything. There were huge areas that were out of bounds. I heard my voice as though it were someone else's, wondering why now, why risk spoiling such a perfect moment.

"That night, at the party, why did you attack me in the barn?"

Gavin was about to bite into an apple, but he stopped and looked at it and then rubbed it on his thigh, polishing the skin. He looked at me, and I could see fear as well as concern in his eyes.

"Kat, I can't tell you how...."

"You're sorry? I know."

He stared at the apple in his hand.

"Sometimes," he said, blinking, "in the dark, something happens and I don't know where I am. It's like I'm back there. I really am. My mind can't tell the difference between memory and reality. It happens in enclosed spaces in the dark."

The tent. The van. He wouldn't sleep in either, preferring to sleep out in the open.

"The emotions I felt back then, I get them and they're just as strong. Sometimes it's fear, paralysing fear. That's what I felt at first when they captured us. But later I felt anger, and that night in the barn, I was angry."

"With them?"

"Yes, with them. With myself. The situation. Just angry. And I was back there, in that place, and when you walked in you were part of it, except that some part of me recognised you and knew that I wanted you. Which is why ..."

He stopped and shook his head.

"It's no excuse. Sorry isn't an adequate word, but I truly am."

I moved over and sat next to him on the rock. I held the hand that wasn't holding the apple.

"I know."

We kissed, a slow soft sweet kiss that left my lips wet.

"Aggie says you have post-traumatic stress disorder. She thinks you need treatment."

His eyes held for a moment, then he looked down.

"Yes, I know she does. She's probably right. She usually is."

"Then...?"

"She brought a doctor, a psychiatrist, round to the flat once, and I hated him. He seemed so smug and comfortable. The distance between him and his easy life and where I had been was so great, I couldn't see a meeting point."

"Maybe you're not ready."

"Maybe."

He bit hard into his apple. I watched him as he chewed and bit again, demolishing the apple in seconds.

"When you feel ready, find someone yourself, someone you're comfortable with."

He half nodded, and I suddenly felt awkward in this role of advisor. I didn't want to be a patient and concerned friend. Self-appointed fount of wisdom. I knew how much Aggie irritated him. And then there was Sheila.

"Sheila wants to cleanse your aura," I said, shifting the role away from myself.

"Does she?" His voice was dry. He lifted his arm and lobbed the apple core out far onto the moor. It startled a sheep, and we both laughed.

"I personally prefer your method of treating me."

He looked straight at me and I grinned.

"What might that be then?"

He pulled me to him, hard against his chest and put his lips right next to my ear.

"Shagging me senseless," he said, and his breath was hot and wet against my skin.

The highest point on Bodmin Moor, and in the whole of Cornwall, is Brown Willy, about five miles from Camelford. We climbed it after lunch and stood on the top looking at the moors rolling in all directions under a blue sky. We were on top of the world. We stood holding hands for twenty minutes and didn't speak.

Afterwards we walked down to Jamaica Inn, the famous smugglers' pub. We stopped there and ate, hungry after the fresh air and exercise. When we'd finished our food we went and sat in the bar for a beer. I watched Gavin buying the drinks, and I thought how different it was from those days back in May, when I'd come into the pub invigorated by my walk and find him sinking. He'd come a long way since then. Now he was generally clean, shaven, and although he still drank a lot, it no longer seemed that whisky ran in his veins. He made a joke with the landlord and they both laughed. He didn't look like a man suffering from a mental condition, he looked healthy and strong. Aggie might be right: he probably did need some professional help in dealing with his memories. But I felt that I was right too. The mind, as well as the body, instinctively knows what it needs, and if you let it, it will help to heal itself.

Tonight in the moonless dark he would be facing his fears, and he'd asked me to come with him. When he sat down next to me with the beer, I leaned against him and bit his ear. His skin smelled of fresh air and cigarettes.

On the other side of the A30, where the Moor stretches southwards, is Dozmary Pool. Legend has it that this is the lake where King Arthur pulled Excalibur from the stone. As we walked the lane that runs alongside it, the sun was setting and the lake reflected it in sheets of gold. We met a few other walkers, returning to their cars. But as it got darker, and we left the lane to strike out onto the moors, there was no one.

The spot where we stopped was on the side of a tor, sloping up to a pile of rocks at the top. This hill blocked from us the sight and sound of the main road, which was only a couple of miles away. We could see the pool. As the sun vanished beneath the horizon and its afterglow began to fade from the sky, the pool changed its sheen from gold to pink to silver, then to inky black. When finally darkness dropped all around us like a cloak, the pool was no longer visible, but I was aware of its presence.

I was surprised by the dark. The moon disappears like this every twenty-eight days, and I thought I would have been familiar with the lack of its light. My eyes did adjust, but even so, in this open and unfamiliar landscape, I had no real idea what any of the dark shapes could be. Gavin and I sat next to each other on a rock, our thighs touching, and I was glad of his presence. The noises of the night would have freaked me if I was on my own. We held hands, and every time something squawked or rustled he squeezed my hand, and I knew that in the darkness he was smiling.

I can't remember exactly what we talked about that night. Not about why we were there, I know that much. Or about the recent past. I think we talked about our childhoods, schools, about books we'd read, music we liked. Getting to know each other chitchat. Nothing tricky.

Eventually I got cold and wriggled into my sleeping bag. The warmth made me sleepy, and I snuggled down next to Gavin, my head against his leg. I couldn't exactly see him in the darkness, only his shape where he sat, as upright and still as one of the stones out there in the moorland. Far off I could hear sheep bleating and then a soft plash of something at the edge of the pool. I could hear Gavin breathing, steady and slow, and high above, the occasional shriek of an owl. I wondered if Gavin would stay awake all night, or if I would. Then I fell asleep.

Chapter Fifteen

They are brought in blindfolded, as always, a guard on either side holding their upper arms and dragging them along. Gavin can smell fear on his own skin. This happens, not every day, but often enough that he can barely notice the days between; beatings, half-naked, tied at the hands and feet, helpless, while these black-clad young men shout, punctuating their voices with the fall of the whip. Unable to communicate through language, Gavin has learned to count the lashes. They are in sets of twenty-eight. On a good day it will be one set, the worst yet was five for him, seven for Bertrand. Gavin knows that by the tenth lash he will be sobbing, pleading for them to stop, as the whip reopens his wounds. This is what he fears the most; himself, his pathetic fear. Bertrand never sobs or pleads.

But today is different. He is pushed from behind, and then in the chest, and finds himself sitting on a wooden chair. His blindfold is removed and immediately retied around his mouth as a gag. He is at the side of a room, on the middle of a row of three chairs. At each end of the row stands a guard, guns held over their shoulders, a selection of knives on their belts.

The room is undecorated, with bare stone walls and floor. The only other furniture is a Formica-topped table in the middle of the room, set with more of the same wooden chairs. The table is twice as long as it is wide. In the middle, Bertrand is sitting, hands tied behind him, blindfold removed and his mouth unimpeded. On the table in front of him is a piece of paper.

Across the table from him, his back to Gavin, stands one of the guards, the leader, with a camcorder. He turns it on, and says to Bertrand:

'Now you speak!'

Bertrand raises his eyebrows.

'Me?'

'You speak it now.' The voice is harsh and angry.

'Oh, I don't know. I've never been good on camera. I get stage fright. Or camera fright, because it's not exactly a stage is it? I mean this room. I suppose it could be a set, for a film, though not a very jolly one. It is a bit dark and gloomy. The lighting will be very harsh on my skin.'

There is a bare light bulb hanging above the table from a wire, illuminating Bertrand's pale face, throwing his bruises into shadows. The guard behind the camera looks questioningly over to the one on Gavin's left, who gives an almost imperceptible shake of his head. The camera man snaps back to Bertrand.

'You speak to camera,' he shouts.

There is one more guard than normal. Although they're rarely together, Gavin knows there are four of them. There are five in this room, and he hasn't seen this young man on the left before.

'I'm not really sure what you're after. Is it a talking head sort of thing? Shall I just say what comes into my mind, then you can edit it later? Like Thora Hird, though I don't suppose you'd know Thora Hird. She's very British. I suppose I can start with school. One's school days are good for stories and anecdotes, don't you think? Schoolboys are both cruel and funny. They can go hand in hand you know. I don't think you've quite mastered that. You're quite good at the cruel, but I haven't noticed you being funny as yet. You should try it. It could enhance your torture technique.'

The cameraman glances again at the new guard, who this time shakes his head quite visibly. Bertrand has turned his head and sees it too.

'You must read the paper,' says the new guard very quietly.

Bertrand picks up the piece of paper from the table in front of him and waves it at the cameraman.

'You want me to read this?'

The guard nods once, and Bertrand looks at the paper and reads it silently to himself. When he gets to the end of the page he lays it down again on the table.

'Very interesting,' he says, 'It could do with some editing and the grammar is appalling, but I suppose it's not bad for a first effort.'

The guard with the camera slams it down on the table.

'I will make you speak!' he hisses.

The other two guards appear from the darkness at the back of the room. They grab Bertrand by the arms and drag him backwards off the chair, which tips and clatters to the floor. The cameraman had taken a bar from his waistband. Gavin can't see what it's made off. It could be wood or iron.

The two guards hold Bertrand while the other beats him with the bar about his back and shoulders. Gavin tries to count, but Bertrand's silence is too distracting. He can't see his face.

After a while the thuds stop and the guards turn Bertrand round to face his attacker.

'You read it!'

Bertrand raises his shoulders and his eyebrows in a shrug that infuriates the guard. He lets the bar clatter to the floor and attacks Bertrand with his fists. His anger is out of control. He punches Bertrand in the face until blood streams from his nose and his eyes are barely open. He kicks him in the stomach, and Bertrand buckles and would fall to the floor if he weren't held up still by the guards on either side. The cameraman flails his arms and legs like a mad dervish, delivering kicks indiscriminately. Bertrand's head drops, and his body hangs limp between his two supporters.

Eventually the leader reaches the end of his anger and stops, resting his hands on his knees. His mask has slipped and more of his face can be seen than normal. His cheeks, his upper lip, one side of his jaw. His skin is smooth and unblemished. He is trying to grow a moustache and beard, but it is wispy and pathetic. Bum fluff, they used to call it at Gavin's school. The man sinks to the floor and puts his head in his hands. The two guards stand impassive. Bertrand hangs like a rag doll.

Then the guard is back on his feet. He snaps an instruction and they drag Bertrand back to his chair. The leader returns to his position across the table and picks up the camera again.

'Now, you will speak.'

Bertrand doesn't move.

The guard on the left makes a small sound in his throat, like a cough. Gavin realises he's saying something.

'Beg.' He is speaking to the cameraman.

'Beg?'

'Beg.' He repeats, with certainty.

The cameraman turns to Bertrand and points the camera at him.

'You will beg! Yes, now you will beg!'

Bertrand lifts his bloody face to the camera.

'Beg?' His voice is hoarse. 'Why didn't you say so before? I can do beg.'

He is overtaken by a fit of coughing during which blood spatters from his face onto the Formica tabletop. Nobody makes any attempt to wipe it off. He looks at the piece of paper for a few seconds, before looking back at the camera. He obviously isn't reading what it says.

'O.K., I beg. I beg whoever is watching this wonderful example of film making' – again he is overtaken by coughing – 'to do whatever they need to do to keep themselves and their loved ones safe and their consciences clear. If that can be made to encompass any form of help to my friend here and myself, we would be eternally grateful.'

The guards look at each other with uncertainty, the cameraman questioning, the other shrugging slightly.

The cameraman looks back at Bertrand.

'You beg?'

Bertrand nods wearily. 'Yes, I beg.'

The guard turns the camera off and lays it on the table, barking instructions to the others. Bertrand is once more lifted from his chair, this time more gently. He is taken out through the door. There is more conversation between the guards left in the room, and then Gavin finds himself being lifted and dragged across the room to the chair that Bertrand has just vacated.

This darkness here is quite different. There are shapes in the blackness. Next to him there is Kat, asleep, the warmth of her through the sleeping bag, her hair falling across his leg. He could touch her. Further off, vague, the outline of the tor against the sky. Even though there is no moon, it is not dark enough to obliterate the shape of the landscape.

There are sounds too. Kat is making a small snickering sound in her sleep. He puts his hand on the outside of the sleeping bag where her hip makes a mound. There are calls and rustlings of small animals and birds. This darkness is teeming with life.

Things changed that day. Or rather, he changed. Was it the brutality that brought out his anger, or the youthful face of his captor that eradicated his fear? He doesn't know. But that was when he changed, that was when he became angry.

'You! You will read the paper.'

Gavin says nothing. They have removed the gag and the leader is pointing the camera at him. He says nothing and he doesn't blink.

'Now. You read it. Speak.'

Gavin swallows. It isn't fear. There is an excess of saliva in his mouth and he needs to swallow before he can speak. He has something he wants to say.

'No.'

There is an intake of breath in the room. The cameraman takes a step forward. Then he lets loose a tirade, gesturing with his empty hand towards the door, making a fist and punching, talking, talking. And although Gavin cannot understand the words, he knows that he is being warned. What happened to Bertrand could happen to him. And they expect him to comply, because he always seems to be the weaker of the two prisoners, the one who breaks down in sobs, wakes screaming in the cell. The one who looks most afraid.

The stream of words comes to an end. He has made his point. Now I have explained, you will do as I say.

'You read it,' he says, reasonably.

'No,' says Gavin.

The cameraman looks astonished, then a bit weary. He gestures to the guards behind, who come and grab Gavin as they had Bertrand. Then to the other two. They will perform the beating; this time the leader will watch.

Gavin finds that it is possible to take his concentration somewhere else. Previously when they beat him, it was the lack of power that hurt the most. With every lash he felt his subjugation. But, he realises, they cannot control the places he goes to in his mind. It is an effort, jolted every five seconds by the rod on his back, but he makes his mind wander until it reaches somewhere safe. He doesn't cry out.

The guards realise something is different. After a while they stop. The leader steps up to him, holding the camcorder out in front, speaking fast, angrily.

'You will read the paper?'

'No. Not now or ever. You can't make me.'

Many hours later he is lain down in the cell on his sacking bed. His body is limp and wet, he is barely conscious. There is darkness, which is normal. Pain. And a voice speaking.

He tries to listen. It seems to be coming from a long way away, but it's speaking to him, using his name.

'Gavin!' The voice, it sounds like Bertrand, but it's so far away. 'What have they done to you?'

They? He wonders what Bertrand means, if it is Bertrand's voice. The rooms turns and shifts and the voice is very near.

'Gavin?'

How long has he been here in this darkness?

Bertrand has spoken to him, but when was that? Has he been to sleep in the meantime?

'Cricket.' The word squeezes out of him in a breath. He doesn't know if Bertrand has caught it. There is silence for a time. His brain is juddering over tracks, nearly at a standstill. Is Bertrand still there? Have they taken him?

'Bertrand?' He tries to raise his head, but he may as well try to lift the building from its foundations.

'What do you mean, cricket?'

Grass. There's grass, which is sometimes parched and dry. And people in white clothes, and a ball. The air is filled with a living stillness, through which noises travel. A shout, and a thwack as the ball hits the bat, and these noises come flying through the air like the red ball, towards him. He looks up. The brightness of the blue sky is dazzling. He runs and stretches and leaps, and the thing is in his hands. Hard, heavy, his palms are smarting with the force of its landing. There is stitching on the leather. And there are other noises flying after it. Out. Out. Someone is shouting. And clapping. A sound like the wings of a flock of geese taking off together.

'In my head,' he whispers to Bertrand. 'Cricket.'

'Oh, cricket.' Bertrand sounds like he understands. Bertrand knows. 'Good.'

He's slipping now. The green has faded and the black is closing in. He has something else he needs to say to Bertrand though. Something important, not about cricket.

'Bertrand!'

'Yes.'

'I didn't beg.'

'I know. I knew you wouldn't.'

How did he know? Gavin didn't know. He slides under and lets the weight of pain lift off to a different level of consciousness.

Gavin can see. It is a dark moonless night, but his eyes have adjusted and he can see. It bears no comparison to the darkness of the cell, where no amount of adjustment could make any difference. He's happy here, in the cold of night, with the owls screeching overhead and Kat asleep beside him. In a different world this would be one of the high points of his life.

There is a locked room. A place in his memory where he can't go. Being here in the night is not going to unlock it for him. It's held tight. And that locked memory is his guilty treasure, his secret poison that will ruin everything. His work, his recovery, his friendships, the clear stillness of the night, his love for Kat. Everything poisoned.

If he could open the door...but he doesn't know how. And even if he did, he might not survive the knowledge it would bring.

Chapter Sixteen

When I woke, the night was just beginning to dissolve. It was still dark, but shapes were slightly lifted, more defined. The silhouette of the tor was something I could trace with my finger against the sky. The silhouette of Gavin too, still sitting, still as the rock, almost frozen to its shape.

I sat up and half unzipped my sleeping bag.

"Gavin, get in here and get warm."

He turned his head, and his neck was so stiff I almost giggled.

"It's OK."

"Get in here," I repeated. "I'm cold too, and we can share body heat."

"Will we both fit?"

"It'll be cosy."

He took off his boots, and got in beside me. There wasn't really room, but we squeezed together and managed to manoeuvre the zip up above our hips. Soon we were both laughing. I got my finger in the zip pull behind him and jerked it up and there we were, vacuum-packed in a sleeping bag, chest to chest, mouth to mouth, my arm stuck up by my ear with nowhere to go. He was beginning to thaw.

"What we need now," he said, "is the other one on top."

"And how are we going to manage that?"

"With difficulty."

He managed to snake out an arm and reach over to his rucksack. He unclipped his sleeping bag from the pack quite easily. But getting it out of its waterproof covering took both our free hands and about ten minutes. It was about nine of those minutes before he realised how close to him my mouth was and kissed me. I don't know where he'd been to in the night.

We unravelled the sleeping bag. It was yellow, with brown insets on either side, and squashed flat like a discarded skin. The bag we were in was blue and bulging with our cramped bodies. Getting our feet into the opening seemed an impossible task, and the first couple of attempts ended in banged knees and laughing failure. We realised we needed to move as though we were one person.

I shifted my body round inch by inch until I had my back to him. His knees in the crook of my knees, my bum in his groin, his arms round my chest, his face in my neck. We pushed against each other. I could feel him right down the length of my body, but there wasn't room for any movement, I could barely turn my head enough to kiss him.

We rolled so that I was lying on top of Gavin, then we lifted our feet together as one, me holding the top of the yellow sleeping bag, Gavin holding me. It worked. I pulled it up over our knees and up to our thighs. After that it was a case of wriggling and rolling.

By the time we were ensconced inside two sleeping bags, we were warm. The sun was bumping underneath the horizon, sending up a peach and orange glow. Gavin was holding me from behind and kissing my neck. I felt sleepy and happy and, as there was no way we could take our clothes off, I soon dozed again.

When I woke the sun was up above the trees and the yellow sleeping bag was dotted with insects. Gavin was asleep. His left arm was out and lying across me. I was too hot with all my clothes as well as his body heat. I needed a piss too. I unzipped both sleeping bags and got out – much easier than getting in.

When I came back Gavin was awake. He was lying flat on his back, still in both sleeping bags looking up at the sky. I walked into his field of vision, and he said, "This is the best morning. Look at that sky, Kat."

We walked back the same way we'd come, slower this time, as we were stiff from our night on the bare ground. Gavin was happy, carefree, making jokes and kissing me at every opportunity, wrestling me to the ground on Rough Tor over a packet of crisps. The sun was shining. I should remember it as a perfect day. But when I think back to it, it's as though there was something missing at the centre of it. There was this great ball of loveliness, of sunshine and fresh air and love. But in the middle it was hollow. And I wasn't sure what it was that should have been there. Something with weight. Something that would keep us grounded, so all that loveliness couldn't get blown away. At the time I barely felt it. Just a slight nag in my brain, something easy to ignore.

We got back in the early evening and went straight to Mel and Sheila's. They'd promised to cook for us. They had a balcony at the back of their flat, above the tattoo studio, and Mel had built a barbecue up there out of bricks and chicken wire. When we arrived the smell of burning charcoal was beginning to waft through the summer air. The idea of burnt food and cold beer was delicious.

Before long we had both, though Mel was a careful cook, turning the meat regularly and removing it before blackened became burnt to a crisp. Sheila had made big bowls of salad and lit candles that added to the fragrant air. We talked about our walk, the exhilaration of standing on top of Brown Willy, the magical calmness of Dozmary Pool at dusk.

Sheila told us stories about strange happenings on its shores, of meetings with people whose existence couldn't be verified, of islands seen in the pool at dusk that weren't there in the daytime, and mysterious boats afloat on winter dawns. Mel was quiet. He turned the food on the barbecue and handed it out, and listened to what the rest of us had to say. Sheila had hung bamboo wind-chimes up on the balcony and the lightest of breezes moved them softly against each other.

I leaned against Gavin's arm, comfortable and happy to be here with agreeable company. Any doubts I'd had during the day faded into nothing.

It was around ten o'clock, when the light was falling and the candles had started to glow, that Mel said:

"Gavin, I was reading some old newspaper reports earlier, from around the time you came back from Iraq. You never talk about that."

Sheila and I looked at each other. I wondered if she knew he was going to say this. Her face was impassive. I wondered if my panic showed.

I could feel Gavin's stillness through my body where we touched. It was thirty seconds before he spoke. Thirty seconds in which the wind chimes touched and parted, the candles glared with a sudden increase in the breeze. "No. It's not something I find easy to talk about."

"But talking is the best thing, don't you think? If you keep things in, they fester. We're your friends, if you can't talk to us who can you talk to?"

I wanted to scream at him to shut up. Couldn't he see that Gavin was dealing with things, slowly, at his own pace? Didn't he realise that that's what this walk had been about, and that Gavin was improving? And it's not as though he and Sheila were lifelong friends of Gavin's, they hadn't seen him for fifteen years.

Gavin smiled and sat forward in his chair so that he was illuminated by candlelight and Mel could look him straight in the face.

"Mel, I really appreciate your friendship, yours and Sheila's, and what you've done for me. You're right, I do need to talk more. And soon I will. It's hard, I don't know the words to use. Don't know what I want to say. I'm thinking it through, and when I can, I will talk to you."

My body relaxed, I almost breathed a sigh of relief. He'd kept his calm, given Mel a reasonable answer, one he'd have to accept. He'd stepped deftly over a stumbling block. I thought of making a flippant comment to break the mood, make us all laugh.

"But there's others involved too, aren't there?" Mel continued, and I turned to stare at him, "like that photographer you went out with, Bertrand Knight. His family. Do they know what happened to him?"

"I think they do." Gavin's voice was level.

"You *think* they do! What about you? Do you know what happened to him?"

Gavin had moved imperceptibly out of the light. He made a small movement with his head, but it was impossible to tell if he was saying yes or no.

"It wasn't in the papers. Just that you'd returned, that you'd turned up at Heathrow, and then nothing. Nothing more about you, and nothing at all about this Knight. It was all suspiciously low key, not like this bloke they've got out there at the moment. Headlines in all the papers."

Gavin had sat right back in his chair and his voice came out of the shadows, tight and strangled, "Sorry, Mel. I can't"

Mel leaned further forward, his elbows on his knees, and he reminded me of a dog holding on to a stick you're trying to take away from it. He wasn't going to give it up.

I grabbed hold of Gavin's hand and cleared my throat, but Sheila jumped in before me.

"Maybe this isn't the best time, Mel."

He looked at her questioningly, but her face was firm, and the eagerness dropped from his shoulders. Gavin's hand in mine was shaking.

We stayed for about an hour after that. Sheila and I did our best to keep the evening going, but Mel had lapsed into surliness, and Gavin was visibly shaken.

Back in our room, we suddenly didn't know what to say to each other. We undressed and got into bed and made love under the covers in the dark. Gavin was gentle and slow.

Afterwards we lay together, my head on his shoulder, his arm behind my head. We didn't speak, but both of us were awake. We stayed like that for a long time. It was beginning to get light when Gavin quietly extricated himself and went to the bathroom. I hadn't slept. He came back after five minutes and sat by the window looking out at the lightening sky. I lay in the bed and watched him out of half closed eyes.

Eventually I must have fallen asleep, because Gavin woke me at seven with some coffee.

"Shouldn't you be at work?" I asked him.

"I'm going in a bit later," he said.

We went for breakfast in the café along the road. I drank more black coffee and nibbled at a piece of toast. I wanted to ask him how he was, how he felt about last night, but the toast blocked the words. A feeling of misery soaked through me.

I had to be in the shop to help Sheila at eight forty-five, so we parted in the high street and went our separate ways: him to the hotel, me to Merlin's Cave.

The morning started quietly in the shop. Sheila asked me to sort out the storeroom as she was expecting a delivery of new stock and needed more space. I went through half empty cardboard boxes, piling their contents on to the shelves, squashing everything up. On the bottom shelf were some items that had been ordered as special deliveries. Sheila said some of them had been there for quite a long time, and could I go through and sort them into date order. Chase up some of the older ones and see if the customers still wanted them. She always took payment with the order, so officially they didn't belong to the shop.

As the morning wore on the shop became busier, and I didn't get time to sort the parcels. At lunchtime, when the shop was full, Gavin came in. I was surprised to see him – he usually worked until after lunch, and he'd started late today. I was busy with a customer and he hung around the shelves for a bit, glancing at the books.

Sheila said to him "Why don't you go through and see Mel?"

When the customer left I followed Gavin through to the tattoo studio. Mel was working, and the buzz of the needle droned through the shop like an angry bee. Gavin was standing on the other side of the screen, looking at the design sheets on the wall. He smiled when he saw me.

"Is anything wrong?" I asked.

"No. Just thought I'd pop in and say hello. Picked a bad time though. Busy."

The feeling of misery deepened, and I felt unbearably heavy. The effort of forcing my voice up through my throat was almost more than I could manage.

"Have you been in to work?"

"Yeah, there's not much to do there today. I bunked off early."

Summer in a Cornish holiday resort. I didn't believe there was nothing to do at the hotel. I smiled.

"That's nice. What're you going to do with the afternoon?"

He shrugged. "Dunno, go for a walk. Go to the beach. I don't suppose you...?"

I shook my head. "You've seen how busy the shop is. Sheila can't spare me for a few hours yet. Sorry."

"Well, just me on my lonesome then." He picked up his bag and slung it over his shoulder. "See ya then, Kat."

He leaned forward and kissed me on the lips, and I closed my eyes. Even after he'd said goodbye to Mel, and called through to Sheila in the shop, and gone out through the door, and the door had closed behind him, shutting off the sudden slice of blue sky and sunshine, and the bells on the door had stopped tinkling, I still stood there, with a tingling in my lips like the touch of a butterfly's wings.

Chapter Seventeen

His body aches from the recent battle. Aches in places where it never ached before. Places he didn't even know existed. He thought he was going to die, that this was the end of his brilliant, but very short, career. He hadn't gone into the contest at his full strength. Not after the long sea trip, the battle on the island, and then another skirmish at sea when Milocrates' brother had a fleet of ships on their tail. They'd dealt with them of course, they were practically invincible by then, but he'd personally taken a blow to the shoulder which had barely healed when they finally arrived in Jerusalem.

And he was carrying an emotional burden too. Beheading Milocrates had affected him in a way he hadn't anticipated. He wasn't sleeping. At night, trying to accustom his body to the roll of the ship, trying to hold back the waves of nausea, he found that every time he closed his eyes he would see the head separating from the body with the slice of his sword. He would see the silver flash, his own hand on the hilt, moving through the air in a perfect arc, and feel the faintest snag as the blade hit flesh, the slight decrease in velocity as the sword carved, not the air, but arteries and bone. It was a good sword. It went through Milocrates neck as smoothly as slicing cheese.

He would open his eyes wide, look fiercely into the night of the berth, trying hard not to see the spurt of blood and the severed hairs clinging to the blade. Trying not to hear the soft thud of the head falling onto the turf on which they stood.

He felt it was a weakness to dwell like this on the slaying of an enemy. If he hadn't killed Milocrates, then he himself would have been killed. That is black and white, certain. Those are the rules of battle, kill or be killed.

He looks out of the window at the road passing by. Tries closing his eyes to see if the image will rise again. Open – motorway, tarmac, speeding traffic. Closed – a flash of silver, a fountain of blood. Why? Why not the battle which came after it? Three full days on the field against the hugest bulk of a man he'd ever see, Gormundus, the Persian champion. When he'd first seen him it had been an effort to keep his face blank, to keep up the pretence of invincible courage. If anyone had looked closely they'd have seen his Adam's apple moving.

But he'd done it. Towards the end of the third day, every scrap of strength squeezed out of his body, felled for the umpteenth time by this unstoppable giant who seemed to know nothing of fatigue, he'd finally got angry. It was the thought of what was being wasted. The years of training, the love and support of first his father, and then the Emperor. The life ahead, which he was so looking forward to, the women he'd not yet met. He was young and it wasn't his time to die. He'd raised himself from the ground with a force that came from somewhere other than his body, and brought his sword down with the might of nations onto the head of Gormundus. Later they told him that he'd shouted, "This is the blow to end it all!"

He doesn't remember that. But he was right. That blow split the giant's head in two, and both contestants fell to the ground motionless. Gormundus in the endless sleep of death, and he, the victorious champion, into a consciousless stupor that lasted for five days.

He shifts his position so his knees point towards the window. Coach seats are always so uncomfortable. Not enough room for his legs without bumping his knees into the seat in front. They have to go to either the left or the right. If they go right, he worries about knocking the person in the next seat. It's a young lad wearing headphones, eyes closed, the sound of his music dribbling out, his own knees pointing out into the aisle. He seems oblivious, but it's best to be courteous.

The position is aggravating the ache in his hip from that final crippling blow the giant swung at him with the hilt of his sword. By the time he recovered consciousness after the fight, the whole of his side had turned black with the bruising. The Christians of Jerusalem had sent him their wisest healers, and he lay and watched as they moved around his tent, silent in their white robes, preparing the potions and oils with which to anoint his beaten body.

He lets his eyes close again, and this time a different image. Kat in the tattoo studio, baring her face for his kiss, her eyes full of hurt and awareness. Taking in the bag he was carrying, the locked-in look on his face, the tightened body language. She knew he was going. She cared too much to try and stop him.

Better the motorway. Better the flash of steel and the tear of flesh. Better the aches from a three-day duel with a giant than that open face.

The noise leaking from the lad's earphones is becoming irritating. Gavin will get off at the next stop. He bought a ticket from Exeter to Chester, but he doesn't have to go that far.

As darkness falls the bus station lengthens into horizontal streaks of yellow light and wet tarmac. The first rain for weeks. Gavin sits on a hard plastic seat and watches the buses coming and going. The queue builds up; a few women with umbrellas or headscarves, coming from bingo or from jobs which kept them cleaning well into the evening; teenage couples, kissing and sliding their hands inside each others clothes; groups of lads out for a beer, moving on to the next place. Never more than eight or ten in the queue.

Then the bus arrives, wheezing open its doors and grumbling with fumes. The people climb into its gaping doorway, and Gavin continues to sit. Occasionally the driver will call over to him when all the other passengers are on, "you getting on mate?" Gavin shakes his head, and the doors complete their electronic cycle, sealing the passengers inside the yellow-lit body, and the bus moves away. The bones in Gavin's arse begin to ache. He feels that he's melding into the seat, becoming part of it. That his skeleton is slowly turning into the same red plastic.

There are no more passengers. Lights in the bus station begin to go out. An inspector walks through the long shelter, and throws a suspicious glance at Gavin.

"No more buses tonight," he says.

Gavin nods, but doesn't move.

"You can't stay here, you'll have to move on."

Why? What difference would it make to anyone if Gavin sat here all night, on this hard seat, bothering no one?

The inspector is looking at him, waiting. It's not worth a fight.

Gavin slings his bag onto his shoulder and stands up. He is stiff with cold and damp. He turns his back on the inspector and walks away. Not as cool as he'd like, due to the stiffness in his hips. But he aims for nonchalance, doesn't look back as he walks out of the shelter of the bus station and into the wet blackness of the city at night.

He can feel the bump of his bag against his side as he walks. The parcel he's carrying is heavy and unwieldy. He doesn't know where he's going. He just walks. It is late August, four months until New Year. He imagines the brown paper rubbing against the inside of his bag. It's well wrapped, with lots of brown parcel tape, but even so, in time that will wear away. The paper will develop tiny nicks that will grow into tears, and the insides of the parcel will begin to show. He doesn't want to give GK something so dilapidated. He will have to find somewhere to store it.

An hour later and he's on the outskirts of the city. He can see a motorway, the lights of its traffic refracting through the raindrops. There's a large roundabout and a retail park with big square, low slung-buildings – a fast food restaurant, a cinema, a cheap goods department store. He walks along the edge of the dual carriageway in the scrappy grass verge. The ache is getting worse down one side of his body. He can't remember why. When he momentarily closes his eyes he sees streaks of red, blood red, plastic red. He can feel the heavy blow of metal against his body. He remembers Milocrates, Gormundus, and the ache becomes heavy, making it difficult to move one leg in front of the other. The lights are off in the retail park too, but he might find a doorway or some other place to shelter from the rain.

The rain doesn't let up. Morning comes in grey and soaked and finds Gavin huddled in the loading bay at the back of the department store. He opens his eyes and hears the traffic swooshing by on the motorway, the tyres spraying, window wipers on full speed. He's hungry. He hasn't eaten a proper meal since he left Jerusalem. The healers in their white robes had given him a breakfast of honey and figs and bread and fish. They had stuffed his pockets with nuts and dried fruit. But that was gone long ago. The ache in his guts is even stronger than the ache in his sides.

It's still early, but the fast food restaurant is opening its doors, hoping to catch early birds on their way to work who stop for petrol. Gavin hasn't shaved or washed for two days. His clothes are crumpled and dusty from the night in the loading bay. But at least he's dry. The girl behind the counter gives him an arch look when he orders a triple burger and black coffee, but she doesn't refuse to serve him.

The food in his stomach and the warmth of the restaurant restore him to some sense of normality. He wonders what Kat is doing, if she's sleeping on the mattress that was their shared bed, or if she's sitting in the window watching the rain falling on the sea. He wonders if the sky is as heavy and low there as it is here, barely skimming the tops of the buildings. The ache in his side is from twenty-four hours of sitting in uncomfortable positions in damp places, sleeping on a concrete floor, carrying a heavy parcel over one shoulder.

He has to do something with the parcel. He asks the girl, when she comes to wipe the next table, if there is an internet café nearby. She replies that there is internet access in the department store, but that won't be open for another two hours. Gavin thinks about staying here, nursing polystyrene cups of terrible coffee in the bright dry warmth, or heading back into the rain, back up the, by now very busy, dual carriageway towards the city.

He needs to be on the move. He finishes his coffee and thanks the girl. She looks pleased and smiles at him. There's only two other customers in the restaurant at this early hour, men with heads down over their coffees, wishing they were somewhere else on this wet morning, somewhere dry and comforting and homely. It must be a crap job, Gavin thinks, working the early shift in such a soulless place. He smiles back at her as he leaves.

By the time he reaches the city centre the rain has stopped, and his lower half is wetter than his upper, because of the spray sent up by the passing cars. The day is beginning to get warm as the clouds thin out and move eastwards. The city looks a completely different place than it had the previous night. There are people everywhere, bustling about, removing raincoats and putting away their umbrellas. The flowers in the municipal planting are glistening with colour and raindrops in the weak sunshine. Later, when the clouds are completely gone and the sun has risen high in the sky, it might be hot. The flowers and the people and the cars are reflected in windows, the reflections hazed over by the glare of the sun. Gavin watches. Once he might have felt at home here, rushing to a newspaper office, an appointment somewhere, busy with things he needed to do. Now he is wet and directionless, with a heavy parcel knocking in his bag, digging into his sides. He feels more at home in the night.

He heads for the central library, a tall glass building shining in the morning sunshine, dazzling his eyes. He wishes he had some shades. Maybe he'll buy some once he's finished on the internet.

There's a message from GK.

>> Hi Gavin, thanks for collecting the parcel. Really appreciate it. Is it a big item? Don't want to put you out too much. You say you're going up north. If you're passing through the Midlands you could drop it off with my girlfriend, Morgan. She runs a bar ...<<

The address is in a town not far from where he is. He could get a bus, be there in less than an hour.

Chapter Eighteen

The bus pulls in just before midday having travelled a roundabout route that takes in all the villages between the city and the town. Gavin is the only passenger to have travelled the whole route. The two hours of bus fumes combined with many bends in the road have left him feeling queasy. Breakfast in the retail park seems a long time ago. He follows some of the other passengers out of the bus station, heads for the town centre.

It's like a million other towns. Pedestrianised in the main shopping area, a fountain standing dry in the middle, littered with beer cans and crisp packets. A busker is playing the flute along to some taped music, a suitcase of CDs at his feet showing his face, looking younger, healthier. Hanging baskets of flowers drip outside a hotel bar, and the sun bounces off the paving stones. It's a hot day.

Gavin enters the hotel, grateful for its coolness, darkness, and takes off his shades. He orders a double whisky and asks the barmaid if she knows where he can find a bar named Wodwo's. She knows it and gives him directions, but she doesn't think it's open at lunchtime.

' … it likes to think of itself as a bit of a nightclub," she says "but it's more like a drinking den really. They have live bands on sometimes – local kids, and old jazz guys. It's a bit sleazy for my taste.'

He looks at her. Dyed blonde hair pulled hard back off her face, pink lipstick and a white cotton blouse taut across her breasts. He orders a chip butty and takes his drink over to a corner.

He stays in the hotel bar for the rest of the afternoon, alternating beer with whisky, sipping them slowly and dozing imperceptibly for half hours at a stretch. The barmaid swaps shifts at around four. The new girl is older, with dark auburn hair in a bob and narrow hips. Gavin sees the blonde girl nodding in his direction, alerting the new one to possible aggravation perhaps. He doesn't mean to cause any. As long as they let him sit here and cause him no bother, he'll cause them none.

And so the afternoon goes. Soon after six he finishes the dregs in his beer glass and heads off to the toilets. He looks at himself in the mirror. His beard is beginning to look intentional. He runs water over his hands and pushes them through his hair. It's short enough that the dirt can't make it lank. His t-shirt probably smells of stale sweat and cigarette smoke, but there's nothing he can do about that now. He probably should have spent the afternoon buying new clothes and visiting the barber, but it's too late. If Wodwo's is as seedy as the barmaid suggests, then his smell will probably be masked by its own.

He leaves the hotel with a nod to the auburn barmaid, who throws him a tight smile. It's still hot outside, and the glare is blinding after the gloom of the bar. He's glad to hide behind his shades.

The blonde's directions are simple enough and he finds Wodwo's without any problems. It's a black door between two shops with a sign that says WODWO'S Open 8.30 – 11.30 Mon – Thurs, 6.30 – 12.30 Fri – Sat, 2-5 Sunday. He still has two hours to kill.

He spends them in a Pizza Hut and returns at 8.45. The door is open now, wedged at forty-five degrees. It leads into a narrow passage and up a gloomy flight of stairs to another door, this one painted glass with a silver monster spitting out fire, the name of the club emblazoned diagonally in gothic script.

He expects it to be dark and full of smoke, but it's not.

Wodwo's takes up the top floor of both of the shops beneath. One half is set out with tables, and is obviously a restaurant of sorts. There is a blackboard on the far wall with the names of Thai dishes and types of noodles. There's a bar running along the far wall, with an open doorway at one end leading through to the kitchen. There are a few high stools in black leather and chrome, and on one of these, at the end near the kitchen door, sits a young man in a long white apron; the chef.

The other half, on Gavin's left, is an open space with a stage at one end. There are a couple of tables and some chairs at the edges, but the middle is obviously a dance floor. Some lads are setting up equipment on the stage and talking to a woman dressed in black. She has her back to Gavin and doesn't turn when he comes in. But he can feel the hairs standing on the back of his neck. She must be Morgan.

He takes a seat at the end of the bar nearest the wall, his bag at his feet. Here, he can turn side on to the bar and watch what's going on. The chef gets him a beer.

After a few minutes Morgan finishes her chat with the band and walks over to the bar. She glances in Gavin's direction, but it's the chef she wants to speak to. They stand together at the other end of the bar, talking quietly. Gavin could hear what they were saying if he paid attention, but he doesn't. He looks at the woman who is GK's girlfriend.

She's tall and slim, her dark hair pulled back from her face into a short ponytail. If it was down it would be just below shoulder length. She's wearing a tight black t-shirt and no bra, and black trousers that flare slightly at the bottom with a short wraparound black skirt over the top, silver jewellery and a collection of bangles on her left arm. From her outfit you might think she was one of the waitresses. It's the way she carries herself which shows she's the one in charge.

Gavin has met women like her before. Independent, intelligent, self-sufficient. He's never really been attracted to them, probably because they haven't needed him. He's always gone for women who have some cracks in their façade, some flakiness, girls who look a little out of place wherever they are.

For some reason, he's more comfortable with that. With a girl like this one, it's what you are that's important, not what you can give. He admits to himself, women like Morgan scare him.

He drinks from his beer bottle. He notices that every now and then Morgan glances across from her conversation with the chef; tiny glances with no meaning. She's probably aware of his scrutiny. He turns towards the bar and looks into his beer. He doesn't feel ready to talk to her.

The place slowly begins to fill up. Couples come and share a candlelit table and a bottle of wine along with their bowls of noodles. Groups of friends push tables together and laugh loudly over stories and in-jokes. At around nine-thirty the band begins to play – covers mostly, of sixties bands like Love and The Doors – with a few of their own thrown in. They're surprisingly good. Groups of people get up to dance, and some of the couples too.

Gavin stays at the bar, sticks to beer, tries out the house noodles, which are spicy, hot and fragrant – the best food he's had in days.

There are two new staff on duty now, both girls, both dressed in black; one with blonde dreadlocks tied back behind her head, the other a boyish short-cut red head. They work the bar and the tables together with an efficiency and cheerfulness that impresses Gavin. Every so often one of them gets him a new beer. If they're surprised to see him staying so long, alone in his corner of the bar, they don't show it. Gavin has been drinking non-stop since lunchtime, but he doesn't feel drunk.

Through the evening winds Morgan. Gavin tries not to, but he can't help letting his eyes follow her as she moves around the bar chatting to customers and helping out waiting the tables when there's a rush. His attention is drawn to her. She isn't the most beautiful woman Gavin has ever seen, but she is one of the most magnetic.

Gradually the crowd starts to thin. At quarter to eleven the band stops playing and starts to pack up. Morgan puts on a

CD of blues music, and the atmosphere changes. No one is ordering food anymore – the few people still sitting at tables are drinking now, wine or coffee. A couple are still on the dance floor swaying slowly, arms draped around each other.

Morgan helps the band with their equipment down the stairs, returning ten minutes later alone. The two waitresses are sitting on the stools at the end of the bar where earlier the chef had been, sharing a bottle of wine. Morgan empties ashtrays and wipes tables. She gives off a constant buzz of energy, as though she finds it hard to stay still.

By eleven-thirty Gavin is the only customer left in the place. The chef and the two waitresses have left. Morgan pours herself a hefty measure of brandy and sits on a stool next to Gavin at the bar. She lights a cigarette – her first of the evening – and takes a couple of long drags on it, drawing the smoke deep into her lungs.

On the exhale she says, "I guess you must be Gavin."

Gavin nods.

She has a swig of brandy and another drag on her cigarette, then she crushes it out, half-smoked, in the ashtray.

"Dance with me, Gavin."

He'd been prepared to be met with either friendliness or hostility, but this surprises him. He hesitates, but really he has no choice but to agree. He drains his beer in one gulp and gets to his feet, offers Morgan his hand, and they walk over to the dance floor.

It's Billie Holliday's 'Don't Explain', slow and dreamy. Not dancing music, smooching music. Morgan moves in close to him, slides her arms around his body, presses herself close. Gavin breathes in sharply, lets his arms rest behind her, his hands in the small of her back. She's nearly as tall as him, and she bends her neck, rests her head on his shoulder, facing inwards so he can feel her hot breath in the hollow of his shoulder blades. She moves sinuously, seductively to the music, pressing against him all the way down his body, and he can feel himself responding, can feel his body wanting her.

Morgan is GK's girlfriend. Bertrand's brother's girlfriend. What she's doing with him is making his cock hard, and they've only spoken a handful of words. He wants to hold back, but feels his fingers curling over her buttocks, pulling her closer. He's breathing in the perfume of her hair, burying his nose in the back of her neck. He doesn't kiss her. He wants to kiss her, but she's GK's girlfriend. This is a really bad idea.

She moves her hips rhythmically, massaging his cock with her groin. She must be able to feel him. She couldn't not notice. He wonders what to do, how he can turn her down without causing offence. If he can turn her down at all.

The song ends and she steps away. There is space between them and the front of his body feels suddenly cold, exposed. She's smiling at him, but that's all it is; a friendly smile. There's nothing lustful in her eyes.

"Thanks," she says. "I often have a smooch on the dance floor when everyone's gone. But on my own. It nice to have someone to dance with."

"My pleasure," he says, and he means it.

"Where are you staying?"

He shrugs. He hasn't thought that far ahead.

"You can stay with me. I've got a sofa bed in the living room."

She's surprised him again. He is trying to think of the right answer, but she doesn't wait.

"I'll grab my coat. Meet me out at the front."

And she disappears into the kitchen. He walks across to the bar and picks up his bag. Is this wise? He could just go now, not wait, walk down the stairs and away. He feels the bump of his bag against his side, the heaviness of the parcel inside it. He wants to get rid of it. He walks heavily and slowly down the stairs, and has just reached the bottom when she catches up, the keys in her hand ready to lock up for the night.

Chapter Nineteen

It's been three days since he left Kat, but all that time he's felt her presence; as though there's a thread connecting them, unravelling as he travels further away from her, but unbroken. He wonders if there will be a time when it stops unravelling, and what will happen if it does. If it will pull taut or break; or if her pull is strong enough to bring him back to her. He tries to think of Kat now, to imagine where she is, what she might be doing. He'd like to think that she knows he's thinking about her, that his thought waves could reach her. But he knows they're not strong enough. He's here in this house with Morgan, and it's difficult to concentrate on anything else.

Morgan is crouching in front of the stereo putting on a CD. There is energy in the pose, as though she could spring at any moment. He's reminded of someone practising martial arts, or of a cat. When she stands up and turns towards him, her movements are slow and controlled. He remembers her dancing and the subtle movements of her hips. Music fills the room, guitars, someone whistling an eerie melody, a woman's voice low and seductive.

"Goldfrapp," she says.

She goes to a cupboard and fetches a bottle of brandy and two glasses, fills them nearly to the top. He watches her as she moves, reaching her arm up to get the bottle from a top shelf, forcing her breasts into relief against the black fabric of her t-shirt; the sideways movement of her hips as she moves the glasses; the slight clench of her buttocks as she twists the lid off the bottle. Each movement is like the thrust of a dagger. He closes his eyes and remembers the white room at dawn, the sound of the sea, the look on Kat's face as she sleeps, her lashes touching lightly onto her summer-tanned cheek.

Morgan sits down heavily at the other end of the sofa. He opens his eyes.

"Here, drink this."

She hands him a glass of brandy and swings her feet up, hugging her knees to her chest with one arm.

"This used to be my parent's house," she tells him. "I grew up here. They died last year, and now it's mine."

"I'm sorry," he murmurs.

"They were old and ill. They were well into their forties when they had me, at the last minute they possibly could. Last autumn my mum got pneumonia and wasn't strong enough to fight it. My dad died two months later of a broken heart."

"Can you die of that?"

"After that many years, of course you can. They'd been together for sixty-five years, all their adult lives. They never spent a day apart. The reason they left having a child so late was so there was no one to get between them. They were like two parts of the same unit. One couldn't survive without the other."

"Did you feel like you were in the way?"

"No. They were very careful to make sure I didn't. But I could tell, when it was time for me to leave home, they were relieved. They loved me to visit, but for the main part they wanted to be together and alone."

Gavin looks around the room. It's a strange mix of stylish and dilapidated. The wallpaper is old and yellowing, tatty in the corners, and has a hideous pattern of flowers growing up dark red diamond-shape trellis. The furniture is dark and heavy and too big for the room, and the window frames need at the very least a coat of paint. But the floor has been recently sanded and there's an enormous sheepskin rug filling up the middle of the room. The stereo system is sleek and expensive, and the sofa is big, modern and comfortable, covered with a dark red silky throw that matches the wallpaper.

"So you live here now?"

"Some of the week. I'm here Thursday to Sunday, the rest of the week I'm with GK. The bar's quiet early in the week. Just food, no music. They don't need me."

"Does GK come here?"

"No." She looks at him curiously. "I mean, he had been here, before, when my parents were alive. But not since ..." She tails off and looks around the room as though seeing it with Gavin's eyes. "It's a work in progress, as you can see. You should see the kitchen."

She chuckles, then she catches Gavin's eye and the smile dies on her lips. He sips his brandy. She has lit candles in the empty fireplace, and the flames are reflected in their eyes. The music is full of soaring violins and the singer's voice is so intimate he can hear the saliva on her lips. A strand of Morgan's hair has escaped and she winds it around her finger as she drinks from her glass, keeping her gaze locked with his. It's been years since he drank brandy. He'd forgotten its smoothness, how easily it slides down the throat, the sweet aftertaste.

"So, you've been in Cornwall."

"Yes."

"You have family there?"

"No, I was visiting friends." He doesn't want to talk to her about Cornwall, doesn't want to open those memories to this dark red room. There's a silence that lasts a few moments too long.

"So where are...?"

"So what are...?" They both speak at the same time.

Morgan laughs. "You first."

"I was just going to ask about the house. What are your plans for it."

She turns the glass slowly round in her hand, smearing brandy up the sides and catching the glow of the candle flames in reflected amber. She lifts it to her nose and breathes it in, raising her eyes to meet Gavin's as she does so.

"I'm doing it up, bit by bit. Bringing it into the present day."

"And then?"

She shrugs, a slow broad shrug that could mean that she's barely thought about the answer, or that she's thought about so much it's become meaningless.

"Who knows? I thought once that I could live here with GK."

"Why not any more?"

Again she gives him that sharp hard stare, trying to read something hidden behind his question.

"You don't know do you?"

"Don't know what?"

"GK can't walk. He's been in a wheelchair for the past eight months."

Gavin starts to say he's sorry, but she's jumped up from the sofa and put on a bright smile.

"Come and have a look at my kitchen," she says.

The kitchen hasn't had any work done on it as far as Gavin can tell. The floor is tiled with red quarry tiles, worn, dirty and chipped. There's a wooden table in the middle, painted pale yellow and covered with a dingy white plastic cloth, patterned with green leaves. There are four matching chairs, painted the same primrose colour. Under the window is a deep heavy sink, stained from years of use, its enamel crazed, a green tear-shaped mark beneath the taps, which are tall and lime-encrusted. Next to the sink is a washing machine, an old twin tub that looks as though it should be in a museum. Opposite, there is a coal-burning stove set into the chimney wall. The cupboard doors are yellow too, a darker mustard colour, and the cooker is an old gas model, two of its control switches taped up to indicate they no longer work.

"I don't use it, except to boil the kettle," Morgan says. "When I'm here I eat at the restaurant, or get a take-away. I doubt anything in here is safe to use anyway. It's a wonder my parents didn't electrocute themselves."

She opens one of the cupboards and starts removing plates and dishes, piling them up on the table.

"This stuff, it's collectable. There's people out there who'll pay good money for it, can you believe. I think it's hideous."

"What are you going to do with it?"

"Sell it. Put it on ebay if I can be bothered, or take it to the charity shop. There's too much for me to do here. I need to pay someone to do the place up."

Gavin walks slowly round the kitchen. On the far side is a door to outside with a large black key in the lock. He turns it and opens the door, peers outside.

"The coal shed," says Morgan.

There is a roof connecting the house door and the coal shed three feet away, fitted with a stable-type door in flaking red paint. There's the sharp wet smell of unburned coal, and Gavin can see the shape of the pile in the gloom. Morgan stands next to him peering out into the darkness.

"The thing is, there's nothing wrong with him. Not physically."

Gavin looks at her, but she's staring straight ahead.

"He just won't walk. Refuses. Says he can't."

They step together back into the kitchen and Morgan pulls the door to, turns the key in the lock.

"Maybe he can't," says Gavin. "The mind's a strange thing, we don't understand the half of it. If there's something the matter in his brain, it might mean that he can't physically walk, even though there's nothing wrong with his legs."

"But I've heard him."

He looks at her questioningly.

"We don't sleep together. That's another thing that's stopped since ... since he's been in the wheelchair. When I'm there I sleep in the spare bedroom, which is directly underneath his. And I've heard him, pacing to and fro in the night. He can walk, he just won't."

"What caused it? I mean, did something happen…?"

The look she gives him then makes his heart plummet and his pulse rattle in his head. He knows what caused it, her look tells him that. GK and Bertrand were close, as close as brothers can be. Eight months takes them back to the beginning of the year. Eight months ago GK found out that his brother was dead, and he took to a wheelchair and refused to sleep with his girlfriend anymore. These damaged lives are the result of Gavin's actions. He is to blame.

"Could I use your bathroom?"

She directs him, and he takes the stairs two at a time, reaching the door and throwing it open just in time before his stomach contracts and hurls out the contents of the evening into the toilet pan. He gasps, out of breath, his shoulders shaking, his eyes closed. He stands like this for some time, letting the tumult in his body subside, keeping his mind empty of thoughts. Eventually his breathing is smooth again.

There's a tap at the door.

"Are you OK?" she asks.

"Yes."

He flushes the toilet and swills out his mouth at the sink. He probably still reeks, but doesn't feel he can use her toothbrush. He looks in the cupboard and finds a bottle of mouthwash.

When he returns downstairs Morgan is sitting on the sofa again. She's changed the music and Sarah Vaughan's deep voice fills the room. She's blown out the candles and lit a lamp that gives a soft rosy glow to the room.

"Sorry about that. Must be the drink. I hadn't realised I'd drunk so much."

She's refilled his brandy glass and hands it to him. They both know it wasn't the drink.

"I see you've done some work in the bathroom."

"Yes. I quite liked the old bathroom. Some of the old tiles were art deco and worth keeping. But they needed cleaning, and it was only one panel. The rest weren't worth the hassle. So I've taken them all off. And that's as far as I've got."

He sits down on the far end of the sofa from her, perching on the edge, sipping at the brandy in his glass.

"I want to keep the bath too. It's a lovely old bath. I can lie down in it."

He nods. The bath was old and stained, but he knows nothing about these things. It may be possible to restore it. He'd noticed the legs it stood on. They could well be art deco too.

"I could help you if you like," he says.

She turns her head slowly to look at him and their eyes meet.

"What, here...?"

"With the house. I'm not doing anything else at the moment. Save you paying out for a bunch of workmen."

Suddenly she's smiling.

"I'd have to pay you of course."

He shrugs. "If you like, but it would still be cheaper than getting professionals in."

"And you really wouldn't mind? Staying here and doing all this hard labour?"

He smiles back at her. "I deserve it."

"I haven't even got a spare bed. There was one, but it had woodworm and I burned it."

"I can sleep on the sofa. Or get an airbed."

"OK," she says.

At the same moment they both raise their glasses to their lips and drink, then she raises hers, reaching her arm out to him down the length of the sofa.

"To us, then. To our new working partnership."

He chinks his glass against hers and grins.

"To us."

Chapter Twenty

I carried on working in the shop until the August bank holiday was over. I couldn't walk out on Sheila at her busiest time. Besides, it kept me occupied and I didn't have time to think. There were so many customers that week we barely had time to stop for a cup of tea, and by the end of the day I was so knackered I fell asleep by ten most nights.

But the week afterwards everyone had gone. The schools had gone back and sucked all the holidaymakers out of Cornwall as effectively as a vacuum pump.

I didn't even have to tell Sheila I was leaving. On the Tuesday night as we were closing, she said, "When are you planning to go back to London?"

I replied, "Later this week, if you can spare me."

She smiled and said "Thank you for staying. I don't know what I'd have done without you."

I left on Thursday. It was still three weeks before college went back but I had work to do before term began, research I'd been ignoring all summer. I could spend those three weeks usefully in the library.

I didn't think there was any point in chasing after Gavin. I didn't have a clue where he'd gone. I sent him emails regularly, telling him what I was doing, where I was. If he wanted me he'd have no problems finding me. I tried not to use too much headspace thinking about him. It didn't get me anywhere and it made me maudlin. But it was difficult. There were many times that month when I'd realise I'd been staring at a paragraph in some worthy tome for ten or twenty minutes not taking in a word, re-enacting scenes in my head: Gavin and me on the beach throwing stones into the sea; Gavin and me striding over the moors; Gavin and me climbing up to the castle and pretending to be a knight and his lady; Gavin and me naked in bed. I'd shake my head to get rid of the images, focus my attention back on the words on the page. Hours in the library, many of them unproductive.

I went to see Aggie. I thought she might be angry with me because I'd spent so much time with Gavin and not forced him to see a psychiatrist. But apparently Gavin had been sending her regular emails letting her know he was OK, and this thoughtfulness on his part she saw as a sign of recovery. Or at least the road to recovery. She wasn't as anxious as the last time I saw her.

"I suppose you're right, and this travelling about is having some therapeutic effect. I don't think it's enough. He still needs proper medical help. But maybe this will get him into a state where he's ready to receive it."

I didn't tell her about the emails I'd been getting from Gavin.

He'd been sending them ever since he left. To begin with I was amused, relieved even, because I thought he was still living in the fantasy we had created together, that it was a continuation of our love affair, and I replied in kind.

He wrote as though he were the knight Surcote from his stories, now travelled from Jerusalem to England to seek out King Arthur and join his round table. But after a month, I was getting a bit fed up of it. I heard about various skirmishes he's had on the roads, and how once he'd followed a travelling party that included Arthur and Guinevere for a number of miles, but he didn't feel ready to ride up and introduce himself. I'd had interminable moaning about his battle wounds from his meeting with the giant Gormundus, his admiration for the healers who'd helped him back to recovery. But not a word about his real self, where he was or what he was doing. I thought if I told Aggie about this she'd be less convinced of his recovery.

The new term began in October and autumn came to the city, and I remembered again why I loved London. It's not a city that suits summer. It gets too sweaty and dirty. But when October comes and the cool air drifts earlier into the evenings, and the trees turn red and orange in the parks and avenues, and the chestnut sellers push their hot stoves through the street, trailing their delicious smell, then I trip along the streets of Bloomsbury, my bag of books slung over my shoulder like a featherweight.

That was my experience most autumns. This year I found there was a drag in my step and a heaviness pulling me down.

My first seminar was with Marcus Sullivan who I hadn't seen since I hopped back on the train in May. I'd phoned Mum and Dad that evening to let them know I was all right, but I'd made no attempt to contact Marcus. I didn't know how he would be with me.

By the end of the seminar I was feeling relieved. He treated me no differently than any of the other students: friendly in a student/tutor kind of way, no significant looks or snide remarks. I thought, great, this is how it's going to be, pretend nothing ever happened, suits me fine. Then at the end of the seminar, just as everyone was packing their books away, he said,

"Kat, have you got a minute?"

My heart dropped, but I owed him some sort of explanation, so I sat on the table and waited while the others left the room and Marcus shuffled the papers on the desk. When they'd gone he made a big deal of cleaning the white board with a cloth, his back to me, and I realised I wasn't the only one who was nervous.

Eventually he put the cloth down and came over and sat next to me, his hands in his lap, his eyes gazing down at the floor.

"Good summer, Kat?"

"Yes, it had its moments."

"Good."

I'd never seen him like this before, diffident, unsure. It didn't suit him.

"And how about college? Are you ready to pick up where you left off?"

I looked hard at him until he lifted his gaze and turned to me. I know the answer to his question was written on my face, but I said it anyway.

"I think I'm up to date with my work. Academically, I'm ready to carry on, yes."

"Oh."

He looked down again.

"But if you want to carry on with anything extracurricular you'll need to find another girl."

He didn't say anything else, so I shifted my bag off my shoulder and got off the table.

As I was walking to the door he said, "I went on holiday to the south of France with my family. Three weeks."

I stopped and looked back.

"Great. Did you have a good time?"

"Bloody awful. I've left her, Kat."

He was looking straight at me now, and the look on his face was offering me things he'd never offered before. Commitment, openness, exclusiveness, love. It was too late. Last term it might have been different, before the summer, before Gavin. I was a different person then. I didn't want him now.

"Sorry Marcus," I said, and I was sorry but I couldn't think of anything else to say, so I kept on walking.

That evening I got a phone call from Sheila. I could tell straight away that she had news to tell me, although she spent at least five minutes chatting about Mel and the shop before she got to the point.

"I was going through those parcels for collection in the store room. You know, you were going to sort them out for me a few weeks ago but there wasn't time."

"I remember."

"Well, I was going through the order book and I saw that one of them was for a Mr B Knight."

She paused.

"Yes?"

"Wasn't that the name of Gavin's friend, the one who went to Iraq with him?"

"Yes, Bertrand Knight. But it's not uncommon is it, as a name. There must be thousands of Mr B. Knights around. It's just a coincidence."

"Yes I know, but you see, when I went through the parcels I found that one was missing."

Another pause.

"Are you sure? It could have fallen down behind something. Or maybe Mr Knight collected it and we just forgot to mark it down."

"I'm sure. I'd remember if he'd collected it. It was pretty distinctive. And expensive. Not the sort of thing we get orders for very often. And I've searched the storeroom. It's definitely not there."

I sighed.

"So Sheila, what are you suggesting?"

"Well, it was there before."

"Before what?"

"Before Gavin left."

"Are you saying that he's stolen it?"

"No, not stolen. Not exactly. But I thought maybe he'd taken it for some reason. Maybe he wants to deliver it to Mr Knight himself."

"I don't even know if Bertrand Knight is in the country. There's never been anything in the papers about his return. He could still be in captivity, or dead. I think it's the uncertainty that upsets Gavin so much."

"Oh no," said Sheila lightly, "he must be back because he only made the order in February."

I nearly screamed at her down the phone.

"February! Why didn't you tell me before?"

"I was going to. I just hadn't got round to it yet. Don't yell so loud, you hurt my ear."

I put the receiver in my lap for a moment and tried to relax my body. I could hear Sheila's voice jabbering away at the other end. I lowered my shoulders and straightened my neck. Breathed. Then put the phone back to my ear.

"Sheila."

"Oh you're still there. I thought the line had gone dead or something."

"Have you got contact details for this Mr Knight?"

"No. I remember the order, he phoned and he paid by credit card, and he said he'd pick it up personally, so I didn't need his address."

"How did you let him know when it arrived?"

"By email. I have an email address for him. Would you like it?"

"Yes please." She told me the address and I wrote it down. "I'll try and contact him, but I doubt it's the same man."

"But Gavin ... "

"Gavin is ill, Sheila. If he saw the name on the parcel he might have made the same conclusion you are doing. It doesn't mean it's right."

"Mmmm, I suppose so."

When I hung up my hands were shaking.

I knew what I said to Sheila about coincidence was true, but I didn't really believe it. Something about it seemed to make sense, to fit into some picture I was a part of, although I couldn't see the whole. It made me feel a bit uneasy, as though I'd let slip a bit of the control in my life and I couldn't tell what was going to happen. I suppose we do that all the time, every relationship we have gives some control to the other person, and we can never be sure how other people are going to behave. But this was different somehow. It wasn't that I thought Gavin was trying to control me, far from it. More that something was going on over which he had no control, and I'd accidentally fallen into it without having any idea what it was.

I turned my computer on and emailed Mr Knight. I said that I worked at Merlin's Cave and a gentleman named Mr Redman had been in to collect his parcel, and I wanted to be sure that this was all right with Mr Knight before we handed it over. I said Mr Redman was coming back the day after tomorrow, and if it was OK we'd give him the parcel then.

Two days later there was no reply, so I emailed again, during the day, saying Mr Redman was in the shop and could we hand over the parcel. This time there was a reply. It said:

>> Thank you for your message. The parcel which you speak of has been received into my keeping. Please thank Sheila Meldon for her kind attention in this matter. I hope you soon recover from your strange affliction and cease having fantasies about the mysterious Mr Redman. Best wishes, Mr B Knight <<

For some reason this message made me furious. I phoned Sheila and told her about it.

"I don't know why he had to be so bloody sarcastic. I feel like a complete idiot now. You must have been wrong Sheila, he must have been in and collected it. Maybe it was when you weren't there, when Mel was minding the shop or something."

Sheila didn't sound convinced. "Mmm, maybe," she said.

"Anyway, he's got his parcel and Gavin didn't nick it, so there's nothing to worry about."

"No Kat, I suppose not."

That should have been the end of it.

Chapter Twenty-one

Three weeks later Marcus asked me again to stay behind after a seminar. He'd not mentioned our conversation, and I'd been impressed at how professional he was, not letting our personal history get in the way of his teaching. It wasn't just a casual observer who'd have difficulty spotting any tension between us, there really didn't seem to be any. So I was surprised when he asked to see me.

This time there was no paper shuffling or board cleaning. Marcus didn't gaze at his feet. He looked me straight in the eye with his old confidence. It wasn't going to work, but I admired his tactics.

"Kat, I've had an email from someone who's interested in your work."

I was thrown by this.

"Oh?"

"He's a photographer with a special interest in archaeology. Apparently he has a lot of photographs of digs from Turkey and around the Mediterranean, and he's travelled in the Sumerian region. He thinks you may be able to help each other out."

I'd been so sure this was going to be about us that I didn't know how to respond.

"How did he find out? About me, I mean. About what I'm doing."

"Internet maybe. The college website. There's information on it about all the postgraduate projects. He probably did a Google search with Gilgamesh and Odyssey and archaeology, and came up with you."

"But why me? There must have been loads of hits higher up the list. It's not exactly an untapped area."

"Not as many as you'd think – it's not something you can do much practical work on at the moment. Not the Gilgamesh part anyway. He might be an interesting person to meet."

"Yes." I was still off-balance from expecting an entirely different conversation. "You say he has photographs?"

"So he says. Do you want his email address?"

"Yes. Yes I do. Is he here in London?"

"Not sure. He says he'd like to meet you though."

He wrote down an email address on a scrap of paper and handed it to me. I took it, but he didn't immediately let go.

"Do you want me to come with you Kat, if you meet him?"

"No, it's OK."

We were both holding the paper, our fingers a centimetre apart. He was looking at me, and I was suddenly reminded of my Dad when I was a kid, telling me to take care crossing the road. Then he let go.

"Well, be careful Kat. Meet him in a public place."

I nearly said yes dad, but managed to hold my tongue.

The photographer's name was Hugh Challenger. I emailed him that evening and got a reply straight away. He said he was particularly interested in the archaeology connected to epic tales, had spent years travelling the Mediterranean and the Middle East and had a whole bank of photographs. We arranged to meet at the South Bank Centre. I said I'd be wearing an orange hoodie and jeans. He said he walks with a stick – 'result of a hunting accident earlier this year, hopefully only temporary'.

I wasn't sure about the hunting. That, along with the name Hugh, gave me an image of a man I didn't think I'd like. Upper class, pompous, avuncular, reactionary. But I decided to put preconceptions aside and meet him first.

I got to the South Bank centre early and found a corner in the café where I could sit and watch people coming and going. I had my jacket on over my top, hiding the orange, so I could spot him before he spotted me. But I'd only been there five minutes when he materialised at my table. I'd been looking the other way, towards the entrance. He must have got there before me.

"Kat?" he said.

He was much younger than I'd expected. Somewhere in his forties probably. Tall and overweight, he held himself very upright, despite leaning slightly to one side on his stick. He seemed enormous, although when I stood up to shake his hand I realised he was only about six foot. No taller than Marcus. Not much taller than Gavin. He was wearing beige jeans and a cord jacket with a brown striped shirt that pulled taut across his belly.

He slung a black briefcase down onto the sofa and sat down. He moved awkwardly, sitting down on the far edge and then sliding his legs around so they were under the table and he was at right angles to me. Both of his legs seemed stiff. I couldn't tell which was the injured one.

I offered to go and get coffee for us both, but he said no.

"They'll send a waitress over. I know it's not strictly waitress service, but they'll make an exception."

I wasn't so sure, but when he caught the eye of a girl behind the counter and beckoned her, she came straight over.

"Can I help you sir?"

"You wouldn't mind bringing us some coffee over would you? It's my leg."

He indicated with his stick, and the girl made sympathetic noises.

"Oh, I'm sorry sir, of course I'll bring some over. Will you be wanting anything else?"

"No, just the coffee, thank you."

She dimpled at him, and I took a sideways look. He had something, even if it wasn't immediately obvious. There was puffy flesh covering his cheeks and dropping down into his neck, where it fell from his chin to the opening of his shirt. His stomach hung over the top of his trousers with the same appearance, loose, unnecessary. He looked as if he could have been ill. There was a hint of something harder beneath, and his eyes weren't the eyes of a lazy or self-indulgent man. Maybe this added fat was a recent thing, as a result of his accident. If he lost it, got fit again, despite the thinning hair he might be quite attractive.

"So, do you think there's a direct link between the Gilgamesh stories and the Homeric tradition?" he asked me.

Obviously not one for making small talk.

"Not direct, no. There are themes which can be traced. There is a suggestion of a Aegean-Mycenaean literature which drew on the Hittite version of Gilgamesh, and which might have survived to reappear in Greek poetry. I've been looking at the texts, looking for links, examining the possibilities."

"And what are your conclusions?"

"I haven't made any conclusions yet. There is the continual resurfacing of the flood story. I've been studying archaeological evidence, some of which suggests there may have been a flood in the region, but it's doubtful whether it was devastating enough to become part of a mythological tradition which spread so far."

"But myths can change in the telling, can they not? Their size and importance grows each time they are passed on. If the flood has a historical germ of truth, that could be just the seed from which a whole forest of tales has grown and spread."

His eyes were grey and sparked with intelligence. Something else too. Despite his words, I felt that he was flirting with me. Twenty years older than me, lame, overweight, he still had sexual confidence. That was what the waitress had responded to. I could feel myself responding to it too.

"If that's the case, trying to find a traceable line which a story has followed is a futile endeavour."

"Do you feel as though your work is futile?"

I sat back in my seat and straightened my back.

"I enjoy it. I find it intellectually stimulating. Are you asking me if I am adding to the sum of human knowledge? If my work is of universal importance?"

"I'm asking you what you hope to gain from it?"

"I don't know. A PhD. Some greater understanding of history, of civilisations and how they tell stories. Whether stories are simply a retelling of history or if they come from something deeper."

"It would perhaps be more rewarding to find that stories can't be traced back from one civilisation to another. If the same stories surfaced independently in different parts of the world and in different ages, that would suggest that they are an integral part of the human condition."

"Yes, and on a general level that certainly seems to be the case. Stories of quests and battles and overcoming monsters appear in every literary tradition."

"If you accept that, what is the point of looking at one particular story? Why does it matter whether Gilgamesh was an influence on Homer, direct or otherwise? Isn't the story itself more relevant than the history of the story?"

I was backed into a corner. And also I felt that what he was saying and what he meant were not the same thing. He didn't really care if my PhD were worthwhile or not. He was asking me something else. Something that involved looking beyond the hanging fat below his jaw which moved as he spoke, and his stiff awkward legs which nudged against the table, making coffee spill from the cups into the saucers.

"Maybe I will find that out. Maybe the point I will discover is that there is no point."

"But you hope you will have become wiser on the journey. Like the heroes of old, returning from their quests disillusioned, but wise."

Now I felt that he was taking the piss, although there was nothing in his face or tone of voice to suggest anything other than sincerity. I leaned forward to get my coffee from the table. He hadn't touched his.

"You said you had photographs. Have you brought any with you?"

"Ah, yes. The photographs."

He opened his briefcase and drew out a slim folder, which he handed to me. The photographs inside were A4 prints. I looked through them slowly.

They were stunning. Most of them were site photographs from digs in Turkey. People sifting earth in trenches, close-ups of pieces of stone and pottery, a couple of site overviews that took in the landscape. It wasn't the subject matter that impressed me, or the composition, which was, without exception, faultless; but the clarity. These photographs seemed to breathe the air of a hot desert. I could almost smell the sun scorching the sand. As archaeological records they were of limited interest, but I was transfixed.

The last photograph was entirely different. It was taken deep inside a forest. The trees were tall, their bare trunks stretching up to reach the canopy high above. At the top of the photograph, the canopy was dark green, almost black, and dense. Sunlight entered though the chinks where trees brushed against one another, and streamed down in glowing columns between the trunks, adding to their number. Where they ended in pools on the forest floor, more trees were growing, delicate fernlike conifers that seemed to be dancing, frivolous and luxurious compared to the solidity of the ancient trunks around them. The trees were packed tight. There was no path, no clearing. It was spooky and primal and stirred some ancient anxiety within me.

I looked up at Hugh.

"A cedar forest. I thought it might interest you. Unfortunately it's not from the right part of the world, it was taken in Idaho. But I guess a cedar forest is a cedar forest. It must be pretty like the one where Gilgamesh went to slay his monster."

I looked at it again. I tried to imagine what it would be like, forcing your way through, not knowing what you might find, certain you were passing territory never touched by human feet. How it would feel when night came down and sounds filled the blackness around you. I could smell the scent of the cedars in the falling light, and understood how Gilgamesh, great hero and leader that he was, was overcome with paralysing fear.

My skin felt cold. I closed the folder and handed it back to Hugh.

"Thank you. They are beautiful. Very atmospheric."

"If you think it would be of any use to you I have hundreds more. A whole library of photographs at my flat in Holborn. You're welcome to go round and look through them. I could give you a key – I'm hardly ever there."

"But ... wouldn't you mind? I mean, you don't know me."

"I know where to find you," he said.

I went straight home. I felt disturbed and uneasy. My flatmate Rhyssa had bought some white wine and we sat and drank it and talked. I couldn't understand why, but I felt as though I had been violated in some way, as though Hugh was aware of parts of me that weren't meant to be seen. Certainly not by him. He had been polite and courteous throughout, touching only my hand in parting with his own large dry one. All the way home I could feel the weight of his flat key in my bag as though it were made of a heavy alien metal.

What I wanted was Gavin. I wanted him to wrap me in his arms and kiss the top of my head, and then all the uneasiness would seep out. I wanted to rest my cheek against the leather of his jacket, or even better against his skin.

Rhyssa and some of her crowd were going out clubbing and she asked me to come along, but I didn't feel like it. When she'd gone I turned the computer on, hoping there might be an email from Gavin, but there wasn't. There'd been one yesterday, brimming with excitement about the jousting contest he was due to take part in the next day. He said he was at a large tournament, all the knights of the Round Table were there, including King Arthur. He'd kept himself disguised, won all the competitions he'd taken part in so far. Everyone was talking about the mysterious stranger. The contest tomorrow would be the hardest yet.

I'd replied telling him about my day, my college work, trying to keep the tone light and conversational. Not mentioning his email, even though I wanted to scream at him.

Now I couldn't do it though. I found my fingers typing the words even though my brain was urging me not to. Don't put pressure on him, let it ride, things will change in due course.

>> Gavin, where are you? I miss you and I love you and I wish you were here right now. I can't stand it any longer. Kat <<

After that I crumpled fully dressed on to my bed and slept until after midnight, exhausted. When I woke up there was a reply flashing on my computer screen. I opened it. It said, >>I love you too. Gavin<<.

Gavin, not Surcote. I wanted to sing.

Chapter Twenty-two

He's responded to her email before he's had time to think. Only as he clicks on the send button does he realise what he's doing.

I love you too.

That's not what he's supposed to say. Keep it friendly. Keep a distance. These are the rules he's set for himself. And she's been responding in kind. Nothing too heavy. Just news about her life, stories about college, as if he were an old mate, or her diary. It seems as though she is reasonably happy, jogging along. That's why this email caught him unawares.

I miss you and I love you and I wish you were here right now. I can't stand it any longer.

He's let slip the control he holds over his mind, and suddenly Kat is in the room with him. She puts her arms around his chest and pushes her face into his shoulder. Taller, he can surround her, both of his arms wrapped tight around her back and his head bent over hers. She is safe with him. She doesn't need to stand it any longer. He squeezes her gently and kisses her hair, smelling the fresh apple outdoor smell no amount of London grime can quite disguise.

Then Morgan calls up the stairs.

"Gavin, are you there?"

The image crumbles and Gavin is alone in the bare room. A small table, a chair, the computer. The walls newly plastered, floorboards stripped bare waiting for treatment.

"Gavin, I'm going into town in a minute. Did you need a lift?"

He goes to the top of the stairs. She is dressed, as usual, in black. Polo neck ribbed sweater, and high-waisted slacks. Her figure looks fantastic.

"No. I'm going to get on with painting the back room. It's ready for a second coat. And I may do some sanding in here as well."

"OK. Well, I'll be back when the bar closes. See you then if you're still up."

She blows him a kiss and he smiles.

Normally, when he's working, he can switch off completely, concentrate on the task in hand to the exclusion of all else. It's taken a while for him to perfect this. To begin with thoughts would creep in, or images, and suddenly instead of a skirting board he'd be looking at Kat's face, or Sheila's, or Aggie's, and they'd be asking him what he was doing, what he was trying to escape from, why he couldn't just talk to them. It was hard to push them aside. He felt cruel, had to remind himself that they were only projections of his imagination. Now they don't come any more and his working time is a blank.

But not today. Today he is plagued by voices. As he paints he hears them, not in his head but behind him somewhere in the room, asking him questions: how long can you keep this up? Has Morgan told GK you're staying here? What will happen when the house is finished? What about New Year?

He tries to shut it out, immerse himself in violet-coloured walls and the smooth action of the roller. But the whispers float through the empty room, wrapping themselves around him like torn strands of cotton wool. He feels suffocated, scared.

He is relieved to get back to the computer room where he moves the furniture out into the hallway and turns on the sanding machine. The noise is loud enough to blast away any whispering voices. When the job is finished and the machine switched off, the house is silent.

Downstairs he helps himself to a tumbler full of Morgan's whisky, knocks it back as though it were water, refills it and takes it up to bed. He sleeps in a small room at the top of the house on a cheap futon bed. The walls are papered with large pink roses and green velvet curtains hang at the windows, pockmarked by moths, so thin in places that the morning sun shines through making mottled light sculptures in the gloom. Morgan suggested he redecorate, offered to buy him a decent bed, but he didn't want to make himself comfortable. He cleared out all the furniture and bought this bed, the cheapest he could find. Cheap enough to be disposable when he's gone.

The whisky sends him off to sleep quickly, but it's not dreamless. The voices have been silenced but have mutated, grown, expanded into technicolour sound and vision, and his dream is made of memory.

He is alone in a darkened room. Darkened, but not dark, because one wall is filled with a screen showing video footage, projected through a hole in the wall high above him. He is on the floor, his hands tied behind his back with rope, his feet chained together. He has his back to the screen, but he can still see it. Every sound carries its own image, which he knows as well as his own face in the mirror. If he opens his eyes, the flickering light on the walls seems to carry a negative of the pictures on the screen. If he closes them, the images resume their own colours and fill up his head, leaving no space to hide. He has been here for a long time. Days, possibly more than a week. Hard to keep track. The video is on a ten-minute loop and has been playing the whole time.

A prisoner in a yard, hands tied, feet tied, gagged but not blindfolded, standing alone facing a row of soldiers on the other side, guns pointing at him. His eyes black with fear.

Another man is dragged into the yard on the same side as the guards. He's not tied, but a soldier holds a gun to his back. His steps are faltering, he stumbles. A gun is thrust into his arms and he is turned roughly so he faces the prisoner. Their eyes meet.

Words are spoken. Gavin knows very little Arabic, but he understands these words. The guards are telling the man to shoot the prisoner, and the man says no, I cannot, he is my son.

The soldier behind jabs the gun into his back.

If you don't shoot we will shoot you both.

The father drops the gun to the floor, words spill from his mouth, his hands move through the air describing the monstrous shape of his anger and grief.

Gavin doesn't know the exact words, but he can understand the essence of what the man is saying.

How could I live if I killed my son? He is my firstborn, the fruit of my loins, my heir and my beloved. If I raise the gun against my own flesh, my life will be over. If I shoot my son I will kill myself also, my blood will spill from his wounds, my honour, and his, will stain the ground. My family will be forced to walk forever more with their eyes towards the dust. No one will ever again look me in the eye. If I kill my son I will carry his loss forever in my heart and the death will be my own.

He is in full flow when the soldier raises the gun and shoots him through the head.

The prisoner, whose back had straightened a little during his father's speech, crumples to the ground, wailing.

Another man is brought out straight away. He is a young man, like the prisoner. He sees the dead body on the floor and a gasp escapes from his lips.

My father.

He tries to kneel, to take his father's limp hand, but the soldiers drag him back. The gun dropped by his father is lifted from the bloodstained floor and given to him. He, like his father, is turned to face the prisoner, the same instructions given to him.

Shoot the prisoner or we will shoot you.

160

The brother does not drop the gun. He holds it in his arms and stares across the yard at the crouching figure. The prisoner had stopped wailing and is watching, still-faced. He knows he will be killed anyway. First he must watch his brother either die or betray him.

Like his father before him, the younger brother begins to speak. But he words are filled with sadness and remorse, not anger. They don't lift the prisoner up, but let him gently down.

I am sorry my brother, but I have no choice. I have a wife and children, who without me to support them will be destitute. And also, if I go against the army now, my family will be persecuted after I have gone. You would do the same in my position. I will bring your wife to live with my household and provide for her and her children. I love you my brother. May God and my father forgive me for what I must do.

And almost as if he were brushing a fly away from his sleeve, he lifts the gun and fires. The bullet hits his brother in the chest and he falls sideways. Immediately the row of soldiers, still as stone up to now, open fire on the prisoner and his body is lifted from the ground by the number of bullets.

The brother turns away, thrusting the gun away from himself, covering his face with his hands.

But the soldier standing next to him is patting him on the shoulder.

You have shown your loyalty and will be rewarded.

This is the film. It ends with a shot of the prisoner lying on the floor, his clothes torn apart by the gunshots, blood running into the dust from his wounds. His eyes are still open, but the blackness of fear has left them. They are dull brown, and the first fly has already landed, crawling along the rim of the left eye in search of a drink.

Lying on the stone floor in the darkness, Gavin knows every movement, every minute flicker of the eye, every inflection, every break of the voice. His mind has no room for anything else. He knows if it were to stop now, it would keep running in his head. It has become a part of him. If he could escape and run, he would take the film with him, carry it forever in his soul. There is no escape. The certainty of this racks his body with sobs, knocking his bones against the cold stone floor.

And he is sobbing when Morgan finds him. Still asleep, his eyes closed, his body shaking uncontrollably like that of a small child. She lies down beside him on the bed and pulls him towards her, strokes the back of his head and speaks gently into his ear.

"Gavin, Gavin. You can wake up now, it's all over. I'm here."

After a few minutes the sobbing ceases and Gavin's body becomes still. His lips are touching her neck, and he can feel the hot dampness of his breath against her skin. The smell of her perfume is musky and enticing.

She gently lifts his head with her hands until his eyes are on a level with her own. They are open and shining in the darkness. She kisses first one eye, then the other, and they close beneath her lips. She touches his left cheek with soft light kisses which trail down his face from his eyes and he can feel the wetness of his tears on her lips. At the corner of his mouth her kisses become more insistent, pushing his lips apart, probing his mouth with her tongue.

She slides her right hand down his body and slips her hand under his t-shirt. Her arm is cool against his hot flesh. She pushes her body against his, squashing her breasts against him, and her hand moves into his groin, rubbing his erection beneath the soft jersey of his shorts.

He groans and rolls towards her, covering her mouth with his own, pushing aside her robe and grasping at her breasts. She frees him from his shorts and he buries his face in her neck, as they writhe together, legs entwined, hands and lips moving, touching every part they can. He lowers his head to her breasts and she pushes her chest forward, closing her eyes, waiting for him to take her nipple in his mouth.

And suddenly he can't.

She opens her eyes and he has rolled away. He's lying on the other side of the bed, elbow bent and head supported by his hand.

"Gavin?"

She reaches her hand towards him, but he shakes his head.

"Sorry Morgan, I can't."

"It felt like you could."

"It's not that. You're lovely, I'd love to, but ..."

"But what?"

"There's someone else."

She sits up and turns on the lamp by the bed.

"Someone else?"

"Yes."

Her gown is open, only the silk sash still tied in a dark band across her belly. Turning to him her face is still charged with desire, her eyes are dark and her features have lost their definition.

"Where is she then?"

Gavin looks down at the pillow so his lids cover his eyes.

"I left her."

She sits up straight and pulls her gown back together covering herself.

"Explain."

He is quiet for a moment, and his voice, when it comes, is fragile as eggshell.

"I have too much shit. I love her, but I can't bring that to her. She's young and full of life, and the darkness inside me is so vast I'm scared it would consume her."

"Does she love you?"

"She says she does." Gavin loses himself for a moment and a small smile flits across his face like a bat in the dark. "Yes, she does."

Morgan wraps her arms about herself and curls up her legs beneath her.

"Well, if she loves you, and if you love her, shouldn't you let her decide if she can cope with your shit or not?"

"She doesn't know. She doesn't know what I've done. I'm scared that if I tell her she'll hate me."

"You have to tell her. There's no other way." Morgan leans over and kisses him on the mouth, then slides off the bed and stands up. "I'm going to bed. If you need me you know where I am."

She leaves the room and Gavin slides back down into the pillows, holding the image of her silk-clad nakedness in his mind, his erection throbbing.

Chapter Twenty-three

I carried the key to Hugh Challenger's flat in my bag for just over a week. I didn't want to use it. My meeting with him had left me uneasy, and this invitation to make myself at home in his home seemed as though it must carry other expectations. Was he really interested in my work, was he offering his photographs in a spirit of altruism? I couldn't quite believe it, although I wasn't sure what it was he wanted from me.

The email from Gavin kept me buoyed up for a few days. I replied immediately of course, full of joy and enthusiasm at this renewal of real conversation between us. But he didn't reply, or rather, when he did it was back to the old fantasy world. He told me how he had won through to become champion of the tournament and how King Arthur had sent word inviting him to become a part of his round table, but that at present he didn't feel it was right to accept. He even asked for my opinion on the matter.

I replied that before he thought of accepting such a prestigious position it would be wise to find out his true identity, as it was hard to communicate with someone who was so deluded. I tried to make my reply light hearted, but my hopeful mood had evaporated.

I decided to return Hugh's key. My life was complicated enough, and although his photographs were fascinating, I didn't see how they could help me with my thesis. I put it in an envelope with a note thanking him, but explaining that I didn't feel comfortable with the arrangement, intending to drop it in the post. But while I was writing the envelope it occurred to me that posting a key to the flat it opened wasn't a terribly safe thing to do. Holborn was not far from college; I could drop it off myself.

So the following Monday morning Rhyssa and I took a detour on the way in. His flat was on a busy high street above the shops. It was one of those lovely Victorian buildings that are invisible from street level, where all you can see are the plate glass and neon advertising of the ground floor shop fronts. It was only when you looked up that you could see the original Victorian splendour. The door to the upper floors, between two shops, was painted dark green and was unnoticeable unless you were looking for it. It had discreet buzzers and an intercom, one each for the flats on the first and second floors. Hugh's, he had told me, was on the second floor, but the buzzer was unmarked. There was a letterbox.

"Someone could still nick it from the hallway," Rhyssa said.

We pressed the buzzer but there was no answer. So we let ourselves in and climbed up the wooden stairs to the second floor.

The door to his flat had no letterbox, and was closely fitted so there was no way we could slide the envelope underneath. There was no choice but to go in and leave the key inside.

I opened the door.

"Wow; smell the money!" said Rhyssa. "He must be loaded."

It smelled of leather, polished floors, airiness. The lines of the floorboards, smooth and pale, led the eye down a length of hall with doors leading off at various points. There was a small wooden table with an empty vase standing on it. On the wall opposite hung a painting of a woman and a black cat. The woman was wearing a red dress and reclining on a black leather sofa with the cat standing on the back of the sofa behind her left shoulder. Apart from the painting and the table, the hallway was completely empty.

I opened the first door on the left and peered into the living room. I immediately recognised the sofa from the painting, standing in the middle of the room that stretched the whole length of the flat. It was an enormous sofa, but the room was so big that it seemed like an island in the middle.

"I'm going to use the loo," Rhyssa said. "I bet it's amazing."

And she walked down the hallway, opening doors, her high-heeled boots clacking on the wooden floors.

In the living room there was a desk against the back wall. I put the key back in its envelope and walked over to put it in the middle of the desk, and saw that Hugh had left me a note.

Kat, sorry about the dusty state of the flat. I've hardly been here recently, so I didn't think it was worth keeping the cleaner on. The photographs I got out for you are in these boxes. I hope you find them useful. I enjoyed our stimulating chat the other day and hope we can meet up again soon. Hugh.

It lay on the top of two box files, the only objects on the desk other than a phone, which appeared to be disconnected. There was a very fine layer of dust covering the desk, the phone and the boxes and, when I glanced around the room, I saw on everything else too.

I hesitated. I'd made my decision about Hugh, but now I was here with the photographs in front of me, it seemed a shame not to have a quick look at them. Just for interest's sake, while Rhyssa was in the bathroom. Then I could leave the key and go.

I stood with the key in one hand, the other resting on the top of the box files. It might be a mistake, but I couldn't help myself. Slowly I removed the note from the top of the pile leaving a clean square that the dust hadn't reached. I wiped away the rest of the dust with my sleeve and opened the box.

As before, the photographs were stunning. Full of atmosphere, the colour and composition perfect. Lots of dust and sand and smiling faces in trenches; occasional close ups of finds they had made.

After a while though, I began to feel that Hugh had made a mistake. Although these photos were good, there was nothing better or much different from what he'd shown me when we met. They were all from the same dig where he had obviously taken hundreds of photos, often many of the same shot. It seemed that these boxes contained the whole lot, and that he'd already shown me the best. I heard the toilet flush and the tap running.

I put the first box aside and started on the second, but it was more of the same. I wondered if this dig in Turkey was the only one Hugh Challenger had ever been on, or if he'd just put out the wrong box files.

Rhyssa came into room.

"Best piss I've ever had. Are you ready or shall we have a look at the kitchen?"

I was nearly at the bottom of the second box.

"Look!"

One photograph that was out of place. No trenches, no archaeologists. Just a young man in a flak jacket laughing at the camera. A young man with shining eyes, dusty hair and two days' stubble on his chin, leaning against a jeep in the desert, looking as though he hadn't a care in the world.

"Who is it?"

"Gavin."

I could feel my heart beating, but my brain seemed to have switched off. I felt like I was being watched, like I'd been caught doing something I shouldn't.

"Come on, let's go."

Running on adrenalin, I slipped the photograph into my bag. I slammed shut the boxes, threw the envelope with the key onto the desk. I grabbed Rhyssa's arm and dragged her out after me, running down the stairs two at a time and into the street. We banged the door shut and leaned against it. Rhyssa was laughing. The street was full of noise and colour: shoppers rushing by, people hurrying too late to their offices, students. So different from the silent empty flat upstairs. My heart slowed down.

"Come on, let's get to college," I said.

"But how come he had that photo?" Rhyssa asked.

"I don't know, but I guess he wants me to find out."

Marcus wasn't teaching me that day, but I saw him in the corridor after my seminar and he stopped me.

"Kat, did you see that chap? Challenger, was that his name?"

"Yes. Good pictures, but not much use to me."

"Oh well. And was he all right? No problems?"

"No problems. Marcus, where did you say he'd found out about me?"

"Didn't say. From the college website I guess."

When I got home I did a Google search on my own name. Now I thought about it I was surprised I'd never done it before. It hadn't occurred to me that I could be found on the internet.

But there I was, on the postgraduate section of the college website. Kat Webster, researching the archaeological background to epic literature with particular reference to Gilgamesh and Homer's Odyssey. There was even a little picture of me, taken two years ago, barely recognisable.

Next I checked my emails; there was one from Sheila. She was coming up to London tomorrow and wanted to meet me for lunch. I decided to leave the photograph where it was in my bag until I saw her.

"I've been doing some searching on the internet and I've found out quite a bit about this Bertrand Knight."

We were sitting on opposite sides of a wooden bench in a basement café in Bloomsbury. I had a cup of ordinary tea and Sheila had nettle tea. We'd just eaten roasted pepper and kidney bean casserole.

"He seems to have come from quite a prestigious family. A manor house in Cheshire, quite a bit of land. They're listed in Who's Who."

"You checked?"

Sheila shrugged and picked up her cup, holding it between her two palms and gently rotating it, one way then the other, so the liquid rocked inside.

"What are you trying to find out?"

"Where he is. If he ever returned to England."

"What about his family? Can you contact any of them?"

"Well, there's the place in Cheshire, I could write there. But what would I say? I'm just writing out of curiosity to see if your son is alive or not. Not very tactful."

"No. What about the people he worked for?"

"That's what I'm in London for. I thought if I turned up at the office in person saying I was his friend it might be more effective than a phone call."

"Have you tried anyone yet?"

Sheila put her cup down in the saucer without drinking.

"Yes, one. They didn't know any more than I did. Said would I let them know if I found anything out, because they really wanted to contact him. His phone's been disconnected, emails aren't answered, letters just disappear into a black hole. They've no idea if he's receiving them or not."

"God!"

We both picked up our cups and drank from them. I put mine down with a clatter.

"What about his brother?"

"His brother?"

"Yes, I'm sure I remember Gavin mentioning that Bertrand had a brother. He had a strange name, or just initials. JK – no it was GK. He was called GK."

"There isn't a brother."

"Yes there is. I remember Gavin saying. We were talking about blogs, and Gavin said lots of journalists kept blogs when they were abroad. I asked him if he did, and he said no. He said Bertrand didn't either, he used to email his brother GK instead."

"I looked in Who's Who. Bertrand is an only child."

"Then...?"

We stared at each other across the table. Suddenly everything seemed much more complicated than it had before.

"Either GK is someone else, not really his brother, or he doesn't exist," said Sheila.

"He must exist if Bertrand was emailing him?"

"The email address must exist, but not necessarily a person."

"Why tell Gavin it was his brother?"

"Who knows? Maybe it made him feel better. People do all sorts of strange things when they're scared."

"What are you going to do next?"

"Try some more newspapers and magazines. Follow up all the leads I can."

"And if you find him?"

"It depends where he is, and how he is. If he's still in captivity, then something should be done about it – something big. But I don't think he can be – with Gavin back, I'm sure there'd be something in the press if Bertrand was still out there – alive. I think either he's dead – and his family have requested that it be hushed up – or he's alive and back in this country. There must be someone out there who knows."

There wasn't much more we could say about the subject. Not until we got fresh information. So instead I told Sheila about my meeting with Hugh Challenger and my visit to his flat. At the end of the story I took the photograph from my bag and laid it on the table between us.

Sheila picked it up and looked at it for a long time. First she just gazed at it, then she started looking in the corners really closely, then she turned it over and looked at the back.

"I was hoping for a date. Sometimes there is a date on a photograph."

"I already checked for that. But I think it must be quite recent – within the last few years. Because he looks ... not the same, but ..."

"The same sort of age. Yes, but this is definitely taken before he was captured. Before whatever happened to him. He looks like he did when he was seventeen – full of fun and daring, ready for anything."

"I wish I could have met him then."

Sheila looked up from the photograph and looked at me.

"Kat, did Gavin tell you about other places he'd been abroad or jobs he'd worked on?"

"No, he didn't really talk about the past at all. I got the impression it was the first time he'd been to a war zone. Though I don't know if he ever actually said that."

"We need to find out. Because if this was taken in Iraq before he was captured, when he was with Bertrand who was a photographer, then it might have been taken by Bertrand."

"But why would Hugh Challenger have it?"

"I don't know."

We'd both finished our tea. I would be late for a tutorial if I didn't get a move on.

"I think we need to see Aggie," I said.

Chapter Twenty-four

Eventually it changes.

The same video footage has been playing on a loop twenty-four hours a day. How many days Gavin doesn't know, as all concept of day and night has gone. Time is broken now into ten-minute pieces, starting with the prisoner standing in the courtyard and ending with his blasted body bloody in the dust. Then the prisoner's on his feet again, ready to die over and over.

Sometimes the episode seems to drag out to the length of a feature film, each nuance of movement filled with pathos, carrying the backdrop of the protagonist's life before this moment, the way the world will continue after he is dead. What his death will mean to his family, and the cyclic reverberations reaching out from this courtyard into the larger world.

At other times the ten minutes of film seem like a bodily rhythm; the prisoner stands, falls to his knees, stands again and then dies in time to a slow heartbeat, a flow which beats through Gavin's body and is almost soothing. The scenes, the sounds of the voices and the gunshots, have become as much a part of him as the air that he breathes. So when it changes, when the screen is suddenly filled with a different image, a different voice, Gavin is as startled as if he'd been kicked in the belly.

The face is Bertrand's. He is staring straight into the camera, and his expression is deadly serious, deadpan. Once Gavin has got over the initial shock, once his breathing returns to normal, he looks at Bertrand's face and wants to laugh. He thinks of comedians on the TV, back in that other life – that time which now seems as unreal as a novel he'd once read, a film he'd watched. Real enough while he lived it, immersed himself in it, but now, in this new reality, perceivable as the fiction it was.

Bertrand's face, this comic serious face, throws him back. Or rather, it brings a little of the colour from that world into the dark space he now inhabits. Why are they showing him this? Why is Bertrand staring into the camera?

After a few minutes Bertrand begins to speak and his voice matches his expression. It's in a low monotone and the spaces between the words are unnaturally even, as though he were reading them in another language or speaking them to someone who doesn't understand. Gavin is still amused, but now he can see what Bertrand is doing. He is sending Gavin a message, carried not in the words he says but in the manner of his delivery.

He says, "Please don't kill me. If you need to kill one of us, kill Gavin. He's the one that causes all the trouble. He won't do what you want him to do and forces you to punish him. If you let him go he will write subversive material which will be damaging to your organisation. I'm just a photographer, and you've taken away my camera. I won't, can't, cause any trouble. I'll do what you say. It makes sense, if you're going to kill one of us, kill Gavin."

They want Gavin to see his friend betraying him. They want to demoralise him. But Bertrand is sending another silent message to Gavin, which says, they're making me do this, but I don't mean it. Don't let it get to you. Don't let them win.

Gavin feels a warmth that he hasn't felt for a long time. Since he and Bertrand were separated he has felt utterly alone and disorientated. Now it's as through Bertrand had reached over and squeezed his shoulder.

The film begins again, and this time Gavin is ready for it. He looks at Bertrand's face, watching for any flicker or twitch that he missed before. He notices how gaunt Bertrand is looking, his cheeks sunken and grey, a growth of beard that mixes strands of white in with the auburn, dirty hollows beneath his eyes.

Bertrand is naturally fastidious about his appearance, managing to shave and wash even in the most extreme of desert conditions. He must hate looking like this. There is no emotion.

The film runs four times, then the prisoner is there once again, hands bound, feet bound, facing a line of guns all pointed at him. The father is brought out at gunpoint, ordered to shoot his son. Gavin has seen this film before.

They're in IKEA. Morgan is buying furniture for the office and the spare bedroom. Bits and pieces for Wodwo's too. She's borrowed a van from one of the bands who play at the weekends and brought her credit card with her.

They've been looking at desks, unsure how the heights of various designs would fit with the office chair Morgan has chosen, so Gavin goes off with the tape measure to check. When he returns Morgan has disappeared. He wanders around amongst displays of coloured box files and faked-up offices looking for her. He's only been gone for three or four minutes.

The next section is bedrooms. She might have gone on ahead, thinking of the spare room. He follows the rubber-tracked trail that leads through the store, looking out for her slim black figure and the enormous orange trainers she's wearing today.

No sign of her in the flat sweep of beds that stretches out in front of him. He turns back and a glimpse of orange catches his eye. Between the two departments, as a natural barrier, there's a group of walk-in bedrooms, enclosed by shelves, screened off with curtains. A tented child's room, spotted with funky bright storage ideas, sprinkled with books and misshapen toys. A king-size room layered with animal prints and fake fur, dark sheets folded back invitingly, pillows and cushions piled high, dark wood furniture. And last, a romantic bridal room, complete with four poster bed hung with muslin drapes, broderie anglais quilts and pillow cases, seaside ornaments and wind chimes, a fluffy white rug on the floor.

It's on this rug that Morgan's feet are resting, orange and solidly urban in this ethereal room. She's sitting on the bed crying silently, her face in her hands.

Gavin sits next to her and puts his arm around her shoulders and immediately her crying becomes audible, a soft snuffling noise punctuated with hiccoughing sobs. He squeezes her gently and she turns to him, dropping her hands away from her face and burrowing into his shoulder.

They sit there for a few minutes, her body shaking slightly. Gavin says nothing. Another customer walks into the bedroom, but when they see the couple sitting on the bed they look faintly embarrassed and walk out again. Eventually Morgan says something.

Gavin has to put his ear right down to the side of her face to catch the muffled words, and even then he can't quite make them out. But as he replays the sound over in his mind it clarifies. She said, "GK would absolutely hate this room."

He can't think of anything to say to her, but after a few moments she sits up straight, moving apart from him on the bed. She wipes at her face with her hands, smearing the tears across her cheeks. She's stopped crying.

"I could never drag him here to begin with, but if he saw this bedroom he'd be horrified. He'd say something so cutting, he'd make me laugh."

He looks around at the white gauze, the chest of drawers thinly whitewashed to give an appearance of age. "Do you like it?" He'd never have associated a room like this with her.

"No! That's the point. Of course I don't like it! It's bloody awful."

"Thank god for that!"

They shouldn't be here, they don't belong. It's as though their bodies, the darkness of their clothes, the flesh and blood life running in their veins are too real, too animal and could contaminate its whiteness. He looks back at Morgan and she's watching him.

He moves closer, and then they're kissing, their arms around each other, their mouths greedy. She leans back and his body follows her movement so that he's on top of her and his hand slides under her clothes feeling the heat of her flesh.

Someone comes into the room and they hear a loud "Bloody hell!" before the footsteps retreat, and they both sit up laughing.

She says "Did you measure the chair?"

"Yes. It fits."

"Let's go and do some shopping."

They straighten the ruffled covers and leave the bedroom. Neither of them says anymore about it, but for the time being at least, their personal spaces have broken down and merged. For the rest of the time they're at IKEA they can't keep their hands off each other. Looking at toilet seats in the bathroom area, Gavin's hand is resting on her bottom. They walk through the children's department with their arms round each other's waists, and stop between racks of oriental rugs for a snog. There is a feeling of temporariness, of play-acting, but Gavin doesn't try to analyse it. Just for the moment they are pretending to be a happy couple.

Morgan finds all of the items on her list, and more besides. They stop at the café for coffee and strudel and under-the-table leg groping. In the long queue at the checkout they lean against each other, nuzzling each other's necks and ear lobes. It looks like it's the prelude to something more and quite soon. But both of them know they're living in the moment.

Gavin drives the van home. Morgan's name was put on the insurance for the day, and she drove on the way to IKEA, but Gavin feels like driving, and when he climbs into the driver's seat Morgan doesn't say anything. She puts her hand on his thigh as he drives, but lets it lay still, shifting her elbow out of the way when he changes gear. Still they don't speak.

It's nearly an hour's drive. They pull up in front of Morgan's house and Gavin turns off the engine. He looks down at Morgan's hand on his leg. It seems like something inert, something fallen or dropped there. She doesn't look at him.

"Why do you call him GK?"

She picks up her hand and twists it over in front of her face looking at it, her silver rings catching glints of light through the window and throwing them onto her face. Gavin watches them, looks at the way her dark hair grows low down in front of her ears, tugging at her skin where she has pulled it back into a tight ponytail. He looks at the strong lines of her jaw and her cheekbone, and how they are not parallel; if they were to continue they would converge somewhere near her other ear. He'd like to trace these two lines with his thumb and forefinger, all the way to their meeting point.

"It's from when he was a kid. Someone told him about the myth of the Green Knight, and as that's his name – Knight – he wanted to be him. Wouldn't answer to anything else until it stuck. Green Knight it stands for. Even his parents call him GK most of the time."

She turns to look at him and he leans over and kisses her softly on the lips before opening the van door and swinging his legs out away from her onto the ground.

Together they unload the van, Morgan directing where she wants things to go, Gavin mostly knowing anyway. When it's empty, Morgan jumps back in and drives the van back to its owner, leaving Gavin to prepare chicken and vegetables for them to eat on her return.

As he slices and chops he thinks about her driving, her concentration on the road and the way her breasts move when she changes gear. She drives fast. He knows that if she chooses it, this time he won't be able to resist her, and he glows with the heat of desire that has been building up all day. But he is also familiar with the sour taste of frustration.

They speak little over the meal. With their return to the familiar house, the spaces around each of them have re-formed. They don't touch each other, even by accident. Passing each other items across the table, pouring the wine, both are careful that their fingers don't meet. Occasionally glancing up from his food, Gavin catches Morgan looking at him, but when their eyes meet she quickly glances away.

Over coffee she says "I'm missing GK. What I used to have with GK."

He reaches over and covers her hand with his, and it's the gesture of a friend and has no heat in it.

"I know you are."

"If we ... If we did ..."

"I know. It's OK."

She smiles at him gratefully and he thinks she looks younger than he has ever seen her before.

"If things were different..." he says.

"If things were different I'd be in there like a shot," she grins, and the sudden glint in her eye makes the blood rush to his groin.

Chapter Twenty-five

>>Kat, did I mention to you that the Emperor of Rome gave a casket into my safekeeping? He told me it contained papers that were of great importance to me, but that I was not to look at them. Indeed, I was to let no one open the casket save King Arthur, King of the Britons, and that until such time came that I should meet this brave and renowned knight I was to carry the casket with me at all times.

It goes without saying that I have carried out his bidding. The Emperor has always shown me the kindness of a father since the sad event of my own father's passing, and I value his wisdom and judgement in all things.

You are also aware that I was recently in the presence of this same King Arthur at the tournament in which I was fortunate enough to exhibit my knightly skills, and that I kept my identity a secret from everybody.

However, once the tournament was over, I felt that I could no longer delay in carrying out the instructions of my benefactor, the Emperor of Rome. On the morning of my departure from the tournament grounds, I summoned a squire and demanded that he deliver the casket forthwith to the King himself, explaining that it was a communication from the Emperor of Rome, carried to him by the nameless knight who vanquished all at the recent games. As soon as the squire returned with assurance that the casket had been delivered, I sat astride my horse and set forth into the barren countryside in the north west of this kingdom.

It feels strange to no longer be carrying the casket. I feel that I have lost something important and keep casting around for what it might be, until I remember. And, try as I might to silence it, a voice in my brain keeps asking me what it might have contained which could be of interest to the King. But the information was not for my eyes. The casket must remain closed to me and those that know me.

I hope that you can understand this. Some things must remain locked away, because the effects of bringing them into the open would be too enormous, too devastating to contemplate. If things could have been different, if I could have opened the casket with a clear conscience and merry heart and shared the contents with my loved ones, I would have done so. It hangs heavy on my heart that this was not possible.

The casket is now in the keeping of the King and my fate rests in his hands. You are often in my thoughts.

Your servant, The Knight of Surcote. <<

"What the fuck does that mean?"

The swear word sounded hard coming from Aggie's lips, the vowel pronounced almost like an a, the consonants brutally dwelt upon. It sounded as though she rarely swore.

"I think he's trying to tell me something, something about our relationship and why he doesn't feel able to continue it. But I wish he would just tell me in plain English, something I could understand and respond to."

We were all three at Aggie's house. I'd decided a tutorial was beyond me today and phoned to cancel. I emailed Aggie to say we wanted to see her and she'd replied immediately to come right over. She lives in Richmond in a big house not far from the park.

We'd quizzed her and found that Iraq was Gavin's first trip to a desert, certainly as a reporter. She looked at the photograph and nodded. Yes, that was definitely from that trip. It must have been Bertrand that took the photo, we needed to get in touch with Hugh Challenger straight away to find out how he'd got hold of it.

I only had an email contact for him, so Aggie switched on her computer and went to the kitchen to make some tea. When I opened my inbox, there was the message from Gavin, or rather, Surcote. I read it, and felt the frustration rising in me like a tide, swelling the cells of my body. I wanted to grab hold of him and shake him, hit him even. My fingers stretched and flexed. There was nowhere for this energy to go.

Aggie came back from the kitchen with a tray and she and Sheila read the message whilst I paced the room, touching the backs of chairs, the edges of shelves, wishing I could slam my hands down hard and break them.

"I'll reply to him later. Right now we need to find Bertrand, and Hugh Challenger seems to be our only lead."

I sat in front of the computer and drafted an email to Hugh, explaining that I'd left the key and had a flick through the photos, which wouldn't be of any use to me, but thank you anyway. Also I was interested to know who the young man was in a flak jacket, smiling in the desert. I clicked on send, and there was nothing more we could do. We drank tea, and then Sheila and I left, promising to let Aggie know if there was any reply.

Sheila decided to try some more magazine publishers. I went to the gym, spent an hour beating the shit out of a punch ball.

There was nothing for three weeks. It was late November and raining nearly every day. The streets of Bloomsbury shone black and the air was grainy with traffic fumes suspended in moisture. Shop windows came into their own, glowing with yellow light, the jewel colours of clothes and books tempting customers inside with the promise of comfort and warmth, the doors wafting cappuccino smells as they swished open and closed.

I hung about with college friends, went back and forth between the uni and the library, occasionally being pulled inside the bookshops, sometimes taking a detour down Hugh's high street and glancing up at the windows of his flat.

But there was no word from him, and, after I'd replied to his Surcote message, nothing from Gavin either. I'd said what I meant, no pretending. I was fed up with this Surcote charade, and though it had been great when he was telling me stories, it was no substitute for reality. I loved him and wanted to be with him, and if he felt this wasn't possible, surely I deserved a proper explanation why.

In return, silence. A blank inbox.

On the first of December I finally got a message from Hugh, frustrating in it's brevity as well as its tardiness.

>> Some chap I met in the desert, Gary he might have been called? Hugh x<<

I replied >> Gavin, not Gary.<<

And he replied >>You know him then? <<

>> You know that I know him. Come on, it wasn't a coincidence you'd put that photo in with the others. You knew the Turkey dig was of no use to me. The whole thing was a set-up so I would find the photo of Gavin. Are you going to tell me what it's all about? And while you're at it you can tell me what you know about Bertrand Knight. <<

More silence.

Two weeks, and the still wet streets glinted with the reflected reds and greens of Christmas lights. Slade and Wizzard pumped out of in-store radio, leaking into the streets to mingle with the rustling bags of a million Christmas shoppers. Usually I loved Christmas, but this year I felt removed, as though the world were carrying on without me when everything should have been put on hold. Rhyssa did her best to pull me out of myself and get me out, but it was an effort. I went to the pub with friends, to the pictures once or twice, but I felt as though I were walking around enclosed in a glass bubble, that although my friends could talk to me, see me, their words and actions were muted, irrelevant, on the other side of the glass. I was terrible company, either sitting silently in corners or putting on a false show of gaiety, which must have made me look like a bad clown. My mum phoned to ask if I was coming down for Christmas and I snapped at her, I don't know, I haven't decided.

Then another email.

>>Look under your doormat and you'll find my key. You should have kept it, you naughty girl. I've left something for you in my flat. Hugh x<<

I phoned Aggie and Sheila. I didn't feel up to a trip to the flat on my own. Sheila said she'd get the next train to London. Aggie was tied up in a meeting that afternoon, but promised to be free the next morning. Rhyssa had gone home for Christmas the day before. I sat at home in my flat, the front door double-locked, wondering how Hugh had found out where I lived and what I'd been doing when he dropped off the key.

When we arrived at the flat the next morning nothing seemed different from when I'd last been there. The painting of the woman in the hallway watched as the three of us came through the door, the cat by her shoulder peering at us as we went into the living room. The layer of dust was slightly thicker, giving everything a touch of dead whiteness. The black leather sofa no longer quite so shiny; the sound system, the CDs, fuzzed over with a softness that was absolutely unbroken.

Hugh must have been here, but he'd touched nothing except the things on the desk.

I was glad the others were with me. Alone, I don't know if I'd even have got through the door. This place spooked me. It wasn't Hugh I was scared of – not in any normal way. I didn't expect a physical or sexual attack. I couldn't have explained what frightened me. Just finding another photograph like the last time would have been enough.

Aggie hung back near the door, but Sheila marched straight into the room ready to start searching. I grabbed her arm.

"No. Don't disturb anything."

She turned to me puzzled.

"It's on the desk. You don't need to touch anything else, he's left it on the desk."

She looked to where I pointed. The space where the box files had been was clear now. There was a large rectangle that had been cleared of dust. In the middle of it was a disc in a clear plastic wallet and, lying across it, a red rose.

Aggie picked it up and brought it over to us. There was a slip of paper in the wallet with the disc, a note for me.

– *Kat, if you want to know more, watch this. Or more sensibly, leave it and go away and forget about the whole thing, Gavin included. Your choice, Hugh x.*

I shoved it in my pocket. "OK, let's go," I said "We can watch this at my flat."

But Sheila was impatient.

"There's equipment here, we could watch it straight away."

"I don't want to stay here."

"But if it's awful, if we don't want to watch it," Aggie this time, "then we could just leave it here. We could just look at the beginning."

I looked at their faces, one to the other, Aggie nervous but brave, Sheila determined. I couldn't explain to them why I felt it would be worse here than anywhere else. Whatever was on that disc would seem more manageable in the familiarity of my own flat. Away from this sterile dust-covered room that contained the presence of Hugh as though he were watching through some peephole.

But there were two of them and only one of me.

"The electricity might be off. He's not been living here for a while."

Sheila answered by flicking a couple of switches behind the TV screen, and the bank of lights flickered into life. She wiped the screen with the arm of her jacket, and the space she cleared was edged with rolls of ragged dust. Pushed aside like this the dust had more substance, became dirty grey rather than white; dead solid dirt. Something inside of me shuddered and I felt my throat close in a convulsive wave. I blinked, stayed dry eyed.

Sheila was pressing buttons. I handed her the disc and she inserted it into the drive. Aggie sat down on the dusty sofa, and I perched next to her.

When Sheila sat down with the remote control in her hand I closed my eyes. I felt as though I was shaking, but my hands were on my knees and neither of them was moving. There was a sudden noise, of static, of rushing air, of a machine being on that previously wasn't, and I opened my eyes and looked at the screen.

Five men in black with masks are standing in a room, one slightly apart from the others. Another man in an orange jumpsuit, gagged, blindfold, bound, is kneeling in front. There's a flash of silver, which I realise is a pentacle on a chain the man in orange is wearing around his neck. The room is spartan. There is nothing to indicate where it is. One of the men holds a piece of paper and reads something from it in a loud voice. Another draws out a knife – about a foot long, ornate, silver – and holds it out to the man standing on his own. This man shakes his head violently, but still the knife is held out to him. Words are spoken, harsh and loud. The man shakes his head again and speaks.

He says, "No. Never."

The voice is Gavin's voice.

I could feel the tightening in the room as Aggie, Sheila and myself all recognised his voice. The sound of him swilled into my lungs and my bowels clenched, my stomach churned with acid. I could feel my fingernails scrape against the denim of my jeans. My eyes stayed on the screen.

The first man, who'd read from the paper, produces a gun from within the folds of his clothes and points it at Gavin. He shouts something and the man with the knife thrusts it at him again. Still Gavin refuses to take it.

The man with the gun walks across the room and puts the gun against Gavin's head. Suddenly the camera zooms in and Gavin's face fills the screen. Only his eyes can be seen, the rest hidden behind a mask identical to the others'. They're eyes I'd looked into so many times, seen filled with sadness, laughter, lust. Eyes which always carried something else behind them, something hidden and ashamed. Not here though. On this screen his eyes were angry and scared, but not ashamed.

He says "Kill me if you have to. I won't do it. Not ever."

The man shouts at him again, a stream of words slapping him like a weapon. He pushes the gun so that Gavin's head is forced sideways. I could see the fear taking hold in Gavin's eyes, and I wanted to cry for him.

He whispers, "You'll have to kill me."

And the knowledge of his imminent death is clear in his eyes, clouding his anger, thickening his fear into something clammy and tangible, which closes his voicebox and paralyses his movements.

The man with the gun hits him hard on the back of the head with the barrel of the gun and he falls to the floor.

In the next shot Gavin is back on his feet and now he has the knife in his hands. The other men are standing in a row again at the back of the room. Gavin moves towards the man in orange on the floor, who all this time has been silent. Gavin's head is turned away from the camera.

One of the men utters some more harsh words, then suddenly Gavin grabs the man in orange and starts to slice into his throat. The victim falls sideways and struggles. The knife cuts into flesh. Although he is gagged the man makes a lot of noise screaming. Blood starts to flow. The men behind watch silently. As the knife cuts deeper into the neck, the noises change to a gargling sound – a bit like a pig – which continues until the head is almost off. The other sound is the sawing of the knife, back and forth. It happens quite quickly – the knife must be very sharp – but it seems to take forever. When the knife gets right through, Gavin picks up the head and sits it on the back of the victim's body. There is blood spreading across the floor from the neck, but the head itself seems unmarked, alive, the blindfold has slipped and its eyes are looking into the camera. The men speak more words and the screen fills again with static, then blackness.

I stayed sitting, staring at the black screen. Vaguely I was aware that Aggie was being sick, that Sheila was crying. But I couldn't look at them, couldn't turn my head.

I heard Sheila saying my name.

"Kat, Kat."

But she was on the other side of the glass.

I stood up and walked out of the room and down the stairs into the street. I don't remember walking through London, don't remember catching a bus or buying a train ticket. But somehow I got on the train from Paddington to Westbury. And somewhere along the way I must have phoned my mother, because when I got off the train she was there waiting for me on the platform, and I fell into her arms and cried like a baby.

Chapter Twenty-six

"I am so fucking furious with GK. Do you know what he's been doing?"

Gavin's in the front room, kneeling behind the sofa which is covered in a white sheet, applying goose-egg-white gloss paint to the skirting board. He looks up as Morgan storms in. He's heard the car drive up, brakes squealing as she turned fast into the drive, the sudden stop and the slamming of doors. She's wearing a red dress and her body seems enormously tall in the room, towering like an angry goddess.

"I thought you were back tomorrow."

"I was supposed to come back tomorrow, but I left today. He's a fraud. He can fucking walk. He's been going away on his own when I'm not there. No wheel chair, he walks with a bloody stick. He'd made his parents promise not to tell me. Why? Why, for fucks sake? He stays away overnight."

"Where does he go?"

"I don't know. It doesn't matter where he goes. The fact is he's been lying to me and I don't know why."

The anger leaves her and the goddess crumples onto the sheeted sofa and begins to cry. Gavin lays the paintbrush across the top of the open can and goes to sit next to her. She turns to him as he puts his arm around her and her sobbing grows louder.

"Why doesn't he trust me? Why won't he speak to me about anything?" Her voice is muffled against his chest and he can feel the damp spreading into his t-shirt from her tears.

He holds her gently and lets her cry herself out.

It's ten minutes before she lifts her head, mascara sliding down her cheeks, the rims of her eyes red and angry.

He pushes a strand of hair out of her face and strokes the side of her head.

"Would you like a drink?"

She nods silently and he gives her a quick tight hug before standing up and going into the kitchen.

He returns with a bottle of red wine and two glasses.

"His mother let it out by accident. She was talking about something that happened last week, some workman that had been round or something, and she said, but that was when you were away wasn't it GK, and he gave her this stare and shook his head without really moving it, hoping I wouldn't see, but I did. Half an hour later I was out of there."

Gavin hands her a glass and she takes a big gulp.

"I want to help him. Why is he shutting me out just when he needs me the most? Does he think I won't love him anymore because he's not perfect?"

She's glaring at Gavin as though she expects an answer, but he hasn't got anything to say. There's an uncomfortable gliding and gnawing feeling in his stomach and he doesn't want to think about GK or the reason that he is the way he is. He empties his glass of wine and pours another, fills Morgan's too.

"It's Christmas in three days and I don't know if I want to go back there. I can't bear to see him."

"Speak to him on the phone. Or email. Tell him what you feel."

"He bloody knows. I yelled it all at him when I was leaving. I screamed I love you, you fucking bastard, can't you see that. I think I'll leave him to stew for a bit."

She lapses into silence. Gavin looks at her. He hasn't told her about his arrangement to spend New Year with GK and his family, and he's not sure if she'll be working or if she will be part of the family group. The house here is nearly finished, just a touch of paint here and there. He was planning to get the last bits done while she was away at Christmas. There will be no reason to stay after that.

She pulls at the sleeves of her dress, covering her hands, then rubs her upper arm.

"You cold?" he asks.

"Mmm, a bit."

"Shall I light the fire?"

"Yes, lets."

In the coal shed he checks, as always, that the package is still there where he's hidden it, wrapped in plastic behind the pile of coal. Ten days, and he can hand it over to GK. Ten days, and then he'll need to decide what to do with the rest of his life.

Lying in bed later on, he thinks about how Morgan looked that evening in the firelight, the clinging red fabric of her dress glowing orange against her breasts and thighs, her wine glass bejewelled with sparks of light against the ruby red. Her face fragile with dried tears. He wanted to reach out and touch her. She would probably have let him. But the snakes in his stomach would not lie still. Even the three bottles of wine they shared would not settle them. And his fingers could still feel the damp coal dust covering the package out there in the darkness.

Unable to sleep, lying first on one side, then the other, he tries not to think about her lying naked beneath her covers just one floor below him. Tries not to imagine creeping down the stairs and into the darkness of her room, slipping into her bed and discovering the oven hotness of her skin as she sleeps. He forces his mind away from the thought of her soft breast beneath his hand, and the gash between her legs drawing him downwards. He thinks instead about Bertrand.

They showed him videos of Bertrand every day after that first time. Always he said the same thing – "Kill Gavin not me" – always delivered in that same deadpan way. Sometimes Gavin thought he could detect a flicker in his face, a faint lopsided twitch that could be the intimation of a wink. But it was difficult to tell under the growth of beard.

Then one day it was all gone, shaved off. His hair was cut short too, and Gavin could see how much healthier Bertrand had become. His face had filled out, he was clean, the deep hollows beneath his eyes were not so dark. And after that the videos showed Bertrand eating, drinking coca cola, once he was even walking outside in a hard baked mud courtyard. Each time he said the same thing – "Kill Gavin not me" – thrown out flippantly, quickly, and although Gavin could still hear the insincerity in Bertrand's voice, he found it hard to still feel the hand of friendship on his shoulder.

Bertrand was being rewarded, but Gavin still wore rags, still bore the festering wounds of past beatings on his undernourished body. Still he was forced to watch the same video of the father and the two sons, the shooting and the shame and the flies. And although he realised that Bertrand knew nothing of this, he found it hard not to let resentment seep in with the images on the screen. Watching Bertrand, his clothes returned to him, drinking a mug of strong black coffee, saying, "Kill Gavin not me", something curdled in Gavin's blood, a sick solid writhing began in his guts. It is the same writhing that keeps him from Morgan's bed.

For two days he doesn't see her. It's the busiest time of the year at Wodwo's and she puts in the time, going out early in the morning to buy food in the markets, staying open until the early hours, watching the Christmas revellers drinking themselves horizontal until she's had enough and shovels them out of the door. Gavin works on the house, painting skirting, window frames and doors. It's looking good. Morgan has chosen light colours with splashes of brightness, and the rooms seem bigger, full of air. The old mustiness has gone, and the few pieces of heavy furniture she has decided to keep seem less overbearing. He wonders who will live here. Will she persuade GK to move in with her as they'd originally planned? Or will she find she can't bear it after all and sell up?

On Christmas Eve he wakes feeling nauseous, rushes to the bathroom and throws up in the toilet. There's not much in his stomach and the acid burns his throat, the taste of bile fills his mouth. He sits down on the bathroom floor, his head between his knees.

He's forced himself not to think about Kat, but now his longing overwhelms him. He stretches out his arm blindly, reaching, wanting to feel the touch of her skin, to taste the sea salt in her hair. His stomach cramps and he feels hollow and burned. Has he done the right thing? Should he have opened up to Kat, told her everything and taken his chances? If she'd heard him out and walked away, could it have been worse than this? This emptiness, this feeling of life being lived at a distance, an echo of what might have been. Is it too late?

His stomach convulses again and he leans over the toilet bowl, but there's nothing to come out. He brushes his teeth, gagging on the minty taste of the toothpaste, then goes into the office and turns on the computer.

>> Hi Kat, just to wish you Happy Christmas. Thinking of you, always, love Gavin <<

If she replies, then he'll take it from there. See where it goes. He has no plans for after New Year, and maybe it is time to take life by the hair.

In the kitchen he drinks a glass of water from the new stainless steel sink. Its freshness feels alien in his body, a stream of clarity flowing where there was none. He feels it pooling in his stomach and waits for the cramping to start again, but it doesn't. He feels empty, but cleaner inside than he has felt for weeks.

He spends the morning painting the back door to the kitchen and the door of the coal shed opposite. It had been a day's work stripping the doors of their flaking red paint, sanding them, coating them with sealant and an undercoat of paint. Now he is applying a thick blue gloss. The colour is the same blue as the alkanet flowers that grew along the base of the wall of the shop where he and Kat had shared their room. Its brightness seems shocking here on the door, but it will dry a slightly darker shade.

At one o'clock he tries a piece of toast and his stomach doesn't reject it. The kitchen door is open for the paint to dry. It's a clear day, with blue skies and a high pale sun weakly attempting to spice the December air with a little warmth. Gavin breathes in deeply, and the cold air is like the water, clean and pure in his body.

He doesn't check his mail just yet. There are plenty of small jobs he can still do about the house. He fits doorknobs to the newly painted doors on the upper floors, and puts the curtain rail back up in the living room. His own room is the last to be painted, and for that Morgan has chosen wine-bottle green for the walls, with brilliant white for the woodwork and ceiling. He spends the afternoon on the first coat, sometimes smiling as he works, keeping his mind empty of thoughts.

At five o'clock he boils an egg and eats it with more toast and a cup of tea. Then he spends a couple of hours putting up shelves in the office, aware of the silent computer in the room with him, its screen blank, lights out. He doesn't look at it, doesn't turn it on.

By the time he has finished the second coat of paint in his bedroom it's half past nine. He pours himself a glass of wine and sits down in front of the computer. Kat might have been out all day, she might not have had a chance to check her emails, might not have seen his message. He sips at the wine while he waits for the computer to boot up, and thinks about the curve of her buttocks as she lay naked on the bed beside him in their white room, the colour in her face as they raced each other to the top of the tor on Bodmin. She might not want to answer him. She's every reason not to trust him.

His inbox is empty, but he clicks on his junk mail and there it is. His own message returned.

>> Failed delivery. The recipient has blocked all messages from this address. <<

He stares at it. Then his stomach cramps, bending him double, and he throws up on the floor. She's shut him out. She's had enough.

He leaves the pool of vomit seeping into the floorboards and goes downstairs to find some whisky.

Chapter Twenty-seven

He wakes on the living room floor, stretched out on his side, one arm under his head, the other flopped forward in front of him. His neck aches like hell and his stomach burns.

His first thought is of Kat. Kat sitting on the train opposite him reading her book, her hair flopped forward over her face, sneaking occasional glimpses at him when she thought he wasn't looking. He'd thought then that he should have nothing to do with her, that if she knew him, knew what he'd done, she wouldn't want him. He'd been right.

He tries to sit up. Someone has covered him with the throw from the sofa and taken off his shoes. He must have been comatose when Morgan got in from the bar. Not what she needed after a late night.

It feels as though his bones are splintered and his head is pounding. He manoeuvres himself up from the floor and sits on the sofa, holds his head in his hands. She must be upstairs in bed now. It's Christmas Day.

In the kitchen he finds the empty whisky bottle and brimming ashtray on the table. Morgan must have picked those up as well from the floor in the other room. He opens the fridge and drinks milk straight from the bottle, then looks through the drawers until he finds some aspirin.

He should have told Kat straight away. She would have been horrified, disgusted. But at least there would have been nothing between them to destroy. He doesn't doubt that she knows the truth, although he has no idea how she found out. Perhaps the video is on the internet.

His clothes smell of vomit, sweat and cigarettes. His hair is lank.

Upstairs the floor of the office has been cleaned and the room smells of disinfectant. The mop and bucket are still on the landing. The computer has been turned off as well. Morgan must have seen the message from Kat.

He gets clean clothes from his room and showers in scalding water, letting the soap run into his eyes and mouth. He scrubs his body hard, forcing the poison out of his pores. He scratches at the pentacle on his hand as though he could wash it off. The wristbands over his scars get soaked and he rubs them with the soap too as though they were a part of his body. He brushes his teeth twice.

It's late, barely morning any more. In the kitchen he makes two cups of tea, and then fetches from his room the chocolates he'd bought for Morgan earlier in the week.

She's still sleeping. He nudges the door of her room with his foot and it swings open revealing a dusk-like gloom. Heavy curtains blot out the blue skies of an un-white Christmas, letting through only chinks of sunlight. He sits on the edge of her bed, and she slowly turns towards him and opens her eyes.

"Happy Christmas," he says.

"Happy Christmas yourself."

"I've brought you some tea and chocolates. A sorry for last night."

The chocolates are in a gold box wrapped with a ribbon, the best quality handmade Belgian.

"How did you find these on Christmas morning?"

"They were meant to be a thank you not a sorry. I fucked up. Did you clear the sick up?"

She nods.

"Just what you needed. I really am sorry."

She shifts herself in the bed so the covers move. She's naked under the sheet.

He can smell himself – soap and toothpaste underlain with alcohol. He knows his eyes are bloodshot.

Morgan sits up in the bed to take the tea from him, pinning the sheet to her sides with her arms. She sips the tea, looking at him over the top of the cup. He should get up and walk out.

She puts down the mug on the bedside table and the sheet slips. She reaches her hand out to him and he lets her pull him gently towards her. He can smell her as well now, her perfume mixed with the smell of cigarette smoke in her hair. With his other hand he lightly touches her breast.

Their faces are only an inch apart. She stretches forward to meet him and their lips touch, move apart, touch again. She slides nearer, presses herself against him, and suddenly the kiss takes hold. He moves his hands behind her back, behind her head, pulling her closer. The taste of her morning breath mingles with the toothpaste and their tongues wind together.

When she puts her hands underneath his t-shirt he pulls away from her to take it off. She moves over to make room for him and he lies down next to her, his left leg covering hers, his upper body bent over, their mouths together as though the kiss hadn't been interrupted.

This time it's going to happen. Morgan puts her hand between his legs and he closes his eyes.

But the world behind his eyes is a different one. It's summer not winter, and she's there again. Kat, standing in the tattoo studio watching him as he walks out of the door, his bag on his back. She looks so young and so sad. He wants to change the direction of his steps, walk back to her. But this is the past; it's already happened and can't be changed.

He lifts his head and looks at Morgan. She has stopped pushing against him and is lying still, her hand resting at the top of his leg.

"You thinking about GK?" he asks her.

Her nod is barely perceptible.

He bends his head and kisses her once on the lips, then gets up from the bed.

"I'll go and get some breakfast on the go."

In the kitchen he puts bread in the toaster and breaks eggs into a bowl. He can hear her in the shower. He still has a hard-on, but he knows the moment has passed. For good this time. He thinks about his flat in London, about the months he spent imprisoned there, unable to go out or to make decisions about anything. Would he have been better off if he'd just stayed there? Then it would only be his own life that was in disarray.

Morgan comes into the room. She's wearing a kimono – black silk with red dragons embroidered up either side and an enormous one winding up the back. She's tied her wet hair up in a knot behind her head. She looks like a goddess again – or maybe a warrior. Gavin looks away.

She throws him his t-shirt.

"You left this in my room."

He catches it and puts it on.

"I'm making scrambled eggs and toast. Do you want some?"

She nods. "Yes. I'm starving. There's some bacon in the fridge too. And ginger marmalade."

They cook the breakfast together, and they've fallen back into their easy way with each other, not mentioning what's just happened in the bedroom. They sit at the kitchen table and eat the bacon and eggs, marmalade and toast, follow it with coffee.

"Close your eyes," Morgan says.

He does so and he can feel warmth from the sun on his arms as it shines through the kitchen window.

"Now open your mouth."

She puts something between his teeth.

"Bite."

He bites and the sweetness of chocolate floods into his mouth. He chews and the taste mingles with the bitter black coffee.

"More?"

He nods, and she drops the other half of the chocolate between his parted lips. She takes another from the box on the table and bites into it herself.

He doesn't say anything. He looks away from her and stares up at the ceiling. The throbbing in his head is starting again. He can't move. The food and the coffee have weighed him down in his seat. She's offering him something – another chance maybe. But he doesn't think she means it. It's been a long time since she's had sex, much longer than for him.

She reaches across the table and touches him on the wrist. She runs her fingers across the wristbands that are still damp from the shower.

"Those scars will fade in time," she says. "You need to expose them to the air, to the sunshine."

He says nothing.

She slips one finger underneath the band and slides it across his skin.

"The scars on your back have faded. They're going white. Soon they will just be a bit shinier than the rest of your skin, barely noticeable."

He feels the fabric of his t-shirt where it touches his body. His back has stopped itching recently. He's not sure he wants the scars to fade. He needs something to remind him of who he is and what he did.

"They're not you. Whatever they did to you, you're still intact, you're still the person you used to be. Those people – they've marked you but they can't change you."

She doesn't know. She wouldn't say that if she knew.

She sits forward, leans across the table and takes hold of his wrist with her hand. At first he resists, then he relaxes and allows her to remove the red band from his wrist. His skin underneath is white and the scars have faded to a colour that is paler than the rest of his arm, the ridges whitening into thin hard lines of scar tissue. She traces them with her fingers. He wants to tell her to stop, not to touch him, but he doesn't.

She takes hold of his hand and closes it into a fist then opens it out again one finger at a time. Then she reaches for the other arm, and takes the band off it too. Gavin stretches out his hand, flexing his wrist and spreading his fingers.

Morgan dangles the two wristbands from her hand. They look grubby, wet and sordid.

"I'm going to throw these in the bin," she says.

He doesn't stop her. She gets up and crosses the room to the bin underneath the sink unit. Gavin watches her open the door and throw the wristbands in with the eggshells and coffee grounds.

She sits back at the table and looks at him with a smile.

"There," she says.

"It's not that easy."

He is holding on to his wrists, trying to cover the exposed scars with his hands.

"I'm not ready. I can't look at them ... they remind me."

Suddenly she looks stricken. She reaches out and grabs at his hands.

"I'm sorry. I'm being a clumsy oaf, trying to fix things. Shall I fish them out again – I could wash them."

He shakes his head.

"No. They were disgusting anyway. I'll find something. There's probably an old shirt I can rip up."

"I'll find you something."

She looks around the kitchen, her eyes darting from one place to another as though she will find something he could use just lying about. Then she looks down in her lap and her eyes brighten.

"My belt," she says.

Her kimono is fastened at the back with a black silk sash that matches the design of the robe. Her hands are already behind her fumbling with the knot.

"No, Morgan. It's all right."

"I want to give you something. You gave me the chocolates."

"But ..."

The belt is untied and she lays it on the table between them. At each end it is embroidered with a tiny red dragon.

"The dragon will bring you strength," she says. "And red is a lucky colour."

"Isn't that in China?"

She shrugs, and gets up to go to the kitchen drawer. The kimono, which had been tightly wrapped around her body, now hangs loose, but there is a lot of fabric and it doesn't open completely. She gets the scissors from the drawer and sits back at the table.

"What are you doing?"

She folds the sash so that it is exactly double, then cuts across the fold making two equal parts.

"There – one for each arm. Hold them out."

Gavin stretches his arms out to her across the table and she ties half of the sash around each wrist. Each piece wraps round a number of times, and when she ties it, a red dragon sits on the back of his wrist.

"I'll sew the ends for you later, so they don't fray."

"What about your robe?"

Morgan shrugs again. "I'll find something. When you're ready to take them off, send them back to me and I'll sew them together again."

He covers the wristbands with his hands, one after the other, squeezing them, feeling the new fabric against the raw skin. It's soft and light and barely feels like there's anything there.

"Thank you," he says.

Later they watch a film together, sitting side by side on the sofa, relaxed, knees curled up, not quite touching, and Morgan sews the end of the wristbands.

When the film is over, Morgan says, "I think I'll go and see GK. We need to sort things out."

He nods.

"I'll drive up this evening and stay for a couple of days. The bar isn't open again until the twenty-ninth."

"I'll finish off in the house. There's not much to do."

"And then what?"

He shrugs.

"Then it will be New Year."

Chapter Twenty-eight

Sheila phoned the day before New Year's Eve.

Christmas was quiet at my parents'. I went with them to midnight mass on Christmas Eve, and they exchanged visits with friends. When they were out I stayed at home, reread Jane Austen and dyed my hair black. On Christmas Day we went for a walk on the downs. The sun was shining and the air was cold in our lungs. When we returned I helped Mum with the traditional Christmas vegetables, made vegetarian gravy to go with the nut roast she'd bought for me in the health food shop in town. I wasn't really hungry but I ate because it was easier. Mum was letting me get on with things in my own way, but she would have had something to say if I wasn't eating. Neither she nor Dad had asked me any questions.

I was half way through *Emma* when Sheila called. Mum brought the phone to my room and I sat in the window looking out at the garden while Sheila spoke to me.

"Kat, I hope you don't mind but I took the CD."

She paused as though she expected me to say something, but I didn't so she carried on.

"I thought there was something strange about it, and I thought I'd try and find someone to look at it. Mel knows people who are into film and home movies and stuff."

She paused again, so I said "Hm-hm."

"Well, it being Christmas, people are away and the tattoo studio hasn't been open, but Mel managed to get in touch with one guy who had a look at it yesterday."

I would have broken it into tiny pieces and crushed them beneath my heels. I wished she hadn't shown anyone. I didn't want anyone else to see it. I wanted to yell at Sheila and throw the phone out of the window.

"And he says he's pretty sure that it's two bits of film spliced together. It's clever, but they might not have been filmed at the same time, or even in the same place."

"What do you mean?"

"Well, there's nothing to identify Gavin in that second part is there? He's wearing a mask and doesn't speak, and you can't see his eyes. If it's a different bit of film it probably isn't him."

"But why...?"

The sun was shining across the back of the house, lighting up the winter jasmine so it shone like a scattering of gold thrown over the bricks.

"I don't know why. It's all psychology. Power games. It's probably on the internet."

"What about the victim? Is it Bertrand?"

"I don't know. But I've found out where his girlfriend lives. Someone at one of the magazines I contacted – an old friend of them both – told me the name of a bar she owns. I phoned it and there was an answer machine message with her mobile number, which I rang. I'm driving up to see her tomorrow. Will you come with me?"

The bricks were glowing orange, and drops of moisture on the jasmine flowers glinted silver in the afternoon sun.

"Of course I will."

I recognised her as soon as she opened her front door. She was the woman from the painting in Hugh Challenger's flat. She was wearing old jeans and a baggy black sweater, her hair pulled back in a ponytail, and still she looked sophisticated.

"Hi, I'm Morgan," she said. "Come in."

We sat at her kitchen table and she poured us coffee from a cafetiere.

"I take it you're looking for Gavin," she said.

"Amongst other things," Sheila answered.

"Well, he's not here any more. I got back two nights ago and found this note."

She pulled a piece of paper out of the back pocket of her jeans and unfolded it, laid it on the table. I looked at the handwriting and thought of that morning way back, in Cornwall after the party.

It said: *Morgan, it's time for me to move on. I think I've finished everything that needs doing in the house. The paintwork is all done, and I've rehung all the blinds and curtains. You might want to put another coat of varnish on the upstairs floor at some point, but it's not urgent.*

Thank you for giving me this time and space – and employment. I really appreciate it. But I don't think it's a good idea to carry on. On Christmas Day –it would have been lovely, but it's not what either of us want. You need to sort things out with GK. And I, well, I've got something I need to do, and after that who knows. Sorry I'm not saying goodbye in person, but I think it's for the best.

Love, Gavin

I read this twice over. There were so many questions I needed answering, I didn't know where to start.

"GK?" I said.

"GK is Bertrand. Bertrand Knight my boyfriend. We've been having a rough time since he came home."

"I knew it!" said Sheila.

But Morgan was looking at me and took no notice.

"He's at his parent's home, their family home in Cheshire. Gavin has been staying here in my house, doing it up for me."

She was so beautiful. Taller than me, self-assured. She held my gaze and I knew she was telling me more than her words conveyed.

"And you…?"

"I split my time. The bar I run, Wodwo's, it's here in the town. I need to be here half the week for that. The rest of the time I've been up in Cheshire, with GK."

"So Gavin's been here alone a lot of the time?"

"Gavin's very troubled. He hasn't spoken about the past at all. He never mentions GK except in relation to me. It's all there still inside him."

Her eyes were deep brown, almost black, and full of a warmth that I read as pity for me.

"He did mention you though Kat."

I looked down.

"Did he?"

"Yes."

"He thinks that GK is Bertrand's brother," said Sheila, and we both turned to look at her.

Morgan was confused.

"Bertrand doesn't have a brother."

"In the desert Bertrand sent emails to someone called GK, a sort of diary. He told Gavin that GK was his brother. Gavin told Kat about it."

Morgan looked back at me and I nodded.

"It's true. Gavin really believes GK is a different person. I think he thinks that Bertrand is dead."

Morgan shook her head as though trying to shake out the confusion.

"But we talked about GK, about what he's going through. How could he not have realised."

"Did you call him Bertrand?"

"No. I always call him GK. Bertrand is just his work name, his official name."

Sheila said, "He's certain that Bertrand is dead. It wouldn't even occur to him that GK could be the same person. Those people went to the lengths of making the film, they might have told him anything."

"Film?" asked Morgan.

So we told her about the disc and how it had come into our hands.

"Where did you say this flat is?"

I told her the address, knowing already what she would say.

"That's GK's flat."

She went into the living room and got something out of a drawer. It was a photograph, which she laid on the table between us.

"This man, Hugh Challenger, did he look like this?"

He was thinner, younger looking, but it was undoubtedly the same man. I nodded.

"Well this is GK. This is Bertrand Knight, the man who went to the desert with Gavin. The man I've lived with for fifteen years."

"And the man who left this disc for Kat in his flat, with footage of Gavin apparently killing someone."

Morgan turned to Sheila.

"You have the CD with you?"

"Yes."

"Can I see it?"

Sheila removed it from her bag and handed it over.

"Do you mind if I stay here?" I said. "I really don't want to see it again."

While they were gone I sipped at the strong black coffee and looked around the room. Gavin's work was all around me. His hands had sanded down this table, painted the window frames, the door. I laid my palm flat on the wood and I could feel the warmth left from my coffee cup. I wondered what had happened on Christmas Day. I knew that Morgan was telling me that whatever it was didn't matter. He had no commitment to me anyway, I knew that. It's not as if I was his girlfriend. I wondered where in the house he had slept. If anything of his was still here.

When they came back into the kitchen Morgan's face had blanched. Her hands were shaking a little. She took a cigarette out of a drawer and lit it.

"It's not GK ... Bertrand, I mean, who died. But someone wants it to seem as though it is. It is him at the beginning, I recognise him. His arms, his neck. I've been with him long enough."

"And the necklace?" asks Sheila.

"Yes, that's his. He always wears it. I gave it to him when we were first together."

She drew deeply on the cigarette drawing the smoke down into her lungs.

"But at the end ... the head," she choked on her words or the smoke, "that isn't him. It's someone else."

She turned her back on us then, the smoke from the cigarette in her hand rising in spiral columns, wreathing around her arm before dispersing into the air.

I went and stood next to her and put my arm across her shoulders.

"What a mess," she said, "What a bloody mess."

Morgan said she'd take her car. She was meant to be at her bar that night – New Year's Eve being one of her busiest of the year – but she phoned her bar manager and told him they'd have to manage without her.

I asked if I could use the bathroom, and when Morgan gave me directions I asked which was Gavin's room.

"Up another flight, turn right at the top," she answered without looking up.

It smelled of fresh paint, which disappointed me slightly. It seemed as though all traces of him had been erased. The walls were dark green and the woodwork and ceiling a brilliant shining white. I couldn't imagine Gavin living in this room.

The futon bed had been stripped, but I lay down on it anyway and buried my head in the pillows, hoping for some hint of his scent. But he must have lived here very lightly. I couldn't find Gavin in the pillows, or in the white muslin curtains, or the stripped pine floor. I even looked under the bed, hoping to find a stray sock or a toenail clipping. But there was nothing.

When I went back downstairs Morgan and Sheila were ready to go.

Sheila sat in the back of the car, me next to Morgan in the front. We didn't talk. I looked out of the window at the countryside rolling by, quiet and still in this mild winter weather, the stripped trees looking naked in the early dusk.

"Is Gavin carrying a parcel with him?" asked Sheila.

I'd forgotten about the parcel.

"What sort of parcel?"

"Wrapped in brown paper, addressed to Mr B Knight." Sheila told Morgan how it had disappeared from the shop at the same time as Gavin. "We wondered if he was taking it to him in person."

Morgan shrugged.

"I never saw anything like that, but suppose it could have been in his bag."

"If it was, he might be taking it to GK."

"He's been gone two days. If that's where he's going he's already there."

Chapter Twenty-nine

I expected something pretty grand, with a sweeping well-lit drive and steps up to an oak panelled door with an enormous brass knocker. Maybe some balustrades, some topiary, even peacocks. It wasn't like that. It was old and large, but it was asymmetric with a modern extension, the older part covered with Virginia creeper in need of cutting. The drive was longer than average, but there was no gatehouse, just a slightly potholed, pitch black lane across a field, a parking area for three or four cars, two of the spaces taken up with a BMW sports car and a battered Range Rover. Morgan parked her car next to the BMW.

"Well, GK's car is here," she said.

Mr and Mrs Knight were surprised to see us, as Morgan hadn't phoned to say we were coming. They were both in the kitchen listening to the radio, he sitting in a rocking chair with his feet in the fire place, his eyes closed in a doze, she standing at the table with her hands in a mixing bowl, up to her wrists in flour.

Morgan didn't knock, she just walked straight in. Sheila and I stood back in the doorway, less sure of our welcome.

"Oh, Morgan dear, we didn't expect you. I hope something hasn't gone wrong at your bar." Mrs Knight held up her floury hands in front of her and waved them at Morgan as an apology for lack of an embrace. Morgan shrugged it away.

"No. The bar is fine. I just need to see GK. I have some things I need to ask him. Is he up in his room?"

The couple glanced at each other, and Mrs Knight coughed a little. Mr Knight shuffled uncomfortably in his chair.

"Well dear, no he's not. You see, his leg has been feeling a bit better lately, and he does need to stretch it sometimes..."

"What are you telling me?"

"He's taken the dogs out for a run," said Mr Knight bluntly.

Morgan sat down heavily in a chair and seemed as though she were counting to ten. Mrs Knight beckoned to Sheila and I to come in.

"OK, " Morgan said, "we'll wait for him. Will he be long?"

"He's been gone about twenty minutes – could be up to an hour, I guess. He was going to drop in and have a word with Joe Green in the village, something about mending the fences in the far pasture. Can I make you and your friends some tea?"

Mrs Knight abandoned the mixing bowl to wash her hands at the low kitchen sink, and Morgan introduced us.

"Kat and Sheila are looking for Gavin Redman." I saw the older couple both flinch slightly at the name. "We wondered if he'd come up this way."

Mr Knight shook his head. "There's been no one. Not since you left two nights ago. Just the three of us and the dogs."

"I thought he was staying with you, my dear."

"He left, while I was up here. He'd left a note. I thought he might have come up to see GK."

"No, like Dad says, there's been no one. Why would he be wanting to come up this way? I shouldn't think he'd come here."

Certainly if Gavin did come here he'd get a cool welcome. I wondered what was his worst crime in their eyes, the episode in Iraq or living in their daughter-in-law's house.

It was an uncomfortable hour. Once the tea was made, Mrs Knight went back to her pastry making, and made some attempt at conversation, remarking on the mildness of the weather and how it was affecting the garden.

Mr Knight didn't try. He'd turned the volume down on the radio when we arrived, but now he turned it up again and sat back in his chair, closing his eyes and putting his slippered feet dangerously near to the burning coals of the fire. The voices on the radio were slightly manic as they built up the excitement towards the New Year countdown, and they were like a muted chattering of children in the background.

I looked around the kitchen. They hadn't decorated for Christmas, but there were a lot of cards standing on the mantelpiece and hanging from strings above the fireplace. There was no sign that the Knights were planning to celebrate New Year.

Morgan was in no mood for conversation, and left me and Sheila to reply to her mother-in-law's comments. I was pretty monosyllabic, but Sheila and Mrs Knight managed to give a convincing impression of a friendly chat. They'd got on to the topic of the best time of year to prune roses when the door opened and GK walked in with two Labradors bounding ahead of him.

I stared at him. His cheeks were flushed with exercise and he'd lost some weight since I saw him in London. He was wearing jeans and a raincoat, and his hair was damp. But he was undoubtedly Hugh Challenger. Was undoubtedly the man who had led us all on this goose chase, and was still leading Gavin who-knows-where. Seeing him there in the doorway, the look of surprise on his face at the full kitchen, my anger suddenly surfaced. I'd been keeping cool up to that point, staying rational. But now anger swept through me like ink in blotting paper, red ink, from my stomach up to my head, blurring my vision and spreading out into my limbs.

GK was looking at me. I didn't hesitate. I slammed my mug on the table, crossed the kitchen and slapped him as hard as I could across the face.

The force made his neck twist and his head turn, but he didn't flinch.

"You bastard! Who do you think you are to play with people's lives?"

I lifted my arm and hit him again and again. He still didn't react. Then I lost control and attacked him like a fury, raining blows on his chest and kicking him in the shins.

I yelled at him between sobs. "Bastard! Bastard! Fucking Bastard!"

He stood as still as a rock. The sobbing began to take over and my attack lost its force, and then I felt arms wrap around me from behind, gently pinning my arms to my side.

A voice whispered hot through my hair. "It's OK. Kat, its OK," and I slumped back against Morgan's body.

All this time GK had not made a sound, but now he spoke.

"Morgan darling, what catastrophic event can have happened to prise you away from Wodwo's on this of all evenings?"

Even I could hear his voice tremble beneath the sarcasm.

GK pushed the door to behind him and stepped properly into the room. I felt the wet nose of one of the dogs pushing into my hand. GK was looking at Morgan. She still had her arms around me, and I sniffed. I couldn't see the others in the room.

"G, it's New Year, you know it's one of the busiest nights."

"So, why aren't you there?"

"We need to talk."

"We need to talk. Fantastic! I'll get the whisky out and we can have a good old chinwag, see the New Year in."

He opened a cupboard and brought out a full bottle of single malt with dust on it.

"G, not like that. There are things we need to talk about."

She let go of me and walked over to GK, put her hand on his arm. He looked at her and smiled, put his arm across her shoulders.

"Come on, darling. Surely it can keep until the morning. It's New Year's Eve. Let's not spoil the party."

He got six glasses from under the sink and spread them on the table.

"Not for me, thanks dear," said his mother.

"Would you prefer a drop of sherry? You have to have something to toast the New Year, to celebrate this unexpected family gathering."

"It will not keep until the morning. We need to talk now."

GK looked up at Morgan and momentarily his face lost its smile.

"We will talk later. It's waited for months; it can wait a few more hours. Now come and sit by me and have a drink and at least pretend that you're having a good time."

He started to pour whisky into the glasses.

I watched Morgan. She stood staring at GK, frustration tightening her body, her hands clenched into fists. Then suddenly the tension vanished. She breathed in deeply and closed and opened her eyes in a slow blink.

"OK, let's have a drink. But we do need to talk, and we need to talk tonight."

She walked over to the table and sat down next to Sheila. Mrs Knight accepted a glass of sherry. Bertrand took a glass over to her husband by the fireplace. He poured a glass for me.

"Kat, shall we be friends for a little while?"

He held the glass out.

I ignored him and walked out of the room.

Outside the night was bitter cold. I sat on the stone steps and lit a cigarette. I tried to see GK through Morgan's eyes. Morgan who'd known him for nearly half her life, who loved him, who knew him before he became ill. She wanted to make allowances for him, to understand, to help him get better. The same as the way I felt about Gavin. She was viewing GK's behaviour with love, whereas I could only feel anger. I tried a few deep breaths.

Inside the excitement was building on the radio as reporters visited screaming crowds gathered in city squares.

We sat around the table drinking whisky at varying rates. Sheila sipped very slowly – I don't think she even liked whisky. GK topped up his and Morgan's glasses liberally and the bottle was disappearing fast. I was somewhere in between, consciously slowing myself down, afraid of getting angry again and losing my self-control, going outside when it got too much for me.

GK orchestrated the conversation, asking Sheila how she'd spent Christmas, me how my thesis was going. And slightly awkwardly, like unwilling musicians, we responded. He talked to his mother about the fences in the pasture, to his Dad about the shenanigans on the radio. He was the image of an irresistible host. Throughout it all Morgan sat silently scowling, knocking back the whisky and smoking.

Not long before midnight I went outside for another cigarette. Mrs Knight assured me I didn't need to – the smoke from mine would hardly make a difference to the smog Morgan had created. But it wasn't just the smoke I wanted, it was the fresh air.

I was gone for five minutes, maybe ten. When I went back in everything had changed. Morgan was on her feet glaring at GK who was pouring himself another whisky.

"Why the fuck didn't you tell me you felt like that?" she yelled at him.

"You never asked. You never said, do you mind if I dump you here with your parents while I get on with my life, I might visit if I have time."

"But you wanted to come here. You didn't want to come to my house."

"I didn't want to be alone."

His voice was barely audible. The quiet that followed his words fell into the room like snow, covering us all with its cold blanket. Even the dogs lay down on their stomach, heads on their paws, tails tucked beneath them. GK's father stopped rocking in his chair.

Before anyone could speak the countdown began on the radio. Ten, nine, eight ... GK did a quick check to see that we all had something in our glasses. Five, four, three ... I looked at the kitchen clock and saw that it was fast, already the second hand was past the hour ... two, one, zero.

"Happy New Year!" GK raised his glass and we all followed suit, chinking our glasses together and drinking. Even Mr Knight got out of his chair and came over to join in. GK kissed Sheila and me on the cheek, gave his parents a hug, then turned to Morgan and wrapped his arms around her resisting body.

His voice was soft now, and intimate.

"I was scared. I needed to know someone else was in the house all the time."

"I wish you'd told me," her voice a whisper.

"I'm telling you."

Mrs Knight's arm jerked and her glass tipped over spilling the dregs of sherry onto the table. She leaped to her feet and got a cloth to clean up the mess. Everyone watched her.

When the table was wiped clean GK said to Morgan, "Let's go to bed."

Morgan agreed instantly and, without looking at any of us, they left the room.

The door clicked shut behind them and there was the sound of feet ascending the stairs, another door being opened and closed above. Mrs Knight rinsed out the cloth at the sink. Mr Knight began rocking again.

"Thank God for that," said Mrs Knight her voice loud in the room, and I realised that the radio had stopped.

We collected up the empty glasses and stood them on the draining board. Mrs Knight replaced the stopper in the almost empty whisky bottle.

"You'll be wanting to stay the night," she said cheerfully. "I shouldn't think we'll see those two again before morning. I'll get some sleeping bags down from the attic, you should be comfortable enough on the sofas in the front room."

She clattered about tidying away bowls and kitchen utensils. Mr Knight was quietly humming Auld Lang Syne. The dogs moved closer to the fire and lay down either side of the rocking chair.

The front room was enormous, with a pristine green carpet, sideboards filled with crystal ware and two enormous floral print sofas, as well as two matching easy chairs and another rocking chair. It didn't look as though it was much used, and I imagined most of the Knights' time was spent in the kitchen. This room had some of the grandeur I'd expected from the house.

The sofas were comfortable though, and Sheila and I settled down in the slightly damp sleeping bags.

"I like your hair that colour," Sheila said before she turned out the light. "It was a bit of a shock at first, but it suits you."

She fell asleep pretty quickly. I could make out the movement of her slow breathing in the moonlight coming through the gap in the curtains. I lay thinking about Gavin, wondering where he was, if he was alone or scared. Wishing I could press my body against his and feel the safety and reassurance made by our shared body heat.

I must have dozed, because in the early hours I was woken by the sound of a car. Someone was leaving. I got up from the sofa and went to the window to look out. I could see the rear lights as the car drove across the field to the road, and the cones of yellow light made by the headlights in front, but the moon had gone now and I couldn't see which car it was.

I tiptoed up the stairs to the toilet, and on the way down I bumped into Morgan just making her way out of the kitchen.

"Kat?"

"Yes."

"Are you awake? Do you want some tea?"

We went back into the kitchen and Morgan put the kettle on. There was still a glow coming from the coals in the fire, and the dogs were sleeping side by side in front of the grate. Once the tea was made we turned the lights out and sat in the firelight, me in Mr Knight's chair and Morgan on the floor with the dogs. She rubbed their ears between her fingers and they sighed in their sleep.

"It's been hell these last few months. I didn't know if we would make it through – together that is."

"And now?"

"We talked. Properly talked about what we've been feeling. We've got a strong base to build on – we've been together for fifteen years. I think we've got a chance – which is a definite improvement."

She was wearing an enormous grey t-shirt and leggings and she was hugging her knees to her chest, the t-shirt pulled over her legs right down to her ankles. Her hair was dishevelled and loose around her shoulders, and although her face was still pale it had a glow that wasn't wholly a reflection from the fire.

"Gavin and I only just met," I said.

She looked up at me and said nothing. Then she looked back into the fire.

"I must apologise to Gavin. And to you. I wanted to make GK jealous, having another man staying in the house, even if it was as an employee."

"Did it work? Was he jealous?"

She nodded.

We sat like that for a while, drinking tea, watching the play of light across the glowing coals, listening to the breathing of the dogs.

"Was that GK driving off?" I asked.

She looked surprised. "Didn't I tell you? He's gone to meet Gavin. They've made an arrangement. He's going to bring him back here in time for breakfast."

The stone that dropped in my stomach immediately began to fizz. Breakfast! That was just a few hours away. I could feel the corners of my mouth curling.

"Where are they meeting?"

"Oh, it's this place that GK loves. A small ravine covered in moss and stuff. It's thought to be the green chapel of the old legends, the home of the Green Knight. The way the rocks have formed, it looks like a face, and people say it's the green knight looking down. It is beautiful. And of course GK feels a special connection with it."

"Why are they meeting there?"

"Sheila was right. It's the package. Gavin has brought it up for GK from the West Country, and he's going to hand it over."

Suddenly I was freezing cold and on my feet. The fizzing had stopped.

"Did he tell you what's in that parcel?"

"No, he didn't." Morgan was regarding me curiously.

"He's meeting him at the green chapel, at dawn, on New Year's Day?"

"Yes. He's always liked that sort of thing, ritual and tradition. Do you think it's strange?"

"Do you know how to get to this green chapel?"

She nodded.

"Well get dressed straight away. We need to get there, and fast."

Chapter Thirty

He wakes in the early hours of midwinter dark and dresses quickly. His sleep has been light and dreamless. He knows where he's going. The landlord of the Rose and Crown had pointed out, last night, the direction to take, and Gavin creeps down the stairs of the inn, out into the freezing air.

The lane winds from the main road away between the hills, and when Gavin looks up he can see black outlines of the jagged outcrops that mark their summits. This is not mountainous country. The hills are gentle and green by daylight, but they are deceptive. Hidden amongst the trees of the woody slopes are rocky cliffs and sudden drops. Not two miles away are sheer rock faces, challenging enough for experienced climbers. The pointed edges to the hilltops give the clue to these secluded dangers. At least the first part of his journey is to be on the road, the trodden tracks. By the time he gets to the ravine the day should have arrived.

It's strange to be walking this road alone in the darkness. There are a few farmhouses here and there but they are shrouded with night, their windows blank and blind. He hears the shuffle of animals in a barn as he passes, a snort of air, but there aren't any animals outside. No dog barks at his passing and the hedgerows are still. The new year is only hours old and the world is sleeping.

He doesn't have a torch. He reaches the highest point on the road, where it slides between three or four houses. By daylight the houses perched here must have a fantastic view, but now they're hunkered down in the dark. He stops and looks, almost expecting to see them gently moving with the rhythm of a sleeper's breath. In front, their apron gardens teem with the secret life of the night hours. Dead stalks stand proud above withered leaves in the beds, and frost-rimed bushes shake gently although there's no breeze. Flowering pansies have thrown off the bright colours of day and shimmer softly in their pots in elegant shades of grey and violet.

He moves on, following the road as it dips, and now he can hear the river rushing along the bottom of the valley. He tries to catch a glimpse of it, but it's concealed by the night. Down here it's darker than it was on the breast of the hill. The valley is filled with a blackness his eyes can't penetrate, however hard he stares. He passes the county boundary without noticing the sign.

He must be nearly at the turning. Following the landlord's instructions he crosses the river, stopping on the bridge to listen to the angry rush beneath. Then the road bends, and here it is, on the right hand side, the track dropping away to the level of the water itself.

He must follow this road for half a mile, until it forks, keeping the sound of the river on his right. He lets his feet take him, his ears guide him.Even so, he misses the fork, and it is only the sudden upward slope of the road that warns him he's going the wrong way. He backtracks, finds the right road and then it seems that he is walking into the very heart of the night.

It's true though, that the darkest hour comes before the dawn. The coldest too. It is only a short walk along this road, and from then on he'll be walking on footpaths. In those few minutes between the fork in the road and his arrival at the Youth Hostel at the end, a change has occurred in the sky. As yet it is barely noticeable. He sits on a wall and lights a cigarette, the flare from his lighter momentarily blinding him. He presses his arms against himself as he smokes. Walking has kept the blood moving round his body, distributing warmth from his muscles, but now that he's still the cold grips him. It reaches up from the stone he sits on, clasping at skin and bone. It wraps around his head and neck, immobilises his fingers. By the time the cigarette is finished he can barely hold it. But as he looks about him he sees that the darkness is lifting from the valley, the landscape is slowly coming into view like a photograph emerging from developing fluid.

And something turns on in his brain. Up until now he has focused only on the moment, on the walk in the darkness, on keeping his footing and finding the way. But with the faint glimmerings of day come thoughts of the meeting ahead of him. Of the package he still carries in the bag on his back. Of the man he is to meet. He wishes he could keep his mind still. Movement backwards or forwards through time seems equally treacherous. He looks at the hostel, empty right now, an echoing shell of a building that must some times ring with life and laughter. He tries to think back to a time when he visited places like this, walking alone or with friends, sharing baked beans and sausages cooked in a communal kitchen. But his memory isn't amenable to control. It flits and darts, circling, forever circling, the thing he's been trying to evade for months, the gaping hole, the emptiness at the centre of his being.

Because there are some things so terrible that the memory won't hold them. He has read that everything we've ever done, every sneeze, every mouthful of food, every smile from a friend, is recorded in our brains, and given the right stimulus can be retrieved. But what sort of stimulus would be needed to bring back the worst thing you've ever done? The brain is a self preserving organism, and a memory so bad it could destroy the brain's balance, its very functions, surely it's in its own interest to destroy it?

He remembers being brought into the room, seeing Bertrand there on the floor, helpless in that stupid orange jumpsuit. He even remembers a moment of amusement, thinking how upset

Bertrand would be at the shapelessness, unstylishness, of what they'd forced him to wear.

Then the awful realisation of what they want him to do.

They'd shown him other videos in the preceding days. Grainy, unclear, amateur. But all of the same thing. Frightened victims, and frightened men in masks with knives. It seems like something from the dark ages and he can hardly believe that the videos are real. After the first time he closed his eyes. When he realised it wasn't going to be Bertrand sitting in the sunshine with a glass of grapefruit juice, or the familiar father/son/brother story that he knows so well. He doesn't want to watch beheading scenes, however badly filmed.

Now he can smell Bertrand's fear, sharp, metallic, animal. As they try to press the knife into his hands, that smell is the worst thing. He's never smelled it on Bertrand before, only on himself. And he wants to tell Bertrand, whatever happens to you it won't be at my hands. But he doesn't trust his voice and is surprised to hear how clear it is when the words come out.

"Kill me if you have to. I won't do it. Not ever."

Inside his head he is screaming no, don't kill me, I don't want to die, but those aren't the words that come out. It's as if someone else has scripted the dialogue, some cold automated part of himself, and this part has taken control.

They will kill him if he doesn't do what they want, and they'll kill Bertrand anyway. He understands that. The barrel of the gun presses into the side of his head, pinching the top of his ear. Inside his body everything has let go. He can feel warmth and wetness on his thighs, can smell the stink of his own urine, and perhaps Bertrand's too. There are no thoughts in his head.

Still the voice continues.

"You'll have to kill me."

But they will. Don't say that because they will, screams the voice inside.

Then there is the sudden movement, the swing of the gun and the flash of pain before blackness.

This is what he can remember. The next thing he knows he is waking in his cell again and the video is showing once more on the prison wall. The son kneeling, the father refusing to kill his child, the pointless death, the brother who saves his own life. This is what he knows. But now things are different. There are things now that he doesn't know, such as whether Bertrand is alive or dead. And the film grates on him like a hair shirt on broken skin. He can't bear to look at it but his brain is incapable of switching it off. Even when he turns away, when he covers his head with his arms, when he shouts and screams loudly enough to drown out the sound, it is still there, playing on behind his eyelids. If only one time there would be no fly, if he could just force his brain to edit out the fly, it wouldn't be so bad. But it is always there at the end, crawling across the dead man's eyelid in search of water in its own bid for survival.

It's hours before they come, by which time Gavin has torn his clothes and gouged at his arms and cheeks with his nails, drawing blood. He is barely aware of them, or of the cessation of the film.

They bind his hands behind him and tie a gag around his mouth. He doesn't struggle. Two of them hold him upright, one each side. The cell door is open and three more of them stand just inside waiting.

The cell wall flashes with light again, and this time different images fill the screen. It's the scene he remembers, with the same dialogue, the same actors, the same blow to the head. But this time he sees how it ends. They show him the part his memory has erased. They show him a video of himself killing his friend. Then they force him into the back of a van and drive for hours through the night before dumping him and his belongings at the side of the road two miles from the city.

Sitting on the wall of the Youth Hostel Gavin sees the film they showed him play through his head. He hasn't let it come before. The memory of it has been hovering just below the surface of his consciousness, butting itself against his brain in a bid to come in, wanting to be played through, to be watched. But Gavin hasn't let it. Hasn't been able to bear it. This is the first time he's brought the memory out and examined it.

It's no better than the first time. He stands abruptly and shoves his freezing hands into his pockets.

The path leads along the river and round behind the hostel into a field. Gavin climbs the stile. The sky is lighter along the horizon, a deep blue against the utter black of the hills. Here at ground level the grass and the trees are touched with a white glow, as though washed in weak moonlight. There are sleeping cows in the field, which snicker slightly as he passes.

Soon he reaches the great beech tree, stretching out its silvered limbs into the coming day. From here he has memorised GK's instructions.

Up behind the beech tree onto a path that leads uphill to the right, until you reach a rocky outcrop. Here the path is signed, and doubles back on the one you've come up. The chapel is a little way down this path, on the right. You can't miss it.

As Gavin walks up the hill the light grows, and colour begins to leach into the landscape. The hills opposite are now touched with green, the trunks of the trees about him mix brown into the silver of their bark, and the day seems a little warmer although the sun is not yet over the horizon.

The rocky outcrop shines in this new light, and he can imagine a different journey, scrambling up to the top to sit and eat his lunch, feeling like the lord of creation. But for now it is a waymarker, a sign that his destination is close. His stomach clenches suddenly, but he breathes through it. He realises his arms are shaking as he walks the path to the ravine, but he puts it down to the cold.

GK is right, it isn't far. He almost walks past, but stops and looks into a gap between the rocks. The ravine isn't visible from here, not until he goes in and down the steps. Gavin traces out the letters of its name on the mossy rock at its entrance. He doesn't wear a watch and doesn't know the time. But it is dawn and he has arrived at the green chapel where GK asked to meet him.

Chapter Thirty-one

The steps have been carved roughly, unevenly from the rock. They are icy and treacherous. The walls on either side are slimy and wet with moss and algae. He touches them lightly with the tips of his fingers for balance and recoils. At the bottom, black water fills the entrance, covered with a thin layer of ice. It isn't deep, but he can't cross it without soaking his feet. His boots are waterproof, but some of the icy water seeps over the top. He shivers.

The ravine curves away in front of him, its walls rising on both sides, slicing out a track of pale sky, way above him. Mosses, algae, liverworts and ferns grow in profusion. The daylight has barely penetrated down here yet, and the air seems as green as the walls. There are crevices and tiny caves, dark secrets hidden in the green tapestry. He treads carefully over the icy rocks and frozen mud.

Round the bend the ravine splits into two smaller channels, the one on the right obviously the most used. Steps lead upwards, and looking towards the sky, Gavin can see the huge face hewn into the rock by wind and weather. The Green Knight. Gavin has read about him and knew he would be there, but still he's surprised at how lifelike he looks. He thought it would be difficult to see him, that you'd need to squint to make out some sort of face, but actually it would be difficult to miss him. He's massive, solid, with a large chin and heavy brow. He doesn't look like someone you'd argue with. He's been hanging there guarding this chapel for centuries, providing the meat of legend, of poetry and nightmares.

Gavin is about to climb the steps to stand underneath the knight when something stops him. A coldness down his right hand side, a freezing of the skin and the roots of his hair. He stands still. Slowly he turns his head to look into the other channel of the ravine.

It is even greener than the rest. The vegetation has spread from the walls to the floor, growing more thickly and upholstering the rocks with fleshy, slimy cushions and tentacles. A gap in the trees above is letting some light through at the nearest end, throwing the farther part into deeper gloom. There are no steps up to it. Getting in would mean clambering over boulders. But although he can see nothing up there, Gavin knows this is the way he has to go.

The moss on the rocks squeezes out its moisture as he climbs up, soaking his knees, shins, hands. He stands up and looks down the length of the channel. It's a dead end. Nobody comes this way because it doesn't lead anywhere. But there is someone here now. At the far end Gavin can make out the shape of a standing figure. The man is as still as the rocks, like the Green Knight himself, but he isn't made of stone. This is the man that has brought Gavin to the chapel, this place of revenge and retaliation, of myth and history.

"GK?"

Gavin's voice sounds as thin as the morning air.

The figure doesn't move, so Gavin takes a few steps forward. As he moves closer the figure becomes clearer. He can see it's a man wearing dark jeans, a duffle coat, a black woollen hat pulled over his head against the cold. Nearer and he can see the hands stuffed into the pockets, the breath issuing in clouds from his nostrils. Still closer and he can see the red patches burned into his cheeks from the cold, the scars on his neck, the tears filling his eyes. Gavin is only a foot away.

"Bertrand?"

The tears rise and run down Bertrand's face.

"I'm sorry," he says.

He grasps Gavin fiercely by the shoulders and shakes him.

"I'm sorry, I'm sorry." His voice is almost a sob.

Although the breath is knocked from his body, Gavin barely registers what is happening. He looks at Bertrand and blinks his eyes as though to clear his vision.

"But you're dead," he whispers.

Bertrand stops shaking him and stares into his eyes, then the two men hug each other tightly. Gavin can feel the rough duffle fabric against his cheek, and where his tears dampen it there is a faint smell of dogs.

"I saw you die."

Bertrand's neck is warm. The scars on his neck point upwards – the visible ends of much longer scars on his body caused by beatings. There is no horizontal scar. Bertrand's head has never left his body. Gavin can feel the beating of his heart.

Bertrand breaks off the embrace and turns away abruptly.

His back turned to Gavin he mutters, "I'm sorry. I'm ill. My mind isn't working as it should"

"I saw you die," repeats Gavin.

He puts his hands to his face. Bertrand walks away, turns, and comes back to stand in front of him again.

The sun has just risen above the horizon, blood orange, sending out a glow of fire. The walls of the ravine behind, where the light is shining in, are bright emerald green. Gavin can see Bertrand clearly, the shape of his features, the pores in his skin, the blue of his eyes, his hands pulling at his fingers.

"They put that film on the internet and I downloaded it. I didn't think you'd fall for it, the join is so obvious. The man with the knife, the killer, he's nothing like you – much taller and broader."

Gavin tries to remember, but it was so long ago. When they made him watch the film he was nearly out of his mind. He saw what they wanted him to see.

"I thought you'd twig a long time ago. And that I was GK."

"You were GK?"

"Yes, GK is me. It's me that's been emailing you."

"GK your brother?"

"I don't have a brother. There's just me, Bertrand, GK. One person."

Gavin's head is whirling. He frowns.

"But why...?"

"I hated you. I hated you for not killing me."

"They showed me the video – I thought..."

"I wanted you to think that you had. I wanted to destroy you."

"I can't believe you're here."

Gavin touches Bertrand's hand, which is stiff with cold, and Bertrand grabs his hand, holds it tight.

"I would have killed you."

Gavin looks into Bertrand's eyes and they hold steady.

"If it had been me, if the gun was pointed at my head and I thought I was going to die, I would have killed you."

Gavin looks away.

"No, you..."

"I would. At that moment, when we were in that room, if there had been something I could have done to save myself, I'd have done it. Whatever it was. Whatever."

Their gazes lock again.

"That's why I hated you. I hated your goodness. Your selflessness. I wanted you to know what it felt like."

"What felt like?"

"To know. To know without a shadow of a doubt that you're about to die. To know that this moment, this blackness, this stench, this stone floor beneath your knees, this green chapel, is the last thing you're going to have. Ever. I want... I wanted you to stare death right up in your face like I did."

"I did. I had no doubt that they would kill me too."

Bertrand pays no attention, but carries on. "I wanted you to believe I was going to kill you. That's why I asked you to bring me the parcel."

"The parcel! I'd forgotten. I've got it here."

231

Gavin removes it from his bag and holds it out to Bertrand, who takes it without moving his gaze from Gavin's face.

"Would you like to see what it is?"

"After carrying it around for half the year? Of course I would."

There's a fallen tree trunk behind Gavin, and they sit on it side by side. The moss covering it is saturated and the water soaks through their trousers immediately, but Gavin barely notices.

The parcel is covered with brown paper, worn in places to a softness like fabric. There are small tears, and at one corner a hole showing the bubble wrap underneath. Bertrand tears off the paper. Whatever is inside is much narrower than the size of the parcel would indicate. There's a lot of bubble wrap.

Slowly Bertrand unwinds it. A wooden handle emerges, a foot and a half long, but the head of the object is still heavily padded. Even when the bubble wrap is all off, there is still an oval case of tough leather hiding its shape. But Gavin has an idea now what it is.

Bertrand undoes the clasps, and removes the axe from its protective covering. It's beautiful. The blade curves out from the handle, the lower edge swooping down into a point. It is shining silver and decorated with intricate Celtic knotwork. The blade is covered with a guard, which Bertrand removes. The sharpened edge gleams and catches the low rays of the morning sun, reflecting them into Gavin's face and blinding him.

"It's lovely."

"It's a replica of a Celtic bearded axe. A battle axe, for fighting and killing."

"You could do a lot of damage with it."

Bertrand runs his finger lightly along the edge of the blade. "You could kill someone."

Bertrand leaps to his feet and swings the axe through the air. Gavin watches the silver blade, fascinated, as it cuts the air in a wide bow from left to right, then back again. Then it stops.

"How have you been getting along with Morgan?"

"Morgan?" Somewhere far off the birds are starting to sing, but he's suddenly aware of the air in the ravine, still and cold in his lungs. "Oh God, if you're GK she's your ... "

"Yes."

Gavin glances at Bertrand, but his face is blank.

"You've been living with my girlfriend. How's it been?"

"I wasn't living with her, not in that sense. I was helping her do up the house. We got along OK."

Bertrand holds the axe out in front of him and rotates the handle between his hands so the blade swings slowly round sending light reflections leaping across the walls of the ravine.

"You must have been a comfort to each other."

"Yes."

Bertrand swings the axe over his head in a full circle and brings it down so it cuts into the tree trunk only inches from where Gavin is sitting. Gavin stares at it. The blade has gone three or four inches into the wood. Slowly he raises his eyes to look at Bertrand who is still holding on to the axe handle, and sweating slightly.

"We talked in the evenings. It was a comfort to have each other's company. There was nothing more."

Bertrand starts pulling at the axe. The blade is wedged quite tightly, but eventually he manages to free it. He holds it in front of him, the top edge of the blade resting on the tree trunk, and leans on the handle as though it were a stick.

"You've been quite the happy home-makers I hear. Trips to Ikea. Late night DIY. It must have been very sweet, the two of you like newly-weds."

Before Gavin can reply, Bertrand has swung the axe again, this time cutting into the wood on the other side of Gavin. Gavin takes a deep breath and feels a calm creeping through his body. He looks at Bertrand who is tugging at the axe, trying to free it from the grip of the tree.

"You know it wasn't like that. I was working for Morgan and I did the work she asked me to do. She wasn't there a lot of the time. We got on well – she's a lovely girl. But she's in love with GK – with you."

The axe comes free with a jerk that nearly pulls Bertrand over. He sits down on the tree trunk next to Gavin and lays the axe across his lap.

"And what about Christmas? Did you have a good time together on Christmas Day?"

Bertrand's voice is level.

"She went to see GK … to see you. I can't get it straight in my head. I can't believe it's you and you're here."

"She was with you first."

What has Morgan told him?

Gavin looks at him but Bertrand doesn't meet his eye. He's watching the axe move in the sunshine.

"I had a hell of a hangover on Christmas Day. I slept until lunchtime – I think she did too. We had a late breakfast together and watched some Christmas telly. I gave her some chocolates."

"What did she give you?"

"Nothing."

Bertrand thrusts the axe at him.

"Here, feel its weight."

Gavin's arm darts out to catch the axe handle, exposing the silk band on his wrist. The embroidered red dragon can be clearly seen. Bertrand lets go of the axe handle before Gavin has time to grasp it, and it drops. The heavy blade cuts into his thigh, slicing straight through the fabric of his trousers and into his flesh. Bertrand makes a grab for it, but too late. Gavin stares at the wound. He feels cold. The cut is nearly an inch deep, the edges of the severed flesh disappearing under the sudden rise of blood.

Bertrand is on his feet.

"Fuck! Oh fuck!"

Blood is soaking into the fabric of Gavin's trousers.

"Jesus, you cut me." Gavin's voice is faint. The blood is running down the skin of his thigh. He can't look away.

Bertrand takes off his coat and removes his sweater and shirt. He rips the shirt in two and Gavin watches as he ties it around the wound, pushing the lips of the cut together, knotting the ends tightly. The pain is intense, much more than when the axe fell. A wave of nausea washes over him and he puts a hand on Bertrand's shoulder to steady himself.

Bertrand ties the other piece of the shirt. The blood is already seeping through.

"Give me those things off your wrists."

Gavin removes them with trembling fingers and Bertrand ties them tightly round his thigh above the wound.

"Do you think you can walk?"

Gavin doesn't know, but he nods his head. There's no other way down from here. Bertrand helps him to his feet.

He can't put any weight on the leg. He leans heavily on Bertrand and slowly they make their way along the foot of the ravine. His vision blurs and the air seems thick with green. He feels like he's pushing through curtains of moss that brush wet against his face. Their translucent leaves fill his nostrils, his throat, his brain.

"Morgan told me you've been a great help to her over the last few weeks," Bertrand says.

The steps will be impossible. He can't make it up the steps.

"Which is more than I've been."

They're at the foot.

"It's not what you think," Gavin whispers.

Bertrand goes in front and puts his arms beneath Gavin's, half lifts him up each step as he himself goes backwards. Half way up, the green air turns red and Gavin knows he's going to fall, but Bertrand pulls him close, holds on to him until the moment passes. This place is too beautiful, too old. He swallows hard and looks into Bertrand's face.

"Morgan loves you."

"I know. And Kat loves you. Can you move yet?"

Kat. There's nothing to stop them anymore, if she still wants him. Beneath the pain Gavin can feel something small inside his chest, something like a bubble or a bead, precious and delicate and he barely dares notice it in case it vanishes.

"OK, now."

Bertrand pulls and Gavin pushes with his good leg and they reach the top.

The walk down the hillside is easier. Bertrand removes his scarf and ties it over the top of the torn shirt, which is already red with blood. He wants to add his sweater too, but it's too bulky. Gavin leans heavily against him, and arms about each other, they make their way along the path as though they were in a clumsy three-legged race. When the path gets too narrow to go two abreast they go sideways.

Twice Gavin begs to stop for a break, leans against a rock, a tree. But Bertrand looks anxious and wants to keep moving. He is carrying Gavin's backpack, the axe inside wrapped hurriedly into its swathes of bubble wrap.

Eventually they are back on a level with the river. They can see the roof of the youth hostel beyond the tress.

"That's where I parked. We're nearly there."

The sun is higher in the sky and the fields are glowing with the newborn colours of day, tinged with white frost, like the down on a baby's skin.

There are two cars parked there, not one. Bertrand's BMW is coated with frost, but the other car is steaming, its engine just switched off. The doors open and two figures jump out and start running towards them.

Through a haze Gavin can make out the flying feet and the worried faces. He hears a voice calling his name, a bird trilling a welcome to the day. He remembers the bead of happiness lodged tentatively within him, and finds that, despite the red sweat of pain, it is still there.

Chapter Thirty-two

"After opening the casket, King Arthur sent his knights out far and wide across the country in search of the young knight who had so impressed him at the tournament, but many months passed and he wasn't found.

One day the Queen was out riding when a flock of birds rose suddenly from a tree and startled her horse. The young colt bolted with Guinevere clinging on to its neck for dear life. Her attendants gave chase, but none of them had a horse to match hers, and within minutes they had lost her. She was slipping in the saddle and certain soon to fall when she realised there was a black horse galloping alongside her. Its rider grabbed at the reins, and they soon came to a stop.

Queen Guinevere was ashamed of her frightened tears, and was inclined to give her rescuer a few coins and depart immediately, but when she looked into his face she gave a start of surprise.

'Who are you?' she demanded.

'I am a servant of your majesty, and of your lord, the great King Arthur. I am grateful and humbled to be of service to you, my Lady.'

She paid no attention to his courtesies, but stared at him all the harder in a way he found disconcerting.

'You are the young knight my husband is looking for. The one who beat everyone at the last tournament.'

Now the young man looked positively alarmed.

'But my lady, I believe, although I personally was not in the audience, that the knight of whom you speak was in disguise, his face covered.'

'Nevertheless, it is you that my husband seeks. You will accompany me, immediately, to the castle.'

The young man obeyed, and as they rode together in silence, the Queen glanced often at her companion, smiling to herself with amused satisfaction.

When they arrived at the castle the courtyard was in confusion with knights and squires preparing to go out in search of Guinevere and her runaway horse. The couple on horseback rode amongst them undetected at first, and even when she was spotted, the Queen paid no attention to anyone, but hustled her companion into the castle and up some stairs to the king's chamber.

She threw open the door and announced 'I've found him.'

Arthur was deep in discussion with Sir Bedevere, one of his oldest and wisest knights, and looked up with some irritation at the interruption, but when his eyes lit upon the young knight who accompanied the queen, he was silent and stared with the same intensity as Guinevere had earlier.

'There can be no doubt,' he said.

He rose to his feet, strode across the room and enfolded the puzzled knight in an embrace which knocked the breath out of him.

'Welcome! Welcome to my home, which henceforth shall be yours also.'"

"But how do they know it's him?" Kat's voice is right in his ear sending a tingle down his neck. He squeezes her tight against him.

"You've no patience! Listen and all will become clear."

She reaches across and gives his nipple a hard pinch, but she doesn't say anything else.

"The young man was taken to one of the best chambers in the castle, where he was given princely robes and servants to wait on him. They told him a feast was being prepared in his honour.

'Why is the King making such a fuss over me?' he asked of the servants. They didn't know, but said the King was wise and always had his reasons.

When he entered the banqueting hall that evening the room was full of people and the noise was deafening. Along each side of the hall were long trestles at which sat the knights and their ladies, all of the Round Table who could be gathered at short notice. At the head was the king's table where Arthur sat with Guinevere at his side, resplendent in their royal robes. Seated next to Guinevere was an older man with a grey beard and kindly face. Next to Arthur was an empty chair, and seated next to that was a woman.

Surcote, for that was indeed the identity of the young man, felt his eyes drawn to those of this woman, and as they looked at each other the voices in the hall began to die away, and within moments there was silence.

King Arthur got to his feet.

'Young knight, step forward.'

Surcote did as he was told, walking the length of the hall until he stood in front of King Arthur with only the table between them. But although he knew he should keep his gaze fixed on the king's face, he found it difficult not to let it slide across to the lady at his side."

"Who is she?" Kat whispers.

"Shh! King Arthur spoke. 'Are you the knight who won the tournament this summer and vanished without revealing your identity?'

Surcote bowed his head.

'I am your majesty.'

And did you, before you left, pass into my keeping a certain casket?'

'Yes, your majesty.'

'Were you aware of the contents of that casket, sent to me by the Emperor of Rome.'

'No, your majesty, my task was to deliver the casket into your hands, not to peruse its contents myself, and I performed my duty as required.'

'Very commendable. Very laudable. This means then, that you have no idea of your identity.'

'Sir,' Surcote stiffened his back and looked boldly into the king's face, 'my name is Surcote and I am the son of Viamund of Italy.'

'Wrong!' said the King.

The hall erupted in a flurry of murmurs and whisperings, which dropped immediately at the king's frown.

'Viamund brought you up as his son, but he was not your father. You are Gawain, son of Lot, grandson of Uther Pendragon, blood of my blood. Young man, I am your uncle, and these fine people sitting here at this table are your true parents, Lot and my sister Anna.'

The noise in the hall swelled again and this time the king did nothing to stop it. Surcote looked at the woman next to Arthur. There could be no doubt. The resemblance between her and himself was remarkable.

She rose from her seat and held her hand out to him.

'Your seat is here, Gawain, between me and the king.' Her voice was soft and low and spoke to him of warmth and comfort and rest after battle.

Lot came to stand beside his wife. Surcote leaped over the table and embraced first his father, then the king his uncle, and then his mother, Anna. Only when he was in his seat did Arthur stand and blow the horn.

'Let the feast begin!'"

When his voice stops she leans up on her elbow and looks down at his face on the pillow.

"Is that the end?"

"Of course not. That's only the beginning."

She lies back and snuggles her shoulder under his armpit, her face into his neck. He closes his eyes and the darkness behind his lids is blotted out by the bright shape of the window burned onto his retinas by the daylight. He opens them and the daylight is still there, filling the room with brightness.